ALYSSA JARRETT

Geek Chic Press LLC

Editing by Kristen Tate at the Blue Garret

Cover design by Nick Jarrett

ISBN: 978-1-963875-00-3 (Ebook)

ISBN: 978-1-963875-01-0 (Paperback)

Published by Geek Chic Press LLC

PO Box 1193

Oakland, CA 94604

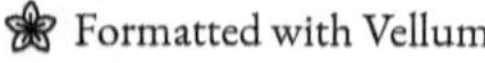 Formatted with Vellum

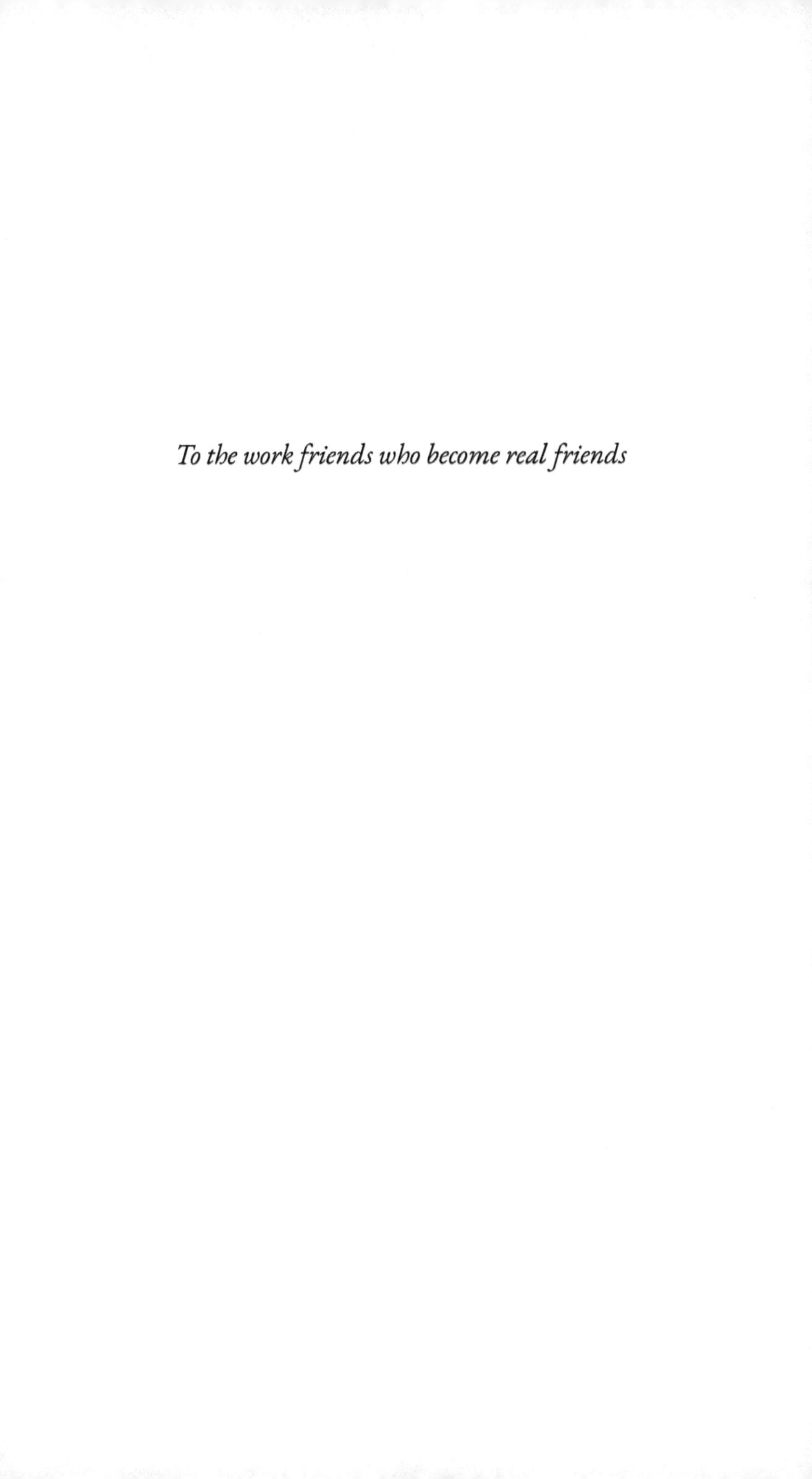

To the work friends who become real friends

content notes

Some readers may find some of the content of this book to be difficult, including childhood emotional neglect (historical, off-page), racial microaggressions, drugging, swearing, alcohol use and intoxication, and explicit sex. Reader discretion is advised.

chapter
one

I'm just going to come out and say it. It's a shame that malls are dying because they're where I feel most alive. Growing up, I practically lived at the Houston Galleria on weekends. While my workaholic parents were at their offices, I was running around the mall with either my two older brothers or a gaggle of friends, an Orange Julius in my hand and an allowance burning a hole in my pockets.

The Stanford Shopping Center doesn't have three million square feet and its own ice rink like the Galleria, but the euphoria of scoring a haul better than I could have ever imagined is just the same. Malls are like Vegas casinos to me—drunk with excitement, I lose track of time and wonder where all my money went. Honestly, I'm extremely lucky that I managed to turn my shopping addiction into a career, so I'm now emptying other people's wallets instead of my own.

Usually that wallet belongs to Alex Waterston-Gardner—aka Princess Alex, the supermodel, socialite, and it girl of it girls—and I'm not emptying it at the mall. Soon we'll be hopscotching across the globe, starting with the haute couture showcase at the end of this month, followed by the blitz that is the Big Four fashion weeks: New York, London, Milan, and Paris. Instead of scanning the mall racks, I'll be collaborating on custom pieces with the hottest designers.

But today's haul is just for me. I always make a point in late January to relish the calm before the storm and head for my happy place, where I can get lost in the crowds, shopping for myself in peace and forgetting for a second that I work for a global icon with hundreds of millions of followers.

The last thing I want to sound is ungrateful, of course. Alex isn't just my biggest client and the world's most adored social media celebrity—she's also my best friend. Our mothers were sorority sisters, so we go back since birth, and despite the Waterston-Gardners moving to the West Coast to build a PR empire, nothing ever broke our bond. Not the distance of growing up apart, halfway across the country. Not those early viral moments that catapulted a teenage Alex into the A-list and her family into the three-comma club. She deserves every ounce of her fame and fortune, and I'm immensely fortunate to have contributed to her becoming a household name.

And yet. Even though I wouldn't trade my life for anyone's, there's a part of me that's always wondered if I would have been as successful if I didn't hitch a ride on Alex's shooting stardom. That line of questioning never catches momentum, though, not when duty calls.

As I head through the courtyard toward the parking garage, my arms sag under the weight of the garment bags that hang on them like anchors, and my legs are so exhausted from closing the exercise ring on my smartwatch several times over that they might fall off before I reach my car. But this is what self-care feels like to me. I play Tetris in the back of my Grand Cherokee with the deals I snagged and peel out of the parking garage toward my Palo Alto apartment when duty literally calls.

"Casey, where are you?"

It's the princess herself, and she sounds stressed. "Hey, I'm almost home," I answer. "Can I call you back once I figure out how to make room for this epic haul I got?"

"No time!" Alex blares through my car phone. "Bring your loot to my place—we've got a major sponcon crisis over here!"

With the sun setting on a deeply satisfying day, I chuckle, unfazed. "Are you sure? Last time you called something a crisis was when that coffee shop up the street didn't carry oat milk."

She lets out a huff. "First off, I stand by that. What kind of business are you running if you can't support a variety of nondairy options? Second, this is way worse than flat whites. Remember that inclusive lingerie brand that wants me to plug their pajamas for Valentine's Day?"

"Of course, I got the delivery notification earlier today. Was there something wrong with the shipment?" With only a few weeks until the holiday, my mind immediately jumps to fix-it mode, calculating how best to coordinate another order if needed.

"I don't know, Casey, you tell me! Were we planning on my tits being out for this one?"

I slam on the brakes in surprise, taking a hard right toward the freeway in the direction of Alex's mega-mansion in Los Altos Hills.

"Okay, take a deep breath. We'll get this sorted out. Open a bottle of red and relax—I'll be there soon."

Alex exhales with relief. "We're already ahead of you on the wine, so you might as well crash here tonight and start catching up."

∽

WHEN ALEX FLINGS open the doors at the Waterston-Gardner estate and envelops me in a tight hug, I sigh, feeling more at home at my best friend's house than in my own apartment—which isn't that surprising. I still refer to the second guest room on the left as mine, even though it hasn't been my official residence since the summer before my senior year of high school, when I followed her out West and became the first member of her glam fam.

"Hope your mother won't mind me storing these for the night." I gesture to the many shopping bags I've dragged to her doorstep.

"Nonsense! I'm just glad you could make it, so take as much space as you need—it's not like we're running out of it." She laughs, throwing a few bags over her shoulder and padding back into the house barefoot.

It's that kind of blissfully privileged attitude that gives celebrities a bad rap, but Alex isn't wrong—there's nothing her family lacks in this ten-thousand square-foot modern day palace. Typical twenty-six-year-olds would be looked down upon for living with their parents, but Alex's got a wing to herself that rivals the grandeur of most art museums.

Sure, the large walk-in storage closet off the foyer where we stash my bags could be considered abundance, but maybe I'm just used to it. To me, true abundance is when I see the rest of the glam fam—makeup artist Som Srisati, hairdresser Glen Cooper, and esthetician by day, jazz musician by night Victoria Townsend—in the great room and know I can finally be myself. Alex and I may put the forever in BFFs, but once the whole gang fell into place several years ago, that's when we became a real family. Because when the five of us are here together, it's like all our problems get locked outside those wrought iron gates and there's no one else in the world.

Except I can tell by the cloying scent of toxic man musk

hanging in the air that someone else has infiltrated the glam fam and thrown the vibes way, *way* off.

"Yo, what up, Case?" a voice calls from the couch, giving me the worst ick possible.

"Dominic." I sink into the plush loveseat next to Glen and do my best to breathe through my mouth. "How sweet of you to join us." Like every proper Southern deb, my mother taught me that if I can't say something nice, I should say nothing at all. But she forgot to cover a major loophole: saying something nice in a tone that's anything but. "I figured you'd be preoccupied watching the NFL playoffs. You know, somewhere else."

He shrugs, oblivious to my bless-your-heart passive aggression. "The boys can wait," he says, either about his favorite football team or the knucklehead friends he watches them with—it doesn't matter. "When my baby has a fashion emergency, I'm gonna drop everything to be there for her."

The sentiment would be touching if I believed a word of it. But Dominic de Silva only plays the gentleman when the paparazzi's around to photograph it, so he must have an ulterior motive to be here. After Glen hands me a glass of pinot noir with a knowing glance, I exchange looks with the rest of the glam fam, all of whom are equally irritated. Seated across the room, Som shoots daggers at Dominic taking up an entire sofa, disgusted at the sight of his sneakers kicked up on the pristine pillows. Tori self-soothes at the grand piano, playing one of my favorite songs of hers, but it's obvious from her clenched jaw it's taking all her strength to keep her mouth shut.

I don't blame them. Ever since Alex brought Dominic back from Miami, Cancún, or wherever you go dumpster-diving for summer flings, we thought surely she'd break up with him before cuffing season. And yet, six months later, we're stuck with a skeezy social climber who's constantly butting into our business.

"That's funny," I say, taking a big swig of wine, amusement nowhere to be found on my face. "Why did she call me then?"

"Because we need to decide what to do about this," Alex declares, digging through an opened package on the living room floor. She holds up a black corset, appropriately themed in red hearts—except for the blank space where the bra cups are supposed to be.

Dominic drops his phone and bolts up, his attention finally diverted from his DMs. "Now that's what I'm talking about! You'd look hot as hell in that, baby."

I hold back a scoff. Of course, he'd be on board. He's such the spitting image of that cartoon wolf with his tongue hanging out that I half expect him to howl *awooga*.

"Alex would look hot in a burlap sack. That's not the point." I don't call out the real issue, which is that Dominic couldn't stay in his lane if he was driving an eighteen-wheeler down California's winding Pacheco Pass. If I want to nip his meddling in the bud, I need backup. "New York Fashion Week and all the rest are around the corner, and this isn't the mic drop we were planning. Right?"

"Quite," Glen quips in his adorably posh British accent. "As much as we say flaunt it if you've got it, Som and I are always going to vote for whatever keeps everyone's eyes locked above her neck. I don't even see any matching panties, and if I'm going to spend hours giving Alex a shag cut, I want the world staring at her fringe and not her minge."

I nearly spit out my drink, expecting Alex to join the laughter, but our giggles fade quickly when she's silent. With how much Alex and her momager care about preserving her impeccable reputation, going topless should be out of the question. The way she's looking at Dominic, however, makes me wonder if his opinion carries enough weight to throw her intuition off-balance.

Dominic shakes his head in disapproval. "This is exactly what I've been telling you, baby."

"Telling her what?" I bark, setting my wine glass down before I'm tempted to toss its contents in his face.

"That you're holding her back! You call yourselves the glam fam, but you've been tied at the hip for so long you've got her stuck in a rut." He points an accusatory finger. "Especially you, Case. You've got her dressed in so much bubblegum and cotton candy, she should get her blood sugar checked. I don't want to be a hater, but if a high-value female is gonna be on my arm, she's not a *princess*." He spits out the childish word with revulsion, as if he didn't call her baby seconds ago. "She's a queen, and what she wears should reflect that."

It's a good thing I'm already sitting because it feels like I got the wind knocked out of me. Sure, Alex has never met something pink and sparkly she hasn't liked, but what's wrong with that? She's a bubbly, blonde beauty, with shockingly blue eyes, angelic curls, and the perfect pout. I didn't go out of the way to turn her into America's sweetheart. She assumed the role naturally, and with half a billion fans hanging on her every word, I didn't question it. After all, I was taught if something ain't broke, don't fix it.

I try to meet Alex's gaze. "Is that true? Is that what you think?"

She avoids eye contact, like it physically pains her to rock the boat. Dropping the cupless corset back into its box, she retreats into Dominic's arms. "It wouldn't be the worst thing in the world to shake things up."

I'm so confused. When Alex called me in the car, she was distraught, like someone had sent her anthrax instead of X-rated underwear. But in the twenty minutes it took me to drive here, Dominic somehow got into her head and supplanted me as her most trusted style advisor.

This isn't the first time some dirtbag Alex was dating had the audacity to throw in his two cents, but it is the first time it wasn't disregarded as chump change. Most dudes are more than happy to be at the service of social media royalty, but Dominic's different. I mean, a sneaker line and a few chart-topping rap singles don't impress me much, but his obsession with Alex's image is now impacting my job, so I have to tread lightly.

"I'm not opposed to baring skin," I clarify, "as long as you're getting what you're worth to show it off. If we're going to make a move this major, let's wait until the whirlwind of fashion weeks is behind us so we can launch a well-orchestrated campaign. I'll get ahold of their influencer marketing team and schedule some time to discuss after we get back from Paris." I look up from my phone after writing myself a reminder and take in Alex's tortured expression. "What's wrong?"

"It's just that . . ." Dominic places a hand on her knee, encouraging her. Whatever she's about to say, they're a united front. "This whole thing is bigger than sponcon. Fashion Week's the ideal opportunity to reinvent myself. I'm already walking the runway for the best houses, and Dom's got connections to streetwear designers that can boost my cred, give me some edge, you know? I know that's not exactly your wheelhouse—which is totally okay, don't get me wrong. You're fabulous, Casey, but I think it's worth exploring other options."

"Other options?" I repeat, dumbfounded.

The idea hangs in the air until Dominic inserts himself into the conversation. "What Alex means is she'll be consulting with other stylists on this trip, so there's no need for you to dress her at the Big Four while she's shopping around."

Alex nods reassuringly, a clear sign that Dominic's come up with this grand plan and she's simply agreeing to it. "At least for this season—and now you're free to sign other clients, too! Whoever you work with is going to fall in love with you. I just know it."

What are you supposed to do when your best friend, the one you've worked for an entire decade, unilaterally decides to open your business relationship? Call me vain, but here I thought we made an iconic duo. Casey Holbright and Princess Alex go together like Law Roach and Zendaya. Except now that Dominic has got her under his mind control, she wants to sow her wild oats, as if that benefits us both equally.

Everyone in Alex's entourage is an independent contractor, and while that technically means we can take other gigs, it's rarely feasible. Not when her agenda dictates our schedules, and her momager cuts our most sizable paychecks. But even setting that aside, we're her closest friends—precisely because we're so involved in her life, both on and off the clock.

I would never tell a soul, but occasionally, when I've had a little too much to drink and need to assert my independence, I have a habit of applying to other jobs. I'd never leave the Waterston-Gardners hanging, but it scratches an itch. A small act of rebellion when I'm feeling like Alex's sidekick and need a reminder that I have a life of my own to consider.

But even if I've blasted off some resumes when my insecurities got the better of me, I'm not the polyamorous type, either personally or professionally. I'm the founding member of Alex's glam fam, and we owe it to each other to stick together.

"Hey, let's not get all dramatic," she says, blissfully ignorant of the bomb she dropped on my life. "We can still have fun and stuff! Dom will be playing at the most exclusive after-parties—you've *got* to come, Casey. Everybody who's anybody will be there."

Alex's words echo in my mind, taunting me. Without her, I'm nobody. She makes it sound like it's no big deal to cut professional ties, even temporarily, but I can't afford to gallivant across Europe for a month without her family footing the bill.

And as valuable as it would be to network in the world's fashion meccas, how am I supposed to explain my predicament in my search for new clients? Alex and I aren't working together at the moment, so I'm here skulking around and name-dropping her for crumbs? Everyone I'd talk to would die from secondhand embarrassment.

I grip the arm of the loveseat to keep myself from doubling over. If I'm not dressing Alex, I feel like a planet off its orbit, untethered and purposeless. She's been my safety net in every way imaginable—not only my primary source of income and my "in" to the fashion industry, but also the arbiter of my itinerary. The reason I get up in the morning, my plus-one every night and weekend. Codependent doesn't begin to cover it. I'm sure if there were a Bechdel-style test for having conversations that didn't have anything to do with Alex, I would fail miserably.

It must be dawning on Alex that she's knocked me off my axis because she leaps up from the couch to take my hands in hers. I hold my breath, waiting for her to take everything back and say that of course she couldn't imagine being dressed by anyone else.

But those aren't the words that fly out of her mouth. "Let me get Anna on the phone," she proposes. "I bet she has a million connections desperate for your help."

Anna . . . as in Wintour? Absolutely fucking not. There are already enough people who think I'm some talentless hack, a nepo baby by association thanks to our mothers' undergrad glory days. I have too much pride to allow Alex to call in a favor and prove them right.

"Don't bother," I tell her, abruptly rising from my seat. "My waitlist is long enough, thank you very much." It's not, a fact which I'm sure is apparent to everyone in the room, but keeping up appearances is literally my job. And although I'm not one to believe in manifestation, if I can call an on-demand clientele into existence, I will.

"Wait—where are you going?" Alex exclaims as I march toward the storage closet to retrieve my shopping bags. I look like an utter buffoon in my attempt to carry all of them at once, but it's less humiliating than making multiple trips back and forth.

Alex follows me out the front door, pacing barefoot as I pack up my car. "Please, don't leave, Casey. Let's inhale some popcorn and watch movies all night, like old times. You're still my best friend, no matter what."

Even if that's true, we can't ever recreate the past—not when the popcorn is now made by Michelin-starred chefs and the movies are projected on a massive state-of-the-art curved screen with 3D immersive surround sound. The old times are long gone, and what's left is a gaping hole in my heart.

I slam the hatch door closed and scramble into the driver's seat before she can come any closer. If Alex goes in for a hug, I won't be able to bite back the waterworks any longer. As I drive through the gates, my face crumples in a pitiful sob, tears flooding down my cheeks.

And when I think I can't feel any sorrier for myself, an incoming call blares through my car speakers. I answer before the caller's name can appear on the dash, because I'm that desperate for it to be Alex offering a heartfelt apology.

"Hey," I gush with palpable relief, ready to put this mess behind us and never speak of it again.

"Hey to you, too!" a surprised man's voice comes through. "Is this Casey Holbright?"

Shit. Girl, get a fucking grip. "This is she," I answer, parroting the way my prim and proper mother answers the phone and wiping the dampness off my face with the back of my hand. "May I ask with whom I'm speaking?"

If the sudden shift in formality throws him for a loop, he doesn't let on. "This is Maxwell Erickson, chief operating officer at Habituall."

Habituall? I rack my brain until I realize why that name rings a bell—it's that buzzy tech startup I applied to in my most recent shame spiral. The one with the executive stylist position to make over their founder and CEO—Evan Chen, that was his name. I saw the job description and thought it would be easy money given how straightforward it sounded, going into an office and working for someone without an ungodly amount of fame or a fleet of brand managers forcing their paid partnerships.

"Yes, hi!" I squeak, embarrassed by my delayed response. "Thanks for getting back to me."

"No, I should be the one thanking you for taking my call after hours. I apologize for dialing so late. We would have contacted you sooner, but—well, our recruiting team thought we were being pranked at first. Do you really work for Alex Waterston-Gardner?"

The awe in his voice hits me like an arrow to the chest. Alex is such a ubiquitous force in pop culture, I'm not shocked that even tech executives know her name. "Mm-hmm," I reply, lacking the courage to correct him with the past tense. "But there's been a change to her schedule, so I'm able to open my availability to select clients."

"Wonderful!" he says, unaware of how my career is hanging by a thread—one that's cheap, synthetic, and about to catch fire. "I could waste both our time by asking you a bunch of extraneous questions, but your portfolio with *the Princess Alex* speaks for itself. Normally for full-time positions, we'd bring you onsite for a round of interviews, but since this a short-term contract and we're crunched for time, we'd like to get started right away. Does that work for you?"

Alex coming to her senses would work better, but I can't afford to wait for that miracle to happen. If I'm being handed an opportunity to take charge as the main character in my own story, I need to take it.

And if my hazy memory is correct, Evan Chen is the closest thing to a Silicon Valley celebrity. Pretty sure that job description mentioned him winning Entrepreneur of the Year, so this could be my golden ticket into the tech industry, where the money is really good, and the fashion sense is really, *really* bad. If this gig is a success, I could change brogrammer culture, one schlubby CEO at a time.

I smile wide to make my answer more convincing—whether it's to my new boss or myself is beside the point.

"Sounds perfect."

~

Archived job posting in the Slack group, AAPI as Fuck!, posted by Wendy Hoang, head of workplace strategy at Habituall

Welcome to our Slack group, AAPI as Fuck! This online community is designed to be a secret, safe space for Asian Americans and Pacific Islanders in the San Francisco Bay Area to escape the racist bullshit we experience every day and celebrate our hella awesome, unique cultures.

Admission into the community is by invite-only. Discrimination against anyone other than Pac Heights Karens is strictly forbidden. Zero tolerance of intolerance #BlackLivesMatter #LGBTQIA #Pride

@WendyHoang (MODERATOR): Job alert! The leadership team at my company Habituall is #NowHiring an executive stylist. This is an onsite contract position at our SF HQ to make over our CEO in the run-up to our annual conference, First Party. My colleagues aren't in this group, so I've added the job description with my honest AF commentary in parentheses—my opinions are my own, blah blah blah. Don't rat me out for being real, or I will use my admin privileges to ban your narc asses. DM me with your referrals!

Executive Stylist - San Francisco, contract

Habituall is an omni-channel marketing platform that orchestrates seamless customer experiences and enables brands to optimize every touchpoint along the customer journey. *(Meaning we track your every move so companies can do a better job spamming the shit out of you.)*

As our executive stylist, you'll be styling Evan Chen, Habituall's founder and CEO. This role includes full wardrobe planning, from everyday business and business casual attire to formal events and special occasions. *(EC is the kind of guy who thinks tucking in his shirt is as fancy as a three-piece suit, so you have your work cut out for you.)*

We're looking for people who maintain a high level of professionalism *(because you won't find it here)*, work autonomously under limited supervision *(because they don't know what they're doing)* and have at least five years of experience styling C-level executives *(but honestly, they're so desperate they'll take anyone with an active Vogue subscription)*.

Most importantly, we want someone who lives by our

founding values of Teamwork *(to do the work we don't want to do ourselves)*, Balance *(of work and life, with a strong preference for work)*, and Loyalty *(so you eagerly accept working all the time)*.

Habituall is an Equal Employment Opportunity employer that does not make hiring or employment decisions on the basis of race, color, ethnic or national origin . . . *(You get the gist, but unless you have a Tiger Mom fetish for whipping into shape a man who embarrasses his ancestors every day with his horrific outfits, this job is best suited for a Becky. You've been warned!)*

Only impostors don't get impostor syndrome.

That's what I remind myself as I knock on Evan Chen's office door. I can't recall where I heard the mantra—probably one of those social media accounts that spits out generic inspirational quotes, to be honest—but it pairs nicely with the etiquette I learned in my cotillion classes. Shoulders back. Head high. Only impostors don't get impostor syndrome. You can do this.

"Come in."

I open the door and stop short. This isn't an office but some kind of exercise space. There's a man sitting cross-legged on a yoga mat in the middle of the room. He's wearing a tight, black tee and khaki cargo shorts, his eyes closed. I'm about to back out slowly and return to the front desk, sure that I've been directed to the wrong room, when the man's eyes flutter open.

"As you can probably guess, I'm Evan. You must be Cathy, the stylist Max hired."

The edge in his voice throws me off more than him getting my name wrong. His expression is pleasant, but he says the word *stylist* the way I might say *telemarketer*. I try not to take it personally, though. Setting aside Alex's recent lapse in judgment, everyone is usually giddy with excitement to work with me, but I can understand when the last thing someone wants to think about is clothing.

"It's Casey, actually. Casey Holbright." He's closed his eyes in serenity again, but I force a smile on the off chance he acknowledges my presence as anything more than a nuisance.

I step further into the room and attempt to perch on a soft bean bag chair near the door, pulling my laptop from my ivory leather Celine tote and booting it up. "Max mentioned you're a big fitness buff, so you'll see I've taken that into account in the looks I've put together for your annual conference in Vegas this year." I'm going to get down to business even if this meeting I've spent the last week prepping for is happening in the company yoga room.

Evan's eyes open in bewilderment like I've said I'm going to kick a puppy.

"Is there something wrong?" I check my notes for anything I might have missed. "Ah, yes. I know Habituall calls the conference First Party as a nod to data privacy, so we can work that into the aesthetic as well. It's such a clever name." Maybe he detects my insincerity—I rolled my eyes when Max first mentioned the name during our follow-up phone convo —because he still looks miffed.

"Casey, there are no devices allowed in the zen room. This is a sacred place for Habituators to unplug."

Says the man who created marketing software that allows brands to send people promotions through every channel imaginable—email, snail mail, push notifications, pop-ups, you name it. His company is now worth hundreds of millions of dollars, so while he has the luxury of unplugging, the rest of us are at the mercy of all the spam sent using his technology.

That's not entirely fair. I'm sure Evan Chen has noble reasons behind bringing Habituall to life. But even if he doesn't, I still desperately need this gig, so I'm in no position to judge.

He pats the mat beside his. "We can't start work together until you've returned to your center. Come, sit next to me."

I tuck my laptop back into my tote, tugging at my vintage Escada skirt, so chic in warm camel and trimmed in black. It's not too short or tight, but now I'm regretting its high slit because I didn't expect to sit across from Habituall's fearless leader on a yoga mat instead of in a conference room chair like in any regular business meeting. There's no way I'm crossing my legs and risking flashing my underwear to someone entering the room to bring Evan a kombucha or a damp towel. Instead, I awkwardly take the princess pose on the yoga mat, with my legs out at my side, crossed at the ankles. Those debutante lessons were good for something, at least.

"Now take a deep breath," he whispers, "inhaling through your nose and exhaling through your mouth."

I follow his instructions, because the sooner we get centered, the faster I can make a name for myself styling Silicon Valley's elite. I thought tech was about moving fast and breaking things, but all I've done this morning has been lollygagging and losing my mind.

"Inhale . . . and exhale . . . and again, inhale . . . and exhale." After several minutes of deep breathing, my exhales are coming out more like exasperated sighs because I so desperately want to get this show on the road. We're fifteen minutes into this meeting, and I haven't even had a chance to identify Evan's favored color palette.

"Wonderful, now open your eyes. How do you feel?"

Evan smiles, disarming me. I almost forget he's running a company of over four hundred people. All while dressed like a gym rat.

"I feel great. Energized and ready to redo your wardrobe!" I gesture at the Habituall logo emblazoned on the yoga mat in front of him—three concentric circles of red, orange, and yellow, like the bullseye targets my two older brothers and I would hit when our dad took us to the shooting range as kids. "I'm guessing you like warm colors? Your logo reminds me a bit of . . ." My brain scrambles for a more appropriate association—I suspect Evan is not a big marksman.

"Of Ibitha, yes." Evan's eyes flutter closed again. "The colors I wear should be found in nature, like those clay tiles I saw on the roofs in Ibitha. I'm visualizing the sun radiating on them, speckled with iridescent reds and browns and golds."

I push down the urge to grab my laptop and take notes on my meticulously prepared client questionnaire. "Yep, I got that. If you're interested in warmer tones—"

"Not just warm tones but bright ones, too, like those old Ibitha homes with their stark white walls . . ."

Lord, give me strength. I foolishly assumed I'd knock it out of the park on my first day, but how can I make any progress with someone who depletes my patience to near-homicidal levels? Despite the sharpshooter training I got from my dad, I never thought I would be capable of committing murder. But if Evan Chen pronounces Ibiza as Ibitha one more time, then I guess I have no choice.

"Um, Evan, do you mind if we move this meeting out of the zen room so I can take notes and maybe show you some swatches?"

He snaps his eyes open. "I said you need to be centered, not self-centered, Casey."

A record scratch goes off in my brain. Excuse me? What did he call me?

"Uh, I'm sorry, I thought—"

"If you thought I'd make for an excellent addition to your portfolio, and you're only going to treat this partnership like a business transaction, then you're not a good fit for Habituall's values."

That accusation stops me cold. Sure, I might be impatient to get the ball rolling, but no one has ever had a problem with my go-getter attitude before. You'd think a Silicon Valley CEO like Evan would appreciate it. I only want him to look his best, but he thinks I'm looking out for number one. I'd seen the company values painted on the walls of the entryway when I walked into headquarters, each with its own cheesy 'culture critter' associated with it: Teamwork (bee), Balance (flamingo), and Loyalty (elephant). I guess I'm not as balanced as Evan would like me to be in the zen room, and he certainly doesn't see me as a part of the team.

So, time to channel my inner elephant then.

"My apologies, Mr. Chen. I didn't mean to give you the impression that I was uninterested in building a foundation of trust with you and your team. I'm just so excited to support you—in any small way that I can—that I got a bit carried away."

Say you're sorry, lead with good intent, then shut the hell up. It always worked in debutante training, especially when I flash a wide-toothed smile like I'm giving Evan now. I just need the ice to thaw between us, and we'll be back on track.

"Alright, then let's try a grounding exercise. Everyone spends too much time worrying about the future, and it's important to be in the present moment."

Easy for him to say. I'd bet Evan Chen has never been betrayed by someone close to him, thrusting him into an uncertain future in which he's scrambling to find another source of income.

Resenting Evan for Alex's actions doesn't last long, however—not when he scoots so close to me that our knees are nearly touching. "I want you to continue your deep breathing," he says, "but with each breath, acknowledge your senses by saying out loud five things you can see, four things you can feel, three things you can hear, two things you can smell, and one thing you can taste."

I hold back a groan and play along, seeing a lava lamp in the corner, feeling the mat underneath me, and hearing light New Age music coming from a small portable speaker. But when I get to what I can smell, it's not the musk of patchouli and weed I expect to waft from a San Francisco hippie like Evan, but a rather intoxicating cologne that distracts me from the exercise. I take in his deep, dark eyes that match his tousled bedhead, and for a moment, I can envision how handsome he could look in one of the many suits I've bookmarked for him. But I definitely can't mention that, so I go with the lavender-scented candle on the coffee table.

"And what's the one thing you can taste?"

Why does he have to speak so low and soft and seductively? No wonder meditation feels like a cult. It sounds downright hypnotic.

"The inside of your mouth—*my* mouth! The inside of my mouth, I mean. I had a caramel macchiato before I arrived."

Evan smirks, and I want my yoga mat to swallow me whole.

But since I sadly don't die of mortification, I clear my throat and power through. "I think it's your turn now."

Evan takes another deep breath, and I expect his expression to revert to its default setting of serene obliviousness, but that lopsided smirk continues tugging on one side of his face.

"Let's see . . . I can see you packing up your Celine bag, hear your Prada heels walking you out the door, smell your perfume dissipate once you're removed from this room, and feel your outrage that I'm telling you this. And the one thing I can taste is victory, because *I don't care*. So now that you're firmly grounded in reality, Casey, you can go."

I can't say I've ever had an out-of-body experience before, but I'm so dumbfounded at what's happened that it feels like someone else has closed my slack jaw, picked me up off the yoga mat, grabbed my tote, and led me out the door of the zen room into the open-concept office.

I've done plenty of walks of shame as a single woman in her mid-twenties, but nothing compares to walking past row after row of cubicles, feeling the stares of dozens of tech workers in company T-shirts and flip-flops as they gape at you in your designer outfit and high heels—like it's a backward version of high school where the nerds are the popular kids, and I'm the try-hard who doesn't even go here. I pride myself on always being so well-dressed for any occasion that I fit in anywhere, but now I'm surrounded by geniuses and I've never felt so stupid in my life.

As I approach the front desk, I see the two women who welcomed me into the building—Lola Nichols, chief of staff and Max's right-hand woman, and Wendy Hoang, the head of workplace strategy—and I take a few deep breaths to steady my voice and avoid bursting into tears. I shouldn't feel this torn up about what a stranger thinks of me as a stylist, but after being pushed away by Alex, my ego's been rubbed so raw I'm questioning whether I'm even cut out for the fashion industry.

"Done so soon, Casey? It hasn't even been thirty minutes." Lola flashes her enviable cheek dimples. She looks like a model dressed for a go-see, in a black blazer over a white tank and dark-wash jeans. She tap-taps her red slingbacks around the desk and gives me a big hug. "I knew you were a miracle worker."

Wendy notices my grimace and slaps her hand on the table. "That little shit!"

My face overheats with embarrassment.

"I know it's not you," she clarifies. "EC is being his pure, authentic, boba-for-brains self."

Wendy looks so sweet with her shoulder-length bob,

round face, and rounder glasses, but she's clearly tougher than she appears.

"Let me guess—you were just trying to do your job, and he shut you down completely?"

I nod slowly, a little intimidated, if I'm being honest. Wendy might sit at the front desk like a receptionist, but according to my research, she runs a sizable administrative staff across the company's San Francisco headquarters and various satellite offices around the country. And with her take-no-prisoners attitude, I'm sure she gets a sick thrill every time a job candidate makes the fatal mistake of acting superior to her because she then gets to harpoon their chances of ever working here. Evan Chen may be the CEO, but Wendy's clearly the HBIC.

She turns to her coworker. "Lola, can you—"

"Already on it." The chief of staff glances up from her phone. "Gave Max a heads-up and told the executive assistants to add this topic to the agenda of the leadership meeting today. Where are they, anyway? The mini fridge in Coit Tower needs to be restocked with nitro cold brew."

When Lola pointed it out to me during the office tour before my meeting with Evan, I thought it was pretty adorable that their conference rooms are named after famous SF landmarks because who wouldn't want to meet in Twin Peaks or the Painted Ladies? But she's a lot less cheery than when I arrived.

Wendy drums her fingers on the table. "Lola, how did you and Max pitch Casey's services to EC?"

She blinks. "Uh, it was pretty self-explanatory. We told him that as one of our keynote speakers at First Party, it would be advantageous to spice up his look."

"But did you make it sound like he was the only one getting new clothes?" Wendy presses.

Lola chuckles. "Evan's wardrobe is the one we need taken

care of. Why waste budget when the others who are speaking know to show up in a nice suit?"

Wendy rubs her temples. "No wonder he bit Casey's head off. Lola, you and Max have only been here a couple of months, but you should know by now that EC doesn't care about First Party, and—more importantly—he hates being singled out for anything, especially for something as personal as what to wear. Max won't mind increasing the budget; tell him there's been a misunderstanding and that Casey will be styling the whole leadership team."

"It's fine. I'll take care of it." Lola purses her lips in a way that says it's not fine whatsoever and turns to me. "Casey, do you have the bandwidth for this? I know it's super short notice to scope-creep this much on your first day, but we need Evan to get on board, and if it takes paying for eight other execs to make our conference a success, then so be it."

Eight? Eight! My brain whirs with mental math as I try to calculate how big this gig has gotten. I had initially quoted a reasonable hourly rate with the expectation of working fifteen hours per week until the day of the event. Even if most of the team needs basic styling, that's still a metric ton of planning, shopping, and fitting. I'll have to work twelve-hour days for the next two months straight, and if I charge overtime, that means six figures, easy.

I take a breath to ensure my eyes aren't bulging out of my head at the thought of making that amount of money on a single project. I anticipated needing to cobble together several clients to replace a fraction of what Alex's family was paying me. It never occurred to me that startups I'd barely heard of would make it rain.

"I think a retainer model would make the most sense in a situation like this," I say, parroting the words I heard so often from Alex's team when they were on the phone negotiating her brand deals. "But I'm confident we can make it work, even with the time crunch."

Lola smiles, visibly relieved, and I find it so strange to consider styling a man who has no interest or desire to work with me. What if Evan doesn't ever come around? What if he spends the next seven weeks being as stubborn as an old mule? What if I fail to finish the job, and he looks like shit at the show, and the company demands their money back or sues me?

Whoa, Nelly—calm down there, Casey. I'm doing Habituall a favor by bringing my type A, 'Best Dressed in High School' energy to the Wild West of tech startups. They need my help, even if Evan wants nothing to do with me. And if I could manage to juggle the hordes of designers dying to dress Alex at the most prestigious events, then I can survive this role-play of *The Devil Wears Patagonia*.

I wish Wendy a great day, and Lola escorts me to the elevator, apologizing that my first session with Evan was cut short.

"He can be a lot to handle sometimes, but now that you're here, everything is going to go wonderfully. First Party will be a runaway success, and we'll soon be a billion-dollar tech unicorn. Just you wait."

Whether she's directing that reassurance at herself or me remains to be seen.

Lola presses the button heading down, and as we wait for the lift to arrive, she claps her hands together. "Oh, I almost forgot—we're doing a team-building thing tomorrow. You should come! You can meet the other SF-based leaders and get to know Evan better. Once you know him more personally, I'm sure he'll stop being such a stick-in-the-mud."

I step inside the lift and hit the button for the ground floor. It dawns on me that I've never attended a corporate team-building event, and the near-constant thought plaguing me reappears.

"Wait!" I burst out, stopping the elevator door from closing with my hand and nearly demolishing my manicure. "What should I wear?"

Lola scans my outfit up and down, wincing with pity. "Yeah . . . it's really casual. Wear something comfortable!"

Withdrawing my hand, I allow the door to slowly close, and Lola adds belatedly, "Love your bag, though!"

"Thanks, it's Celine—" But by the time I get the words out, the elevator is descending. When it dings open into the marbled lobby, one particular detail flashes like a lightbulb in my mind.

Unless Evan had superhero powers to read the tiny logo at the top of the tote, he already knew the designer—not just of my handbag, now that I think about it, but also my shoes. So he either has a woman in his life with the exact same accessories, or he knows way more about fashion than anyone here gives him credit for. *That little shit, indeed.*

~

HOMEPAGE DESCRIPTION of SeriouslyFun.com

ARE you a Silicon Valley startup that likes to move fast and break things, including your team's will to live? Are your employees so tired of being on-call 24/7 without getting paid overtime they'll bail after their two-year tour of duty? Do you love investing in superficial office perks like ping-pong tables and nap rooms to distract your workforce from asking for real, tangible benefits, like 401(k) matching and health insurance that doesn't suck?

Then you should partner with Seriously Fun!

Seriously Fun is an elite team of play practitioners that hosts onsite and virtual interactive group games and team-building activities. That's right—while you were getting your Harvard MBA so venture capitalists would fund your Airbnb-for-hamsters idea, we're making millions sharing LEGO with twenty-three-year-old tech workers who are racing toward IPOs and major anxiety disorders.

Interested in learning more? Here are a few of our most popular Seriously Fun programs:

Paper Airplane Proletariat: In this real-life reenactment of how startups function, employees take turns as individual contributors folding airplanes without any instructions, then as managers teaching others their clueless techniques. It's a great way to foster leadership skills because no one knows what they're doing, and success is completely arbitrary!

Bridge-Building Bourgeoisie: Our bestselling activity for budding entrepreneurs who want to architect their own destinies. By using household supplies and the kind of big-picture thinking that comes from generational wealth, you too can build a bridge with as much structural integrity as San Francisco's Millennium Tower.

Educational No-Escape Rooms: We can turn your conference rooms into houses of horror featuring the kinds of terrifying challenges Millennial and Gen Z tech workers know well, including "Combating carpal tunnel syndrome" and "Explaining your job to your parents." And with our special BOGO offer, you can receive the soul-crushing entrapment of capitalism—for free!

So the next time your six-figure salaried team gets disgruntled over their meaningless work and the sad truth that they still don't earn enough to buy a Bay Area home, reach out to Seriously Fun by calling us at 1-800-BURNOUT.

We're like Squid Game *for those slowly dying inside!*

"There's plenty of room, everybody. Come in closer and take a seat!"

At nine a.m. sharp the next day, I'm back at Habituall HQ, toward the front of the company's all-hands area where Laura Lackner, vice president of employee experience, is waving her hands to get everyone's attention.

Not one to disobey directions from a client, I'm wishing I had a seat to take, but the room must have been torn apart early this morning in preparation for today's team building. The lunch tables have been folded, the chairs have been stacked, and the sofas have been shoved to the sides, so what's left is a wide-open space that spans half of the floor. Except we're hovering around the edges because we don't know what to do—that is, until Laura and a handful of folks in brightly colored baseball jerseys usher people to the center.

"That's it—we're getting in touch with our inner child today, so please sit crisscross applesauce."

I wait for her to reveal that this instruction is a hilarious joke, but nobody laughs. Instead, over one hundred of San Francisco's best engineers and go-to-market gurus start planting their butts on the carpet. All of the execs, too. Even

Kevin Elmore, vice president of customer success—who, according to my frantic research last night, is pushing sixty years old and recently had a feature in *Harvard Business Review*—is sitting sans cushion like he's attending a kid's summer camp.

Resigned to my fate, I sit down toward the back, putting my double coffee order next to me to reserve some extra space. I'm mentally congratulating myself for wearing pants today when I spot the man I'm determined to win over.

"Evan, I saved a spot for you!"

As he swivels his head toward the sound of my voice, I take in his signature outfit. That too-tight black T-shirt may succeed in showing off his tanned biceps, but those khaki cargo shorts and flip-flops have got to go.

When he recognizes me, his face falls, and if I'm not mistaken, he's cursing under his breath. By now, he's lost this round of musical no-chairs, and the only available slice of carpet is next to me. He begrudgingly sits down when I pick up my drinks, and I flash him my most victorious smile.

"Why, hello, Casey. Who let you back into the building? I'm looking forward to terminating them later today."

I refuse to let Evan rattle me with his insensitive wise-cracks, so instead, I focus on the more intriguing matter at hand.

"You remembered my name this time—looks like I made an impression, after all." I offer him the other coffee cup. "Iced caramel macchiato?"

"I'm intermittent fasting, actually," he replies with a smug smile.

I want to smack this elitist hippie into the sun, but I know how important it is to remain unfazed. Instead, I turn to the guy on my other side and hand the drink off. He lights up at the gesture, and I'm glad at least one person in this place appreciates me.

Evan rolls his eyes. "I've never seen Doug from accounting so happy. It's like you gave him the end to tax season," he mutters.

I beam. "That's the plan—literally sweeten up these lovely folks here, and then you'll never be rid of me."

"Is that how you approach everyone in your life? Your boyfriend must be suffering from a constant sugar crash, if that's the case."

That comment flies out of left field. Is Evan trying to figure out if I'm taken?

"Bold of you to assume I'm straight," I point out, "and disappointing for me that you're right. Most men are as hopeless in the dating department as they are in the department store." I've used all the apps and sifted through my friends' social circles, but try as I might to land a Met Gala–worthy man, my recent dates have come from the bottom of the bargain bin.

Evan scans me from head to toe, but not as if he's sizing me up. After making the mistake yesterday of showing up like an ostentatious #girlboss, I decided to tone it down with a crisp, tailored white blouse tucked into olive linen pants with a paper-bag waist. And considering the boyfriend comment, there's no subtlety in the look he's giving me. Evan's enjoying the view.

"What?" I demand, taking another sip of my coffee.

"You look . . . comfortable," he says, his gaze lingering a little too long, as if he was about to give me an honest compliment, but his fragile ego stopped him. It's not exactly flirting, but I'll consider it a win anyway.

"Thanks!" I wiggle my toes, which are peeking through clear, strappy sandals, showing off my rose gold pedicure. As someone who soaks up the sun like a basking lizard, I always appreciate how mild winters are on the West Coast, and today is particularly warm for February. "A step up from the typical tech uniform, don't you think?"

Evan scans the sea of staff, divided into sales bros in puffy vests over button-downs and sloppy engineers, some in actual pajamas and slippers.

"I'm sure it works in Venice Beach, the Hamptons, or wherever you flew in from, but here we're too busy changing the world to care about clothes."

From what I can glean from our interactions so far, Evan Chen is the kind of asshole who relishes in pissing people off, but I take the bait anyway.

"I'll have you know that I've lived in the Bay since I was sixteen," I hiss. The weight of that statement hits me. Has it really been a decade since I unpacked my suitcases in Alex's guest room? What do I really have to show for those years? I moved here to make Alex the best-dressed person on the planet, but if she's going to be bewitched by her toxic boyfriend with terrible taste, then it's time for me to set out on a new mission.

A loud *shhh!* interrupts my walk down memory lane, followed by something flying across the room and hitting me in the face. Appalled, I pick it up off the floor—a crisp, white paper plane with a scrunched nose where it crash-landed into my forehead. Evan laughs way too hard, and everyone turns around to stare at us.

Then someone clears their throat, and to our right I see Wendy folding another plane. She gestures, pointing two fingers to her eyes and then to Evan—the universal message of, "I'm watching, so make my fucking day, I dare you."

"I love your eagerness for today's activities, Wendy," says Laura, plastering on a fake smile. "Now, let's run through the plan, so we can get started."

She introduces the consulting group assisting us—

branded as 'Seriously Fun' facilitators. If Evan continues to be a pain in my ass, today will be anything but.

"All of you will rotate between three play stations purposely designed to encourage collaboration with your colleagues. We've set up separate zones for each station. The biggest conference rooms in the back will be where you'll build bridges both literally and figuratively to test your teamwork. The rooms on the right are where you'll break into small groups and do some arts and crafts to foster your creativity and storytelling. And here in the all-hands area, we've cleared the space so we can practice giving and receiving feedback by making and throwing paper airplanes. Now who's excited to have some serious fun?"

The crowd claps unenthusiastically while a few managers try to *woo!* it up with their teams.

"Is there a prize for whoever wins?" someone on our left shouts.

"Yeah, Chad, not getting PIP'd for missing your Q4 quota!" another dude sneers, and like on the playground, the room breaks out into exclamations at the supposed sick burn I don't quite understand. But since they're acting like children, I guess the team building is off to a great start.

"Watch it, Darryl," barks a man with aviator sunglasses hanging off the pocket of his dress shirt—John Simmons, the vice president of sales, according to my research. "If your next demo's as shit as your last one, you'll be the one getting PIP'd."

More hoots and hollers from the puffy vests until Laura waves her hands to get everybody back on track and directs them to stand up so the facilitators can break everyone into groups.

"What does getting pipped mean?" I whisper to Evan, not wanting to be out of the loop. He sucks in his breath at me leaning in a bit too close, but he doesn't scoot back either.

Now if I could get my hands on that captivating cologne of his . . .

"It's P-I-P: Performance Improvement Plan. It's basically when a manager gives you thirty days to get your shit together, but it's commonly referred to as Paid Interview Prep because rarely does anyone make it through without getting fired at the end."

"Wow, that's rude to bully employees by joking about stuff like that."

"It's sales, standard boiler room, macho guy stuff. They know what they're getting into when joining a startup. Hey, I wonder what your equivalent of qualifying for a PIP would be—wearing Crocs or white after Labor Day?"

"Har har." I roll my eyes. "More like underestimating your stylist whose time is spent around needles, scissors, and other sharp objects."

"You're not my stylist," he growls, but I smile back, undeterred.

"I know. I'm much bigger than that—I'm the *company's* stylist, responsible for the entire executive team. But you already know that since it was made very clear in yesterday's leadership meeting, isn't that right? So you're getting new clothes whether you like it or not."

I suck my drink dry and throw it over the heads of several people and into a trash can ten feet away. Applause breaks out, and Evan stands there, mouth agape.

"Took roping lessons at an equestrian summer camp," I explain. "I lived in Texas before I moved here. So you better shut that mouth before it catches flies, as my mother would say, and follow me."

"Hell no," he groans, stopping in his tracks. "Team-building activities are meant to distract employees from how much they hate their jobs; they're not for executives who need to get real work done. So if you'll excuse me—"

Before Evan can make a break for it, a blond man in his early forties with unnerving blue eyes slaps him on the shoulder and steers him toward the arts and crafts area.

"EC, my man! Aren't you excited to channel your inner *artiste* and get your creative juices flowing? This is exactly what Habituators need to harness the power of their most innovative ideas and cross the chasm, don't you think?"

"Casey, this is Maxwell Erickson, our new chief operating officer," Evan says, deflecting his question. "He joined us last month, but you already know that if one of the first items on his agenda was hiring you to style the leadership team for First Party."

"Lovely to meet you in person, Mr. Erickson. Glad I can match the face to the voice." I stick out my hand, which he shakes energetically, and I appreciate his ensemble: a quarter-zip navy sweater over a collared shirt and tailored gray chinos. "I'm so excited to partner with you. Although I'm not sure how much help you'll need—you look great."

He brushes off the compliment. "The credit goes to my wife, of course. And just Max, please, we're family here! The pleasure is all ours, Casey. You look positively radiant, so I have no doubt we'll be gracing magazine covers in no time."

It's not just Max's clothes that set him apart from the tech bros; his looks and charm are giving off vibes I associate with entertainment and fashion industry types. As much as I want to maintain the same take-no-shit attitude I've established with Evan, Max has me chatting and laughing as we walk down the hall and enter the conference room labeled Alcatraz.

"Welcome, friends!" says a dude with a red jersey, a nametag that reads Trent, and—no joke—frosted tips, like Guy Fieri ready to throw down in a Little League game. "We've got some chairs open in the back, so take a seat, and we'll get going."

We walk past a bunch of folks admiring the cornucopia of

materials on the long table in front of them: colored pencils, pens, highlighters, and markers; stacks of old magazines; samples of textured fabrics like lace and velvet; jars of buttons and sequins; even some peacock feathers and rose petals strewn across the surface. Whatever is about to happen is my jam; I can already tell.

"Come here, Casey," Max says, pulling out a chair, "and meet the dream team!" He introduces two middle-aged executives: Paul Barry and Natasha Mason, vice presidents of engineering and product, respectively. At first, I took Max's tone as jovial, but it doesn't take long to realize the undercurrent of sarcasm. Because from the way Paul and Natasha are shooting death glares at each other, it's clear the dream team finds working together to be a nightmare.

The fact that Paul and Natasha don't get along isn't shocking, of course, in the grand scheme of things. I've spent many a first date listening to pompous product managers complaining about the engineering team not understanding their roadmaps or aggrieved brogrammers decrying the product team's lack of technical knowledge—each side fighting about what to build and how to build it.

I can only hope Laura and the rest of HR know what they're doing, forcing collaboration between colleagues who can't stomach one another to save their lives. We take our seats between Paul and Natasha, with Habituall's CEO and COO on either side of me. Evan slumps in his chair, already exhausted before the battle even begins.

"Please pass these down, so everyone has a copy," Trent says, sending a stack of documents down each side of the table. "What's printed on these papers is an outline of a person who represents you as a superhero. Right now, they're blank canvases—no clothes, capes, or even genders, because being seriously fun is not about norms or limitations. Your instructions at this station are simple: Imagine yourself as a superhero. Think about the costume you'd wear, the powers you'd have, even a kickass catchphrase if you're so inclined. There are no right or wrong answers. We've got all the supplies you need to help you bring your superhero self to life, so let your imagination run wild. I'll give you twenty minutes, and then we'll go around the room and showcase your works of art."

Determined to get into everyone's good graces with unflappable positivity, I grab handfuls of art supplies and slide them over to our side of the table. "How cool is this? The week I join the Habituall team to redo your wardrobes is the same you're sketching your superhero costumes. Aren't you excited?"

My question isn't directed at anyone specifically, but Max tenderly squeezes my shoulder, mirroring my enthusiasm. "That's the spirit! And not a moment too soon, I'll say." He reaches across me to slap Evan on the back, his hands-on chumminess clearly par for the course. "Remember, EC, we're meeting the board at seven p.m. at that dim sum place I was telling you about. Casey's here to make sure you clean up for once, ha!"

Even if he's masking his resentment, Max laughs as if we're in on the joke. Habituall's mean-spirited camaraderie is disorienting as an outsider, especially one who was raised to believe that if you don't have anything nice to say, you don't say a peep, missy.

Segueing from ribbing to wardrobes, I grab my phone out of my pocket. "Ooh, where are you headed?" I ask him, ready to pull up the restaurant's website and match Evan's outfit to the ambiance.

"Don't bother." Evan holds up his hand in protest, shooting daggers at Max. "State Bird Provisions may serve small bites on carts, but it sure as hell isn't real dim sum." Suddenly aware that people in the room are hanging on his every word, he swallows what I'm guessing was about to be a ruthless rant against overpriced cultural appropriation—the same one I'd heard Tori give when the glam fam made an appearance at the trendy restaurant.

The epitome of chill, Max is unfazed by Evan's animosity. "Hey, call it whatever you want. All I know is the place has a Michelin star, so I can't complain. I'm just glad we were able to fit in the meeting after your class, EC."

I perk up, imagining an executive MBA program or advanced computer science degree. "What kind of class? Something at Stanford?"

"HIIT class, Holbright," he sneers. "The board should feel lucky because it means I'll have to shower beforehand. Otherwise, I'd show up like this."

I open and close my mouth, horrified at the thought of Evan arriving all hot and sweaty to a world-class restaurant, however whitewashed it may be. And yet I'm more aghast to find myself imagining that tight T-shirt sticking to his well-defined pecs . . .

Am I getting turned on by a tech bro who spends more time at the gym than putting consideration into his clothing? Swatting the thought away, I grab a pack of primary-colored markers and hand it to him. "I'm going to pretend you didn't say that."

"I find creating art so relaxing and therapeutic," says Paul, interrupting my inappropriate thoughts. The engineering exec has abandoned his superhero entirely and started filling in the background with trees. "That's why adult coloring books used to be all the rage, right? I like to fall asleep to Bob Ross on Netflix, so I'm going to surround my superhero with a forest because I feel strongest and most like myself when I'm in nature."

"Your passion for Bob Ross makes a lot of sense, Paul." Natasha pulls colored pencils out of their box, one by one, until she finds the color she likes. "Given how many bugs—

excuse me, 'happy little accidents'—came out of the last scrum."

Paul's hand slips, causing him to press down too hard and turn one of his wispy, light gray clouds into a harbinger of thunderstorms. "Yes, well, there wouldn't be any accidents if the product team under-promised and over-delivered on the roadmap instead of the other way around."

Natasha purses her lips but doesn't dignify Paul with a response. She grabs three markers—red, yellow, and green—and holds them out in front of her.

"Casey, what do you think of these colors? Committing to a product roadmap is my superpower, so why not use these to represent the projects that are on track, delayed until they're just right, or blocked by the engineering team?"

Paul butts in before I can give an answer. "Better make her shoes green, Natasha, since what's on track should be the smallest part of the costume—for appropriate scale."

By now, it's not just me who's uncomfortable at this sparring. Other employees are sneaking furtive glances and whispering to their peers.

I'm used to playing the mom role with my friends and usually have no problem ordering adults behaving like kindergarteners to take it outside, but I don't want to cause an even bigger scene.

Instead, I let them squabble and turn to Max, the only exec who's not in dire need of an attitude adjustment as far as I can tell. He exudes major dad energy, spending the session cheering on the employees closest to us while recreating Superman's costume so he has something cool to show his ten-year-old son. I treat the assignment like reconnaissance, asking whether Max's favorite colors are also primary.

"I haven't really thought about it," he muses. "Do you think they'd be flattering on my skin tone?"

Evan observes our conversation with a curious glint in his

eyes. Is Max's interest giving him a change of heart about working with me? Likely not, but I might as well seize the opportunity for a little fashion education.

"It's a question I get a lot, but I'm against the concept of 'flattering' as a whole, especially regarding size or skin color. Style should be about wearing what makes you feel good."

"If that's the case," Evan interrupts, dripping with entitlement, "then why can't I wear whatever I want to First Party? As long as I'm comfortable, who cares what anyone else thinks?"

I try to ignore the eyes on me as Evan celebrates his gotcha moment. "I agree you shouldn't acquiesce to what society deems acceptable based on patriarchal, racist, size-biased bullshit, if you'll pardon my cursing. But feeling good is about more than that—it's about putting your best self forward. While nothing about style should be painful, there is such a thing as being *too* comfortable. Growth happens outside of your comfort zone."

Max enthusiastically taps his marker on the table, and Natasha stretches to give me a high five. "Now that's a mic drop!" she says. "I like her, Evan, so you may need to let me cut your place in line so she can make me over first."

He gestures at her to go right ahead before holding my gaze. "I didn't expect an answer like that from a Southerner. I'm impressed."

"And why is that?" I scoff, steam practically coming out of my ears. I may be in polite company, but I'm no pushover when it comes to people belittling where I was born and raised. "Because you think a woman from Houston is destined to be a Karen? That San Francisco is the only city with a monthly subscription to wokeness? Puh-lease, you are giving the South more reason to condemn you as coastal elites with that kind of cultural gatekeeping."

He grins, and I note the irony. While I'm trying to make a

cape out of trimmed peacock accents, he's relishing every chance to ruffle my feathers.

"I'm from New York, so that's Mr. Bicoastal Elite to you." Unlike the other executives who are making good-faith attempts at crafting, Evan must be determined to create the ugliest, most heinous superhero portrait possible because he's picked the least compatible materials available: cheetah print for a deep V-neck shirt; a puke-green silk tie; red lace leggings underneath black mesh Hammer pants; scraps of denim for a quilted cape; bunched-up cotton balls for slippers; and a tiny sheet of aluminum for a tinfoil hat. Oh god, is he a conspiracy theorist?

Finally, Trent's timer goes off. "Alright, colored pencils down, folks. Let's see the superheroes you've brought to life!"

Everyone goes around the table, showing off their works of legitimate art. Their superheroes are wearing everything from badass leather masks to dazzling disco outfits. Many celebrate with rainbow-colored Pride accessories or flags from their countries of origin. Even Paul and Natasha managed to pause their bickering and finish pieces nice enough to be put on the company fridge.

And the team's superpowers are wholesome and moving, with expressions of passion, hard work, and perseverance. They discuss how they use these powers to protect their loved ones, spread joy to the people around them, and leave this world a little better than when they entered it.

Until it's Evan's turn to be a total asshole.

"Isn't this group so lucky that we get to hear from the one and only Evan Chen?" Trent says with sickeningly sweet deference. "It's a little difficult for us to see in the back, so please stand up and show us your superhero."

Pushing his chair back, Evan slowly stands, holding his art over his crotch as if he got caught with an erection in class. When I meet his glance, I realize he's embarrassed. Everyone shared their earnest insights and vulnerabilities—he'll look like a prick by ridiculing the assignment. So when he lifts up his hideous paper to the wide-eyed concern around the room, I can't help but giggle at his expense.

"Wow," Trent gulps, "That's so . . . unique, Evan. Can you please walk us through the inspiration for your superhero?"

What's he going to say—he's a jerk who tackled this task ironically? From what I can tell in a couple of days, Habituall considers their value of Teamwork a grave matter, so I doubt they would forgive him for being a troll.

Evan clears his throat. "Thank you, Trent. While my costume may seem outlandish to most, every choice was a conscious effort to speak my truth. The cheetah-printed shirt is bringing out the animal within, harnessing its will to survive in the wild. The tie represents my servant leadership to this company, while the red lace and black mesh bottoms remind me to balance my masculine and feminine energies. My denim cape is about the strength of being salt of the earth, and my fuzzy cotton slippers are because who doesn't love being cozy when saving the world?"

He pauses for dramatic effect, lasering in on me. "I've been told style is about putting your best self forward, and my best self doesn't allow anyone to dictate what I'm wearing."

The group chuckles, giving a soft round of applause, and I'm fuming in my seat, pissed he thinks he can get away with playing the part of hippie halfwit. His team may give him a pass for acting like a loon, but I certainly won't.

"And what about the tinfoil hat?" I ask pointedly as Evan moves to sit down, and all heads snap to attention.

He taps his temple knowingly. "As the great Fox Mulder said in *The X-Files*, 'The truth is out there.'"

He sits down smugly as if he's just run a victory lap, and I roll my eyes. *The X-Files* premiered before he was even born. The eccentric founder is a Silicon Valley cliché, and it's infuriating I can't tell if Evan's persona is authentic or affected.

I'm the last one to present, so all I can hope is everyone will be so enamored by my heartfelt art that they'll forget about Evan's nightmare fuel.

I take a deep breath, tapping into the reason why I'm here in the first place. "Evan's right," I begin. "Style is about putting your best self forward. But as much as we say to ourselves that we shouldn't judge books by their covers—or superheroes by their spandex—the harsh reality is first impressions mean everything, especially in our attention-deficit digital age. In a split second, someone has already decided how smart, capable, and talented you are simply by evaluating your outfit."

I swivel my paper around, showcasing my superhero in a gold-sequined pantsuit, peacock-feathered cape, and bright red lipstick and heels.

"My superpower is guaranteeing people see your best self in all its glory. This gold costume isn't about dressing rich or expensive but about being the confident badass you were destined to be. A stylist's job is to make you feel like a million bucks, but word on the street is that Habituall is a soon-to-be unicorn, so my goal at First Party is to make your leaders look like a billion bucks. Wish me luck!"

The room erupts into raucous claps and finger-snaps, and I start to feel the weight of this burden in the pit of my stomach. If Evan keeps blowing me off and acting like an idiot, he's not just letting his investors and executives down, but also everyone on this team who wants their stock options to be worth something after the hours they've toiled, day in and day out.

I can't ever let Evan win if it means everyone around him loses.

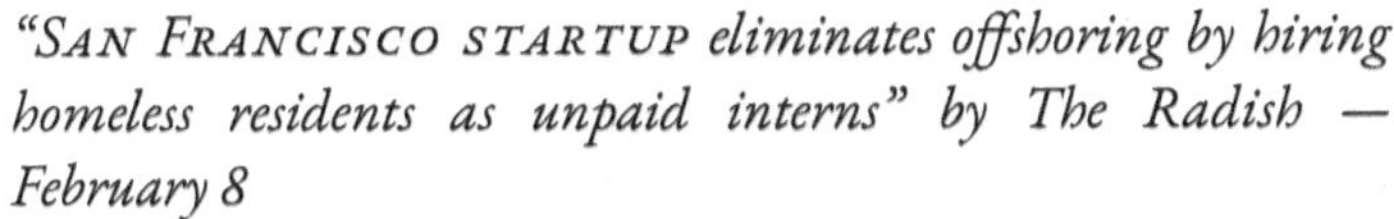

"SAN FRANCISCO STARTUP eliminates offshoring by hiring homeless residents as unpaid interns" by The Radish — February 8

IN A MOVE CELEBRATED by progressives and the alt-right alike, San Francisco technology startup Bubblr announced today that it's putting America first and eliminating its global offshoring practices by hiring the city's estimated eight thousand unhoused residents as unpaid interns.

"After spending an exorbitant amount of money bringing in a consulting firm to analyze our inefficiencies rather than give back to our community, we learned that instead of paying foreigners pennies overseas, we could get the same subpar work done and support our great nation by paying homeless Americans nothing. They're already used to not earning a wage, and we saved 10x on our operational costs, so it's a win-win," said Randy Maladick, founder and CEO of Bubblr.

The sentiment from San Franciscans has been overwhelmingly positive, as seen in the following soundbites we've cherry-picked for this article.

"This move has already improved the character of our neighborhood, and property values are skyrocketing," said Gary Oldman Delacloud, director of NIMBY organization Off My Lawn.

"Technically, we've eradicated unemployment, which is a phenomenal benefit to this city and my upcoming run for reelection," said San Francisco mayor Paris Brand.

"A job gives people dignity. Even though they're working for free, and nothing has changed, just the concept of earning the right to exist offers this underserved population so much hope and purpose," said Barbara Sanderson, a member of California's Democratic Capitalist party.

As for the specific jobs they'll be given, only time will tell. The company's website describes Bubblr as "an inflatable modular technology platform" that allows consumers to immerse themselves in outdoor environments without having the hassle of interacting with anyone else they may encounter. Hailed by TechCrunch as "the Uber for personal space," Bubblr recently raised a $175 million Series A led by Hard-Bank and plans to use the investment to literally roll out its latest prototypes in cities across the Bay Area.

"Ever since the movie *Bubble Boy* premiered nearly twenty-five years ago, I've always dreamed of making that world a reality," continued Maladick. "We're excited for our new interns to accelerate testing of our Bubblr+ edition, which includes a powerized motor in addition to its unparalleled ambulatory technology. They've already been rolling down Lombard Street, and we've only had a few accidents so far, but unpaid interns can't file for worker's compensation, so it's fine. You can't be disruptive without taking risks on others' behalf."

Notably, the environmental impact of this hiring initiative cannot be denied.

The San Francisco chapter of the Environmental Pandering Agency issued a statement that read, in part, "The fact that we can now see—but not smell—the homeless is already making a significant difference. Bubblr is literally changing the climate for the better in real time, and we thank their team for their contribution to society."

I've only been at Habituall for two days, but I can't let another sun set without making some sort of progress. So after completing the team-building activities and grabbing catered lunch from their fully stocked kitchen, I set off to San Francisco's Union Square. It's not my usual stomping grounds, but since I'm already in the city, it'll be a nice change of pace.

Naturally, I have direct lines to personal shoppers from every luxury retailer, but as much as I would love to treat myself to high tea at The Rotunda after doing major damage at Neiman Marcus, it won't be that kind of haul. Lola already suffered sticker shock when my retainer expanded from styling one executive to nine, so when she handed me a corporate card to borrow, I swore to keep the cost of the clothes themselves within a reasonable budget. I consider it more of a challenge: It's easy to look good when the sky's the limit, but only stylists worth their salt can make Banana Republic shine as bright as Balenciaga.

So instead, I march across Market Street, making sure to look both ways lest I be knocked over by one of those ridiculous Bubblr balls terrorizing the city, and head into the mall.

I haven't spent enough time with Evan to understand his preferences, but at least I have his measurements. All his gym rat clothes—save for his bicep-hugging black T-shirts—deserve to be burned to a crisp, so anything I pick out will be a massive improvement.

Powered by plenty of caffeine and the sheer determination to knock this assignment out of the park, the afternoon flies by. When I perk my head up to check my watch, it's seven p.m. and most of the stores are closing.

My tiny apartment already has so many designer samples and brand PR packages packed to the brim, it's more like a retail warehouse with none of the appropriate square footage. I'd like to avoid bringing these purchases home and adding to the chaos, so I call Lola to see if she's in the office to take them off my hands.

"Sorry, Casey, I had to get home to feed my fur babies," she says, "but Tania should be able to let you in. She's always burning the midnight oil. I'll give her a heads-up you're on the way!"

I extend my gratitude and hang up, marching back to Habituall headquarters. I haven't met this Tania, but each executive assistant has to juggle three VPs, so I wouldn't be surprised if she's one of them if she's holding down the fort this late.

When I exit the elevator and knock on the glass entrance to Habituall's lobby, a woman, I'm guessing in her early thirties, unlocks the door. She's wearing a monochromatic black outfit, from her Habituall puffy vest and long-sleeve tee down to her jeans, socks, and Allbirds sneakers. The EA team must be run ragged if she's got her mousy brown hair pulled tight into a ponytail and not a smidge of makeup on her face. But I have to remember not to judge because a woman this secure in her appearance isn't clamoring for help from a stylist.

"Hi, are you Tania?"

She smiles, putting on a friendly face despite her obvious fatigue. "Yes, Tania Beecher. I'm the director of brand and content marketing. Lola told me you were dropping by. Are you a new hire? I haven't seen you around the office yet."

I've heard job titles are inflated in the tech industry, but I would've never guessed by Tania's wardrobe that she was the director of an entire marketing department. Kicking myself for making a snap judgment, I walk through the entrance, hoisting the haul over my shoulder as she leads me to the supply closet. "I'm a stylist, actually," I say, gesturing to the clothes as I find a safe place to put them. "I was brought on to make over Evan Chen, but the contract snowballed to include the rest of the execs, so I've got my work cut out for me."

Suddenly, Tania's demeanor changes, brightening up like I told her she won the lottery.

"Fuck yes!" She fist-pumps the air so enthusiastically I have to jump back to avoid taking a hit on the chin. "I am hella stoked to have you on board. Super pumped, seriously."

"Wow, thank you. I wish every client could be bursting with this much excitement to work with me, to be honest."

After properly storing the clothes for safekeeping, Tania steers me into the kitchen to show off the wall of snacks, and I pretend I wasn't already given a welcome tour of the shelves upon shelves of treasures in clear, plastic jars.

"If *I'm* being honest"—Tania helps herself to some cheese crackers, peering around the corner to ensure we're not overheard even though there's no one else in the office at this hour — "this is a long time coming. I've been recommending ways for us to level up our brand—executive coaching, media training, the whole shebang—so it's nice the leadership team finally took one of my suggestions to heart."

Now that's news to me. After meeting Lola, who looked like she walked right out of Paris Fashion Week, I assumed she was the brains behind the beauty upgrade idea.

"I'm surprised you didn't interview me then." I grab a handful of yogurt-covered pretzels and pop one into my mouth. "It would have been great to get feedback from someone on Max's team."

Tania glances down at her shoes, deflated like a balloon with the air let out of it.

"Ah, it's no big deal. Max's so busy, as you know. He doesn't have time for all his direct reports. I'm lucky to get thirty minutes with him every two weeks, but Lola has daily standups, working lunches, and Max on speed dial. I usually float my ideas by her so she can run them up the chain."

My heart breaks a little. You'd think from the way Tania's talking that she's some lowly entry-level worker, but she and Lola are peers reporting to the same manager. The superficial side of me wonders whether Max gravitates toward ultra-feminine women, and Tania's got the tech uniform so locked in that she fades into the background . . . but again, I can't go making assumptions based on appearances. Sure, Tania doesn't fit the description of most PR professionals I've met—especially Alex's mother, who's dressed to the nines at all times—but that doesn't mean she doesn't kick as much ass.

"Anyway," Tania segues, moving on to the kettle popcorn as quickly as she's shifting the conversation, "how's it going so far?"

I might not work in marketing, but as someone who also cares deeply about putting a positive spin on things, I hold back a grimace. It's my first week, and I don't want to admit my working relationship with Evan is already rocky—especially to an employee who reports to the man who hired me.

"It's been an . . . interesting start," I hedge. "We're working out some of the kinks, but what startup doesn't have growing pains, right? Not like I need to remind you, of course."

Tania chuckles in solidarity, a dark, hollow sound that indicates she's seen some shit. "You have no idea. I joined

Habituall four years ago as the very first marketing hire. If my preteen legs had the same growing pains this company does, they would have snapped in half."

I'm startled by the imagery, clamoring to find the silver lining. "But Lola mentioned Habituall's on track to becoming a unicorn this year. So that must be exciting!"

Tania bobs her head into a half-nod, half-shrug. "Sure, it means we're a hair's breadth away from achieving a billion-dollar valuation, which would be thrilling if the hair on my thirty-one-year-old head wasn't rapidly turning gray because of it." She points matter-of-factly at the thick, white streak through her ponytail. I don't condone the tech industry's bad habit of burning out young overachievers, but I have to admire a woman with a presumably sizable salary throwing up a middle finger at beauty maintenance and spending her dollars on anything other than root touch-ups every four to six weeks—even if I treat my monthly salon appointment with Glen as sacred.

I'm about to compliment her fuck-it attitude, but she's already drilling deeper. "So what's it been like working with Evan? I'm so intrigued to hear how he's handling this style transformation."

I have yet to see Evan handle anything without an undercurrent of hostility, and I can't help but take it personally.

"He's been good. Super smart!" I chirp, my voice an octave higher than it should be. "I haven't had a chance to spend much time with him, to be honest, but a CEO can't be bogged down with shopping details when there are a billion dollars at stake, as you said." I jerk my head in the direction of the supply closet. "But I picked out a ton of potential outfits at the mall today, and I'm sure he's going to love them."

Tania raises an eyebrow, as if she knows exactly how challenging it is to work with Evan. With such a long tenure at the company, I don't why I thought I'd be able to pull a fast one on her.

I sigh, my upbeat façade fracturing into a million pieces. I guess the jig is up. "Okay, fine. It's going terribly, alright? Every farm animal I've ever met is less stubborn than Evan Chen."

She laughs, not out of patronizing pity but real empathy. Here I was afraid she was going to rat me out to the higher-ups, but in a short time, we've found common ground. And bonding over a mutual frustration is immensely more satisfying than sharing a superficial hobby.

Tania reaches into the fridge and pops a bottle of sparkling rosé, as if celebrating the fact that we've moved beyond pleasantries and have connected on a deeper level of commiseration. This time, there are no conspiratorial looks down the hall to see if anyone disapproves of our after-hours drinking. I've heard about the laid-back culture of startups, but part of me wonders if grinding with a wine glass in one hand is just another Tuesday for Tania. Not so much letting loose as distracting yourself from the loneliness.

I'm glad I can keep Tania company tonight, regaling her at one of the round cafeteria tables with my less-than-ideal introduction to Evan. She's the consummate conversation partner, listening intently and laughing at my jokes as we sip our bubbly, until she plays devil's advocate—the devil being Evan, of course.

"Don't get me wrong," she says, "it's validating to hear from someone else that it's not easy working with EC. Try coordinating press interviews for a CEO who can't be trusted to show up without a stain on his shirt. But then I remind myself Evan founded Habituall when he was twenty-three, the age most newly minted college grads spend partying away their paychecks. Startup founders are usually deeply flawed, way more than the average person, from what I can tell. And why wouldn't they be? Their growth is stunted because building a billion-dollar company requires investing every waking moment into the mission."

Before Evan's drive-by comments about my designer shoes and bag, I would have said the only deeply flawed thing about him is his piss-poor fashion sense. But now I'm not so sure—he may know more about style than he lets on, and I have no idea why.

"So what's your advice for me, then?" I ask her, gulping down the last of my wine.

She pauses to gather her thoughts. "I know I sound like I have Stockholm syndrome, but don't give up on Evan just yet. He'll get on your every nerve, but he's whip-smart and his passion for our platform is unparalleled. That's how he's skated by looking like a skater guy. Nobody would have believed in a dude in sleeveless shirts if the product he brought to life didn't sell itself. That's not hyperbolic—Habituall's software gets a bad rap for making it easier for marketers to get their promotions into your inbox, but I am a marketer and trust me, the second I join another company, I'm taking it with me. It's *that* good." She considers what she's said. "That's probably why I'm still here after my stock options have fully vested. I'd die if I had to go back to using Marketo or Pardot again."

She senses she's lost me with her musings on marketing automation platforms. "My point is, I know it sucks you and Evan aren't seeing eye to eye, but he'll come around in time. Great minds think alike, and if he's getting under your skin this badly after two days, that means you're on track. He'll eventually admit you were right all along, but not after you drag him, kicking and screaming."

I frown, my optimism splitting right down the seams. "If Evan was a clueless engineer who didn't know how to pick out pants with a reasonable number of pockets, I could work with that. But some of the things he's said make me think there's something off about him, and I can't put my finger on it. It's like he knows precisely how to dress like a *GQ* cover model, but he chooses not to. It's infuriating."

"Hmmm . . ." Tania ponders, twirling the curls of her ponytail. "If there's anything EC is known for, it's digging his heels in for the hell of it. But it's impossible to dispute real results. You need to get him in one of your finest outfits—once he sees how good you make him look, he'll have to concede."

I stare at her, dubious. The pieces hanging in the storage closet are exceptional, I'll give myself that, but I'm not a magician, conjuring acquiescence out of thin air. "But he doesn't trust me to try on a hat I pick out, let alone a whole ensemble. How the hell am I going to convince him to do anything? You've worked with him for years, and you're a PR pro. He'd be much more willing to listen to you than me."

Tania shakes her head fervently. "I wouldn't go that far. Now Max, on the other hand, I bet he could convince anyone of anything. When he joined, it's like the whole company sighed with relief. I keep saying he's the adult in the room. He dresses well, speaks eloquently, and has the charm we need to woo Wall Street investors and Fortune 500 customers. If anyone had a shot at persuading the brain of the company, I would place my bets on the new face of it."

She gets up from the table to wash our wine glasses and put them away. "You know, we've been so busy prepping for First Party that we haven't formally announced Max as our COO. What if we put together a photo shoot for them both? Two high-powered men running the next unicorn, suited up like the bosses they are—what news outlet could resist an exclusive like that?"

Tania tilts her head like the idea she's proposed is so good it surprises herself. After witnessing Evan's animosity toward Max during our team-building today, I'm less convinced he'll clean up his act for his COO, even if it gets them into the *New York Times*. But I'm desperate for Evan's style journey to reach its destination, so I'll take all the help I can get.

We brainstorm the logistics, and after I explain how I can supply my own equipment and run point as photographer thanks to years of training as Alex's right-hand hype woman, Tania is off to the races. She pulls out her phone and makes a call. "Lola, I'm with Casey, and we need you to clear Max's calendar tomorrow. It's urgent business."

I can hear several tiny dogs yipping incessantly in the background, so I'm not surprised when Lola runs through a list of reasons why she can't shuffle around their boss's schedule: It's late, he's meeting some important clients, and face-time with enterprise execs is hard to come by.

But on speaker phone, Tania and I go on the offensive to break down her resistance point by point. The marketing director name-drops the heavy hitters on the press list she'll pitch Max to—Emily Chang from *Bloomberg*, Nilay Patel from the *Verge*—which is an effective appeal to the COO's ego, but we need an offer she can't refuse.

Based on the chief of staff's penchant for wearing heels to headquarters—in a city known for its steep hills, no less—my guess is Lola cares more about a chic wardrobe than a front-page story. "Lola, please hear me out," I plead. "I've got a pair of next season's Bottega Veneta pumps with your name on it if you can make this photo shoot happen." I don't mention that the designer shoes are in my possession because Alex is no longer interested in taking my style suggestions, but neither Lola nor the brand's influencer marketing team need to know that.

"Okay," she relents. "I can give you a half day, but it has to be first thing in the morning. His lunch meeting is nonnegotiable."

After we nail down the logistics and hang up, I thank

Tania profusely in a flood of gratitude. "To do this for someone you've just met, you are the literal best. I mean it."

She gives me a hug before escorting me back to the lobby. "You're doing us a favor, Casey, not the other way around. Habituall's IPO is at stake, so we've got a lot on the line. I'm not physically flexible in the slightest, but I would bend over backward to get EC to look as competent on the outside as he is on the inside."

Tania's right. If Evan Chen doesn't start dressing like a real leader, then Habituall won't be taken seriously. As she's shown me tonight with her quick thinking, when it comes to Silicon Valley startups, unicorns aren't born; they're made. And it's my job to give this regular old horse some fancy accessories—no matter what its founder throws my way.

So bring on the sparkles and glitter and rainbows and magic. It's unicorn time.

~

TRANSCRIPT OF EPISODE 1,882 of the Bo Logan Podcast: *"The Supermodel Minority" — February 9*

WHAT UP, jerks! It's your boy, Bo Logan of the *Bo Logan Podcast*. It's a legit, beautiful day today—the sun is shining, the bulletproof coffee is flowing, and the haters are hating. We're about one week into the Chinese New Year, Lunar New Year, or whatever it's called where you live, which has got me thinking about the Chinese zodiac. Now I don't know much about Asian astrology, but if I had to pick, I'd say tigers are the best sign. You guys be hella simping for dragons, but they aren't real, so they don't count. But tigers are savage, man. Tigers are one of the most powerful apex predators out there, and they don't take shit from nobody. Sounds like somebody I know!

Side note—Discovery Channel, where is Tiger Week, amiright? Sharks are fucking rad, too, but tigers? I would pay to stream a whole week of tigers low-key murdering people in the jungle. One hundred percent, I'd be down to get high and watch some tiger murder. So get on that, Discovery, and have your people call my people because I would plug the shit out of Tiger Week.

My point is, you gotta channel your inner tiger and be the savage beast you were born to be. Check out our 'New Year, New Tiger' flash sale going on at Bo Logan dot com, slash merch, to get up to fifty percent off all my holistic Eastern supplements and remedies. Get your mind clear, your body jacked, and your dick hard using ancient, natural ingredients that the FDA and Big Pharma don't want you to know about. Use the promo code TIGER to save big on your next order.

Alright, enough about tigers. That's not all China—CHY-NUH, hashtag throwback—has to offer. Our special guest today is none other than Olympic snowboarder and mega-babe Erica Wu. Born and raised here in San Francisco, Erica stirred up some major controversy by choosing to compete for China in the last Winter Olympics, so I invited her to the studio to share her honest thoughts on sports, culture, and patriotism. Is she a product of the American Dream or a traitor to her country?

All I know is she's an absolute smoke show, and if you're watching this live on our channel, we've pulled up some fire pics of Erica from the latest issue of *Sports Illustrated*. Fuck-able of the highest order, and I can say that because she turned eighteen last year, so she's totally legal. Don't come at me, you feminist killjoys. You wish you could look this good. Mmm, damn, so hot. Okay, down boy. Up next is my interview with Erica, after this short break from our sponsors . . .

It's so satisfying to watch Evan cycle through emotions when he exits the elevator where we're waiting to ambush him in the Habituall lobby the next morning. He's too busy taking in a debonair-looking Max and the team surrounding him—Tania, Lola, Wendy, and all three executive assistants—that he doesn't notice me off to the side.

I'm not offended since I did my best to appear as inconspicuous as possible: my long hair tied up into a loose bun, signature red lips swapped for clear gloss, and keeping it business casual with a loose-fitting white blouse and a pair of tailored black cigarette pants.

Max, on the other hand, is soaking up the attention like a sponge. For all of Lola's pushback about the photo shoot, he doesn't seem to mind adjusting his schedule if it puts him in the spotlight. In the midst of meeting with me this morning about his shoot wardrobe, he easily juggled competing priorities, debating the details of the press pitch with Tania and dictating action items to Lola while the assistants answered his emails and kept him caffeinated.

He exudes the confidence you'd expect from a C-suite executive, thanks to the winning number I curated. I've got

Max looking slick in cool, blue-gray trousers on bottom and a crisp, white dress shirt and navy blazer on top. It's not like he couldn't have picked out these pieces without my help. They're not particularly unique, exclusive, or expensive, but professional tailoring and attention to detail can make all the difference.

By the way our founder's tugging at his distressed basketball jersey, Evan is abundantly aware of that difference. He and Max are about the same height, but dressed like a former NBA player down on his luck, Evan doesn't have the same stature.

Max waves off the assistant powdering his nose. "Thanks for gracing us with your presence, EC," he jokes, slapping him on the back with a tad too much force. The COO isn't good at hiding his irritation, and a pang of guilt hits me even as I stifle a chuckle. I don't like wasting time as much as the next person, but I also know we needed to catch Evan by surprise in order for this plan to work. Given a heads-up, he probably would have filed a restraining order to keep me from entering the office.

Tania speaks up, playing her part perfectly. "Evan, did you not get the memo I sent?" she says aghast, knowing full well the memo is nonexistent. "This photo shoot is a big deal. Not only are we formally announcing Max joining the company, but we'll also be pitching you to every top-tier media outlet. The *Forbes* 30 Under 30 is coming up, and we are way overdue on getting a quality headshot of you." She gives him a once-over. "I should add you're eligible for the enterprise technology category, not sports, no matter how hard you try looking the part."

Oh snap. Evan looks down, mortified, at his basketball shorts and a pair of high-tops so grimy I can't tell their original color. I want to double over laughing at the fact that someone other than myself is calling him out to his face, but I don't dare move a muscle to avoid breaking the spell and directing Evan's attention to my presence.

Laura Lackner, the VP of employee experience, walks behind the front desk to grab a couple of water bottles from the mini fridge, which is reserved for guests. And when Evan Chen sees an opportunity to avoid his public-facing responsibilities, he takes it.

"Hey, Laura!" He waves her over. "Isn't our diversity and inclusion agency coming in today?"

She lights up, as if this is the first time Evan's ever taken an interest in HR. "Yes, they'll be here any minute now. Will you be joining us?"

Tania doesn't miss a beat, cutting in before Evan can weasel his way out of the photo shoot. "Perfect timing, actually. We're walking over to Chinatown so we can get a head start on pitching Evan for Asian Pacific American Heritage Month. I know it's February, but May will be here before we know it, and reporters need to finalize their features well in advance. You and the team can come with us to craft our AAPI-specific pitch while we're on location."

I have to hand it to Tania. She can spin anything at the drop of a hat, making a one-mile trip sound like we're shooting a blockbuster film. And it works: Laura asks one of the EAs to enable her out-of-office autoresponder, eliminating Evan's last-ditch attempt to bow out.

"That sounds great," he says, buckling under the pressure. "It's just that I, uh, don't have a change of clothes at the moment."

Tania and I exchange a victorious look. "That's why Casey's here," she says, and I take a step forward, waving at Evan with one hand while holding up the garment bags I brought in yesterday with the other.

I brace myself against his fury, wondering if he's going to kick me out, regardless of what the crowd in the lobby thinks.

I'm taken aback, however, when all I see from Evan's expression is appreciation. He's dressed like a hooligan, but he can tell I'm here to save the day, to make him look competent in front of his C-suite and staff. As much as I want to give him the juicy 'I told you so' he deserves, I settle for a businesslike nod. "Let's walk you through the options I've brought and get you changed."

It pains me to hold back, but the 'I told you so' can wait.

A SHORT WHILE LATER, after we've successfully rallied the troops and taken care of Evan's hideous attire, we make the ten-minute walk to the corner of Bush and Grant where Dragon Gate, the entrance to Chinatown, awaits. Between the spontaneous addition of the HR crew and Max's natural ability to monopolize as many administrative staff as he can pull into his orbit, we've got a bigger crowd than I anticipated. Max will love the audience; Evan might not.

But whenever something goes sideways, I take stock of the good, the bad, and the ugly—because what white girl from Texas doesn't have a dad obsessed with Clint Eastwood?

The good: I did a damn good job styling Evan, and he knows it.

The bad: I might have done *too* good a job because I can't stop sneaking glances at him when I think he's not looking. And he often is.

The ugly: If I keep checking him out, not only will I get sidetracked from finishing the photo shoot on time, but it will also be harder to deny that I'm . . . attracted to him?

Oh lord, I put one nice outfit on him, and it's all going to hell in a handbasket.

Getting him into this outfit has done wonders for Evan's attitude, more so than his appearance. He may not care about my expert opinion, but at least he'll comply to avoid letting down his team. Not once did he argue as I made him try on different options, and now he's downright gorgeous in the winning selection. Both men are wearing similar white dress shirts, but whereas Max's styling is more traditional, I've chosen to give Evan an edgier look, with a black leather jacket with gold accents, slim-fit slacks, and a skinny tie in deep purple to cascade over his rippling abs . . .

Okay, that's enough, missy, I can hear my mother admonish. Close that mouth of yours before you catch flies.

I do my best to admire my handiwork without ogling, and it helps that Max and Evan complement each other so well: the seasoned executive and the eccentric founder, the moderate and the troublemaker, mister 'been around the block' and the rebel without a cause.

After taking some test photos at the gate to check positioning and lighting, I place Evan and Max exactly where and how I want them while Tania engages the others in a conversation about what the team should read for the company's business book club next month.

"What would you recommend, Evan?" she asks as I take my place behind the tripod. "What books have been helpful as you've scaled Habituall?"

"Uh . . . I guess I'd have to say *Dare to Lead*."

"You read Brené Brown?" I exclaim, distracted from snapping away. The surprises keep coming today. First, he looks better than I ever expected, and now he's capable of picking up a book on vulnerability?

"Why do you sound so impressed?" Evan retorts. "I saw her on Netflix one day and got intrigued. You know, you're not the only blonde woman from Texas who gets it right occasionally."

Here I was fascinated for a moment, but that jibe breaks the spell. For the next shot, I walk over to make a few adjustments, cinching Max's belt a tad tighter to get the fit just right, before moving on to his photo shoot partner.

I direct Evan to take off his leather jacket and toss it nonchalantly over his shoulder, but it looks awkward on camera, so I decide to switch it up.

"Let's try it without the jacket this time and roll up your sleeves." I take a cuff of his dress shirt between my fingers and start slowly sliding it up his toned forearms. Everything about this interaction feels too intimate—I'm standing so close to him, I can catch the amber and citrus notes from that addictive cologne lingering on his chest—but each square inch of skin I reveal pulls me in like a moth to a flame.

Yet again, I try sneaking a glance, but the moment I look up, he's staring back at me with a level of intensity that's in no way professional.

"What's the last book you read, Holbright?" Evan smirks. "Let me guess—were you disappointed by *Fifty Shades of Grey* because you thought it was about color swatches?"

If he wants to fuck with me, two can play that game. I roll his other sleeve, grazing my nails across his arms, which prickle with goosebumps. "No, but I did pick up a few tech industry favorites to prepare for this gig, and I happened to enjoy that Horowitz book every founder goes nuts for . . . the one with the strangely sexual title? What was it called again?"

The heat builds between us as Evan croaks out the answer. "It was titled *The Hard Thing . . . About Hard Things*."

"That's it! I had a feeling you would know what I'm talking about." I glance down at his strained slacks before giving him a shit-eating grin. "Did I not get the right pant size? They look awfully . . . tight."

I'll admit that was a bit over the top. It was worth it to see Evan blush for the first time, but I need to focus on what I was hired to do. I've got six figures on the line with this contract, and now that I can't count on styling Alex, every dollar counts. Evan's the key to proving I'm not a one-trick pony, that I can support myself outside of my innermost circle.

Nothing brings me back down to earth like the fear of paying my bills, so I spend the rest of the session keeping my distance, instead catering to Max's whims on which remaining poses he'd like to capture. The spotlight naturally follows him wherever he goes, but outside the office is where the COO's personality truly dazzles. As I undo one button on his collar, it's like he literally loosens up, cracking jokes and making everyone feel lucky they got to escape their cubicle this morning.

When I'm confident we've got the winning shot at Dragon Gate, I turn the camera around so Max can take a peek. "Holy smokes! Who is that supermodel?" he enthuses as I show off the images. "If this doesn't land me on the cover of *Fast Company*, I don't know what will. Thank you, Casey, for coordinating this shoot. Once the word gets out, every leader in this city will be begging you to take them to the next level."

To emphasize his point, he places his hand on the small of my back, and I tense up, surprised. It's a platonic gesture as far as I can tell, an old-school attempt to build rapport. But when I catch Evan's expression, it's clear he disagrees. The move is way too close for comfort, and it bothers him. A lot.

At first I assumed I wouldn't get Evan to commit to being styled if I kept provoking him. But what if he commits precisely *because* I'm provoking him? If how quickly his pants stirred at the slightest touch is any indicator, he's into me, so I might as well use that to my advantage. Nothing like a little harmless jealousy to get a man to do—and wear—whatever I want.

"Every *smart* leader in this city, anyway," I reply with a pointed glance at Evan, insinuating that the CEO doesn't qualify as long as he ignores my guidance.

Pitting Evan against Max pays off when the latter is

dragged off by Lola to get to his lunch meeting. With the competition out of the way, Evan steps up to the plate, proposing to take a few more photos at the nearby park in St. Mary's Square. As overjoyed as I am to have an opportunity to get Evan to open up, if I don't find a way to ditch everyone else, especially Laura Lackner and her lackeys, I'll be sent home empty-handed.

Being mindful of the time we have left, we pack our equipment and make our way up Grant Avenue. I hang back with Tania and Wendy as the group marches forward. "Hey, Evan's looking pretty stiff in the photos," I say conspiratorially to the ladies, channeling all my willpower not to laugh at the double entendre. "I think he'd be more relaxed without everyone watching. Could you both keep the team entertained while I finish the job?"

"You mean HR's killing the vibe? Imagine that," Wendy deadpans. We stop in front of a tea house across from the park. There's a big red sign that reads BOGO BOBA and a line that snakes down the block. "We could use an intermission anyway. Go on ahead—we got this."

"Alright folks, it's boba break time!" She makes a big commotion and corrals the others toward the end of the line. "Laura, you've never had their Hong Kong milk tea? That's an abomination, and I will not stand for it. No, this can't wait another second. Don't worry, Tania will work with the DEI agency on the AAPI pitch while Casey and Evan get everything set up at the next site. What are you talking about? The line's not that long. Come on, trust me, it will be worth it, I'm telling you—"

I grab the tripod with one hand and Evan's arm with the other, dragging him through the intersection and into St. Mary's Square lest we get derailed any further.

"Hey! What about me?" I look back at Evan, who's pointing at the tea house, and chuckle. One minute we're locking eyes over rolled-up sleeves, and the next he's afraid of missing out on a delicious beverage.

"I thought you were intermittent fasting?" I say innocently, recalling how he refused my coffee offer yesterday.

We stop in front of a large ginkgo tree. Other than a few folks off in the distance practicing tai chi, the park is fortunately quiet and empty—because everyone is in line for boba.

Evan refuses to acknowledge that I caught him in a lie, instead walking up to a plaque nearby. I pause behind him to read the inscription.

WE SALUTE THESE AMERICANS OF CHINESE ANCESTRY WHO GAVE THEIR LIVES FOR AMERICA IN WORLD WARS I AND II.

"There are ninety names," Evan says quietly. "I used to come here to meditate and count them."

We stand at the memorial in a moment of silence, and I feel like dirt. I came to a sacred place, not some tourist trap that's only good for snapping photos for the 'gram. People must travel far and wide to pay their respects here. Especially when there's no equivalent where I live, a fact that suddenly sticks out like a sore thumb.

"Why aren't there more Chinatowns in the South Bay?" I wonder out loud. "San Jose has a tiny Japantown, but that's about it."

Evan raises an eyebrow. "San Jose had five Chinatowns during the Gold Rush. All of them were burned down or demolished. Immigrants had to build tunnels to get home from work because they were banned from walking down the street after dark. The Bay Area likes to present itself as progressive, but anti-Asian hate runs deep, ever since our ancestors arrived here."

I let out a long, anguished exhale, horrified by white America's actions but even more by my ability to put my foot in my mouth. I could blame my ignorance on my Southern roots, but I've lived on the West Coast for a decade and never bothered to learn its history.

"I'm sorry." Awash with shame, I wish I had the right words to express myself, but a meek apology is all I can muster.

"You should be." He stares heatedly at me, my mouth agape, then waves his hands in frustration. "Jeez, I'm not talking about San Jose—I've got plenty of opportunities to school your white ass, but not if you're too busy fawning over Max."

"What the hell are you talking about? Max and I are friendly, but nothing more. I'm honestly insulted you'd think otherwise."

Evan takes a step closer. "I saw the way he leaned in and touched you." His voice is angry, but there's an undercurrent of sadness, like he knows he shouldn't be hurt but he can't stop it from seeping through.

"Max is the one who hired me, so he's practically my boss —and one who's almost twenty years older than me, might I add. There is *nothing* romantic going on between us. I'm just trying to do my job," I insist, trying to sound earnest instead of exasperated. I was going for low-stakes simmering jealousy, not the kind of high-heat possessiveness that makes a pot boil over.

Evan crosses his arms. "Is that why you're parading him in my face—to show me what a real leader is supposed to look like?"

"Well, if you're going to put it like that—yes! Tania was so overjoyed by how great Max's photos turned out that she's convinced Kara Swisher will want to interview him. And do you know why?"

I don't bother giving him a chance to answer. My mother would be horrified to hear that I'm arguing with anyone out in the open, let alone a client, but Evan's got me so fired up I can't help it.

"Because he *listens*. And that's what's so frustrating! Unlike most hapless straight dudes, you already know what you're doing. Your colleagues may be oblivious, Evan, but I'm not. You knew every designer I was wearing the first day we met. I have no idea how, but I'll get to the bottom of that, trust me. You know how to dress well—really well—but for some ridiculous reason, you're being a dipshit and choosing not to. And as much as I like to think I can work miracles, I can lead a jackass to fashion, but I can't make him like it."

My bastardized proverb takes him off guard, because instead of matching my indignity, he falters and breaks into a smile.

"Dipshit and jackass, wow." He puts on a ludicrous drawl and pretends to clutch his chest. "I didn't think a proper Southern belle such as yourself could utter such profane language. What's next—you're going to call me a douchebag?"

"I'm quite fond of the word chode, actually."

He laughs hard at that, and the way his eyes scrunch makes my heart do a backflip. For a minute, we appreciate the peace of not tearing each other's heads off. The group nearby stops gawking and resumes their tai chi, and if it weren't for the camera equipment, we could be mistaken for two well-dressed tourists enjoying a day of sightseeing in San Francisco.

"I'm sorry for behaving like a chode," Evan says, placing his hands on my shoulders. Like the wardrobe adjustment earlier, it's undeniably intimate, and I bask under the warmth radiating from his palms.

"And I'm sorry for making you feel like the second-in-command. You could be my number-one client if you stopped making such a fuss and enjoyed having me around."

He leans in closer. "Who said I don't enjoy having you around?"

My breath hitches in my throat. If we were anywhere else, I'd let his hands linger on my shoulders, his thumbs lightly brushing the delicate skin near the collar of my shirt. But Evan's a client, and we're technically at work. With Habituall keeping my career from careening over a cliff, I can't be doing anything I'd come to regret.

I force myself to step back and reestablish my personal space—just in time, too, as I catch Wendy and Tania out of the corner of my eye, walking toward us, alone.

"Where is everybody?" I'm grateful for fewer onlookers to potentially catch Evan and I acting inappropriately, but the plan was to shoot in multiple Chinatown locations. "HR wouldn't get off our backs all morning, and now they disappear?"

Tania shrugs. "We weren't seeing eye to eye with the DEI agency about the direction of our AAPI pitch, so we decided it would be best to craft it ourselves."

"Why?" I ask, concerned. "Were they worried about tokenization?"

Tania exchanges a look with Wendy, as if she doesn't want to be the one to deliver any further explanation. The head of workplace strategy rolls her eyes. "No, they started going off on some bullshit, questioning if it was a good idea having EC do an AAPI photo shoot in the first place. They had the audacity to declare that he, quote, doesn't present as Asian, end quote."

"What the actual fuck?" Evan shouts. "I'm half Chinese!"

Wendy holds her hands out, distancing herself from being killed as the messenger. "That's what I said! Don't get me started on white women telling me how to champion diversity. So I said if they're going to ignore how our founder identifies because he's multiracial, then we were done here. Grabbed their boba out of their ignorant hands and told them to get lost."

She lifts up the to-go bag and hands us each a drink, which Evan guzzles with a vengeance. When he sucks his drink dry and tosses the empty cup into a nearby trash can, I consider offering to intervene with Laura to rectify the situation. Shoot, I'm tempted to give him a giant bear hug so he knows that despite our bickering, I'm on his side, but that could make things worse. Evan's a grown man who must deal with discrimination on the daily. I don't need to be his savior, especially if the only ways I can think of supporting him involve proving to him I'm one of the good ones.

With the photo shoot abruptly wrapped, Wendy and Evan take the lead on lunch plans, debating which restaurant has the best Peking duck until they land on the winner, R & G Lounge. At first, I fret about being an outsider since I'm no expert on either Chinese cuisine or the trials and tribulations of working in tech. But as I told Evan at yesterday's arts and crafts, growth happens outside of your comfort zone. Sitting with a little discomfort—like when I first paired stripes with polka dots—can be a good thing.

Thankfully, conversation flows easily, and as we finish lunch and head back to headquarters, I feel lighter, grateful to know Evan as his own person and not just as Habituall's quirky founder. Evan hangs back at the entrance while Wendy and Tania take the elevator up, and I appreciate having another moment of privacy before I make my way home.

"Other than HR butting into our business, today went better than I thought it would. It feels good to be on the same page for once." I nudge Evan's elbow with mine, still cautious of any colleagues who might be entering and exiting the building.

He tilts his head. "And what page would that be, exactly?"

"You agreeing to be styled, of course!"

Evan snorts. "You assumed because I don't hate having you around that I'm suddenly on board with giving up my athleisure?"

"W-why wouldn't you accept my help?" I stutter,

distressed that the progress I thought we made might be circling right down the drain. "If you don't, then there's no point in me being here!"

For the sake of my own financial stability, I want to dive into a diatribe about his company's obligations to our contract, but I don't want to lose him this time. Even though the silence is tortuous, I refuse to relent.

"Fine." Evan sighs, throwing his hands up in the air. "I will allow you to make a few tweaks to my wardrobe for First Party. I'm not saying I'll like any of it, but I will tolerate it for your sake. However, I have one condition."

His steely tone brings my happy dance to a screeching halt. "What is it?" I ask, not sure if I want to hear the answer—which works out since he refuses to tell me.

"If you want me to follow your rules," Evan says, "then you're going to have to follow mine. And that means proving yourself to be a team player. You in, Holbright?"

Well, when he puts it like that, I guess I am.

~

"12 THINGS BAY AREA Zoomers Would Rather Do Than Pay for Therapy" by FuzzBead – February 11

WE GET IT—ADULTING is *hard*. How are you supposed to heal your inner child when your twenty-something self is being slowly crushed to death by student loan payments and a full-blown housing crisis?

Sure, you could talk through your existential anxiety with a licensed clinical social worker . . . *or* you could try one of these fun activities just to feel something.

Come on, it's for the ~ *experience* ~

1. **Ax throwing**. It's like hunting, but for liberals—
    just as primal, but without any of the (satisfying)
    carnage.
2. **Oyster shucking**. If almost slicing your hand
    open to eat Bodega Bay boogers is "living off the
    land," then Hog Island is cottagecore on steroids.
3. **Cedar baths**. Who among us hasn't spent $250 to
    sit in some hot, fermented mulch because the
    website touted the benefits of "unique synergy"
    and "spiritual elation"?
4. **Indoor mini golf**. You aren't truly living the
    single life until you've nursed a beer for ninety
    minutes on a first date at Urban Putt. I don't
    make the rules.
5. **Day drinking**. Oh, so when the man with holes
    in his socks does it in the Tenderloin, it's tragic,
    but when Amanda from marketing does it in the
    Marina, it's classy?
6. **Sound baths**. You haven't attended a church
    service since Easter circa 2009, but you won't miss
    out on bringing your yoga mat to Grace Cathedral
    for some auditory healing.
7. **Meat sweats**. Chinese hot pot, Japanese shabu-
    shabu, Brazilian steakhouses—whatever your
    preference and price point, there's no tapping out
    until you have to be rolled out of the restaurant.
8. **Competitive races**. You're not at all qualified to
    run a marathon, so you'll dress up like a sexy
    bumblebee for Bay to Breakers instead.
9. **Float tanks**. If sensory deprivation worked for
    Eleven to enter the Upside Down on *Stranger
    Things*, then it's good enough for you.
10. **Flea markets**. You absolutely do not need another
    succulent, but there's something about haggling

with the plant lady at Treasure Island that makes you feel alive.

11. **Rage rooms**. You can't take a sledgehammer to your sales manager's face for assigning you a shitty territory, so you'll settle for Hulk-smashing old office equipment.

12. **Museums after dark**. Sometimes you want to take an edible and wander around the Exploratorium while tripping balls without tripping over any children. Fuck them kids.

chapter
six

"Are you kidding me right now?"

It's eight a.m., and I'm standing outside the Habituall office, more perturbed than I ever was inside of it. One of the executive assistants stares at me blankly, seemingly not put out by my irritated tone. She must be used to taking the heat for the leadership team's tiny annoyances. But this is straight-up ridiculous.

"I'm not, ma'am. Evan decided to drive himself to the offsite."

Here I thought we had come to a truce in Chinatown two days ago, but Evan has to go and be a jerk for no reason. I suck down the last of my iced coffee and toss it above a group of Habituators into a trash can six feet away. So now, on top of Evan not being here like he said he would be, he's also missed another kickass shot of mine. Why have this useless skill if CEO b-boy isn't here to appreciate it?

"First off, you seem like a great person, but I'm not that much older than you, so you can cool it on the 'ma'am' thing. It's just Casey. And second, when exactly did Evan send you that update?"

She dutifully checks her phone. "Hmm, 7:14, so almost an

hour ago. He texted, 'Change of plans: I'm taking my car. See you there.' Why, what's the problem?"

The problem is that little shit waited until I was already up to my ears in Bay Area traffic and never sent me the memo. The problem is that I live in fucking *Palo Alto*, which is not that far away from Half Moon Bay, so why the hell would I suffer through the weekday morning commute to drive an hour north to the city, only to turn my ass back around and ride for another hour south?

I was willing to make the trek when I thought it would give me a chance to connect with Evan. But now I'll be crammed into the kind of musty charter bus I haven't had to endure since my sixth-grade field trip to the Houston Space Center, and Evan's nowhere in sight.

But I don't bother telling his assistant this because it's not her fault her boss is an inconsiderate turd. Like I tell myself it's not the customer support rep's fault that my cable company is price-gouging me, that my bank charged me an unnecessary fee, or that health insurance when you're self-employed is a goddamn joke in this country.

I take a deep, slow breath, determined not to spiral into being a negative Nancy. "No problem, it's fine. I get to ride the bus with the team—it'll be fun!" It won't be because I'm only on my first coffee of the day, but I don't dare run off to the nearest café because I have no idea if this bus has a restroom, and I'm not about to find out.

The assistant walks off hurriedly, looking for anyone who's not as grouchy as me, leaving me on the sidewalk to continue stewing until we make our departure.

Evan made a big fuss about me being a team player, but that's pretty hypocritical when he couldn't be bothered to tell me whatever's on the agenda today. Since I'm not an official employee, I don't receive companywide communications, so I have to rely on Habituall's overworked staff for the most basic of information. All I was told was to meet outside the office at eight a.m. and once again dress "comfortably," which is about as useless a dress code as "country club casual" or "Brooklyn formal."

I decided to go with a safe option: a light camisole under a cream cashmere sweater, high-waisted, wide-leg jeans, and ballet flats. Comfortable, yes, but also cute and professional. And because I don't know if we'll be indoors or outdoors, I brought along a large tote with sunglasses and a hat, just in case.

Employees continue to emerge from the building to board the bus, but I haven't seen any of the executives—not even Laura, who you would think would accompany the team because she's in HR. It's her responsibility to make sure everyone behaves themselves.

"Hey, Casey! Are you looking for someone?"

I turn around to see Tania, who's broken away from the other marketers after a round of team selfies. My mood lifts, comforted by her company-sponsored ensemble. I have zero interest wearing head-to-toe swag emblazoned with Habituall logos, but after Evan's abrupt itinerary update, I'm grateful for some predictability by at least one person here.

"I was wondering where the leadership team was . . . they're coming to the offsite, right?"

She laughs darkly. "Against their will, yes. They can't be bothered being among the plebs for too long, so they coordinated their own transportation."

I tap my foot in impatience and envy, wishing I had a heads-up so I could have done the same. "That's a shame. It's rare that the entire organization is in one place, and I was hoping to use the ride down to chat through wardrobe options and learn more about what makes each executive tick."

The marketing director brightens, an expression I'm all

too familiar with when I'm excited to be of service. "I can help!" she chirps, already unzipping her backpack and shuffling through a series of folders. "I'm no fashionista, obviously, but I'm fluent in the C-suite. I did a round of mock interviews with the execs recently, and I've got a *lot* of thoughts about where you could be of the most assistance . . ."

BY THE TIME the bus rolls to a stop, I'm struggling to absorb all of the information Tania has divulged. We sat in the back, and she pulled out all the receipts—going bullet point by bullet point on the execs, from their filler words and speech patterns to their pet peeves and favorite conversation topics. After these detailed dissections, I'm no longer surprised Tania has been rapidly promoted through the ranks.

The only problem is that Tania saved the best for last, and before we could get to Evan, the drive was over. I can't stand being in traffic for one minute longer than I have to be, but I was ready to demand we make circles until I could get the lowdown on EC, as the Habituators call him.

So now I still know very little about Evan and way, way too much about everyone else. Just my luck.

"I'm so excited for this offsite," Tania says as we exit the bus and follow the rest of the team to our meeting spot. "This has been on my Bay Area bucket list for years."

I expect to see, you know, a bay in Half Moon Bay, but we're not even close to the coastline. Instead, all I see is a long dirt road lined with bales of hay and a barn off in the distance.

"What exactly are we doing today?"

Tania's eyes bug out. "You didn't get the memo? We're doing goat yoga!"

No. No, no, no, *no*. "Whose idea was this?"

"I don't know, but it will be a blast. I promise."

Someone nudges me in the arm, startling me so bad I almost karate-chop them in the neck.

"Whoa there, Holbright. Save those extensions for the session, will ya?"

My nostrils flare, taking in the sight of Evan embodying his quintessential yogi persona in a black, V-neck tank top and Golden State Warriors basketball shorts in team gold and blue.

"Heed your own advice, EC," I spit, failing to ignore his tanned biceps. "How a CEO gets away with showing that much armpit hair is beyond me."

Evan laughs, wrapping his arm around my shoulders and rubbing my cashmere sweater between his fingertips. "Mmm, EC," he whispers into my ear. "I like the way that sounds coming from your mouth. You sound like you're a real Habituator now."

I aggressively shrug him off. It's bad enough my brain has our most intimate moments on replay: knees almost touching in the zen room, inching his sleeves up his forearms, nearly kissing in St. Mary's Square. I don't need to get caught up imagining his fingers dancing around the rest of my body. Thank goodness we're pulling up the rear because I'd hate for anyone to mistake us for acting inappropriately—or worse, *chummy.*

"Let's get one thing straight, Evan: you are my client, not my boss, and I am not your employee. Although I must admit that would have made it easier for me to learn today's itinerary. Thanks for informing me, by the way. Real classy."

He smirks, enjoying my fashion faux pas. "It's supposed to be an abnormally warm day for early February. I must say I love watching you sweat."

"And when the hell are we going to get any work done?"

I accidentally bump into somebody, and everyone glares back at me.

Whoops. I said that last part a little too loudly, and now

I'm getting dirty looks like I'm some Goody Two-shoes who complained to the teacher that the class wasn't given enough homework.

"Casey's got a point, Evan. Not sure who planned this offsite, but the beginning of the fiscal quarter isn't exactly the ideal time," says Natasha, who's flanked by the rest of the leadership team. Did I miss their arrival, or do they have secret teleportation superpowers?

"If you'll remember, Natasha," Laura interjects, "my team conducted a survey, and this was the day that worked best for the majority of the office."

"Yeah, Nats, don't be such a wet blanket," says John Simmons, who I think I remember is the vice president of sales—not to be confused with John Gibson, an almost identical older white man who is chief financial officer. He pulls out a flask from his jacket and takes a hearty swig. "The beginning of the quarter's certainly better than the end, amiright?"

Yep, definitely sales.

"Tell that to the teams who still have to be on-call," says Kevin Elmore, the VP of customer success, pointing at the employees who have already planted themselves on nearby picnic tables and pulled out their laptops. Does this farm have Wi-Fi?

"Let's look on the bright side!" says Max, ready to escort middle schoolers through a busy intersection in a neon orange baseball hat and matching jersey. "We've got the whole team together in the same place for once. Even Drew descended from his cabin to join us."

A burly mountain man with a bushy, snow-white beard waves his hand from the back of the group. He's the only executive I haven't met yet, meaning he must be the chief information security officer that Tania told me lives in the Santa Cruz redwoods.

Laura gasps. "Drew, did you seriously bring Bigfoot with you?"

For a split second, I expect to be confronted by the dangerous mythical creature until I see Drew's holding a long leash—though at first I can't see what's at the end of it. Tracing the leash up the tree closest to us, I spot a baby leopard stalking a small flock of birds perched on the branches.

Oh, wait. Not a baby leopard, phew. Just an impressively sized Bengal cat, as if that's a completely normal pet to bring to a company gathering.

"He has separation anxiety! I couldn't leave him at home. He'd wreak havoc on my house plants and try to attack the fish in my aquarium."

"And what makes you think he'd be more well-behaved on a farm . . . full of other animals?" asks CFO John, the one everyone refers to by his surname Gibson.

Drew waves off the concern as if it's nonsense. "He's fine around livestock. As long as his companions are larger than he is, they'll be best friends."

A bird squawks angrily, and we jerk our heads up to see it narrowly escape Bigfoot's clutches. Uh-huh, let's hope Drew's right on that one because otherwise, HR has its work cut out for it. Pretty sure Habituall's employee agreement doesn't address cat murder.

"That's enough," Evan says, and I perk up, remembering he's still here. Because even though the execs are dressed casually, he looks more like a personal trainer than the figurehead of Habituall. "The team's being rounded up, so let's get started. Drew, keep both eyes on Bigfoot at all times. That's an order."

Drew gives him an enthusiastic salute, tugging the cat down from the tree. "You got it, boss!"

We follow everyone into the barn, and my shoulders

slump. Because if you googled 'barn,' the stock photo you'd find is exactly what this place looks like. Fire-engine red, white trim, strewn with hay—fine for goats but impractical for yoga.

And I don't say this to insult either Californians or Old MacDonald barns. Even though my family never owned or operated a farm, we lived on a ranch-like estate of several acres in the country outside of Houston. My brothers and I learned the fundamentals of horseback riding and often badgered our parents for the occasional chicken or rabbit. And most of my friends were in 4H or FFA, so I'm used to being around live-stock, and the idea of getting my zen on among grimy, grunting animals boggles my mind. The farmers around me never even bothered to name their animals, because they learned from a very young age that you don't humanize crea-tures meant for consumption. While I wasn't that detached, I was also never one to integrate the great outdoors with my fitness regimen. I love goats and yoga, but they're by no means peanut butter and jelly. As my mom would say, not on god's green earth do those two things go together.

That's what kills me the most—I can't vocalize this without sounding like the Valley girl everyone thinks I am. Anyone who sees me in my cream fucking cashmere sweater isn't going to think I know anything about farms; they're going to think I'm a Hollywood diva smelling fertilizer for the first time. The curse of being a Southern girl in West Coast packaging.

"Welcome to the Painted Goat!" booms a weathered but cheery man in his sixties, next to a similarly aged woman in athleisure, cradling a baby goat in her arms.

"I'm Dave, and this is my wife, Margot. After thirty years working in corporate America, we escaped the grind and opened this farm to get back to nature. For the past decade, we've been operating it full time, and while our pumpkin patch and Christmas tree farm are big hits during the holidays, by far everyone's favorite attraction is our goat yoga. People from around the world visit us to disconnect from the stresses of life and achieve the greatest form of nirvana with our bleating buddies here. We've got mats for everyone, and Margot will run through our ground rules . . ."

I zone out, not needing to hear the finer details of farm life. The barn's not large enough for the whole team to have stretching room, so I'm hoping they'll split us up into smaller groups. Especially considering how stuffy it is in here. Beads of sweat are rolling down my sides, and I'm regretting not dressing in something breezier. I turn my head toward Evan, and he catches my eye, dramatically pulling at his collar.

"Feeling hot yet, Holbright?" he pants at me, rubbing it in. I can only imagine how pathetic I look, a layer of sheen on my forehead and my wavy hair frizzing in the humidity.

Ignoring his teasing, I try to channel a meditative state. Sit with the discomfort, Casey. You can do this. Don't let him get to you.

"Alright, those are the rules," Margot concludes. "Does anyone have any questions before we break you up into groups? We've got plenty of activities for everyone—hayrides, a corn maze, even bumper tractors!"

A timid engineer raises his hand. "Do the goats bite?"

Margot chuckles, setting her kid down to bounce around her ankles. "Unless you stick your fingers in their mouths, you should be fine. They may nibble on your shoelaces, though, so watch your feet as you move through the flow."

"What about the poop?" another employee yells from the back, to the giggles of everyone around him.

"It happens," admits Margot with a shrug, "but goats poop out small pellets, so it's not messy at all. Shake off your mat and keep it moving. Okay, one more question, and then we'll get a move on. Yes, you in the braids?"

I look over where Margot is pointing, and oof, it's not the

braids that stick out but those horrific baby bangs that give feminists a bad name. Makes me want to dial up Glen for a hair intervention, stat.

"Doesn't this count as animal cruelty to keep them around for our amusement?"

I shake my head at the ignorance of Baby Bangs' question. Girl, clearly you haven't ordered dinner directly from a butcher if you can't see the only cruelty happening right now is two inches above your eyebrows.

Margot addresses the accusation with much more tact than I ever would. "Of course not. Our yoga classes are not a mandatory performance for them, and we keep the barn door open, so they're free to come and go as they please. And we don't encourage anyone to force our animals to stand on your back, do tricks, or take selfies. But goats are naturally friendly and genuinely like being around people, so don't be afraid to shower them with affection."

I'm too overheated to suffer through the particular brand of Bay Area entitlement that's itching to be offended on another's behalf. My feet are slip-sliding around in my ballet flats, and I have to stretch my arms out to avoid losing my balance and taking a tumble. Ugh, why did I decide to forgo socks in these things?

I hear Evan stifling a laugh behind me, and I glare, daring him to say something. But he has no shame holding my gaze, which only makes my cheeks hotter.

Fuck it. I'll give him something to stare at.

Even though I want to rip off my sweater as desperately as Carrie Bradshaw wanted to get out of that wedding dress during her panic attack at the bridal shop with Miranda, I force myself to slowly peel it over my head like I'm giving Evan a private burlesque show. And instead of gasping with relief once it's no longer smothering my body, I sigh and shake my hair for good measure.

That's right, assface. I'm not wearing a bra.

Evan blinks and runs his hand frustratedly through his hair. In any other circumstance, I would be mortified to strip down to a camisole with the thinnest of linings to support my chest—especially at a work function—but I can't spend another second broiling from the inside out.

Plus, it's Evan's time to sweat, and I plan on payback.

"Okay, let's hit the mats! Everybody to my left can stay here for the first session, and everybody to my right can follow Dave out of the barn and enjoy the rest of the grounds. Meet back in an hour, and we'll break for lunch."

I purposely select the mat in front of Evan to torture him with the view of my glorious behind. Under the guise of a warmup stretch, I bend at the waist and give a good shake. Evan breaks out into a coughing fit, so I dig into my tote in front of me.

"Thirsty, EC?" I hold out my water bottle not-so-innocently. I can't help myself, squeezing a suggestive squirt into my open mouth.

It's difficult to decipher the emotions on Evan's face, but his eyebrows are furrowed and he's biting his lip, so I'm guessing it's a blend of anger, frustration, and lust. It's such a good look I'm tempted to douse myself with water and give him a real show.

No, you're at a corporate event, remember? You can't go full wet T-shirt contest and expect anyone to take you seriously.

But as we move from downward dog to cobra to pigeon, I realize that even better than turning the tease dial up to eleven is this battle between desire and willpower. It feels like the whole world falls away, and it's just the two of us.

We spend an unknowable number of minutes following each other through the yoga positions, eyes locked like we're at some Regency ball sharing our first dance. The air, already hot, feels electric as I'm entranced by the hills and valleys of his muscles, stretching and straining throughout the flow. I've seen Evan in athletic wear this entire week, but today I can't be offended because he's dressed appropriately for the occasion. Instead of being annoyed, I can admire what he's working with, which is quite a lot as far as I can tell . . .

"Ow! What the—" Something's pulling on my hair. That's when I notice a brown and white speckled baby goat chewing on my blonde strands like they're a delicious bunch of hay.

"You little shit," I hiss, breaking out of my wide-legged forward fold. I consider swatting the kid away with my hand, but its teeny hooves and clueless, sideways eyes thaw my heart. How can you get mad at a face that cute?

I overhear chuckling behind me, and when I turn around, of course, Evan is enjoying my unexpected confrontation. That's when the eerie similarity hits me—he drives me nuts, but I let him push my buttons when he looks like that.

Is that how he gets away with everything?

~

"How to Craft the Perfect Name for Your Software Product" by Adventure Capitalist – February 11

IF YOU'RE an entrepreneur who thought naming your startup was hard, then you clearly offer only one product. That's like naming only one baby—pretty easy when you've been obsessed with calling your firstborn "Noah" for as long as folks have known about the ark, but a lot more challenging when you've got a quiver full of people or a suite full of SaaS to manage.

You don't want to end up like Elon Musk desperately

trying to rebrand everything he comes into contact with as X, so heed our advice on how to come up with a name your customers won't be embarrassed to say out loud.

1. *Embrace the weird.* Let's face it. An entire human generation has passed since the advent of the modern computer, and all the easy names have been taken. Apple could get away with adding "i" in front of words and calling it a day, but you'll need to put in more of an effort. The quirkier the better, so power through the cringe. If we can use "Google" as a verb with a straight face, anything is possible.

2. *Double-check yourself before you wreck yourself.* You may have the most ideal string of letters imaginable, but all bets are off once acronyms enter the chat. Calling yourself the Krazy Koupon Kween isn't as fun when potential customers are asking for discounts on pointed hats.

3. *Consult your team before they risk losing their minds.* You may think matters of capitalization, punctuation, and plurals aren't that important in the moment, but trust us, your SEO will be fucked if your first search result includes "one word or two?" Think we're overreacting? Go ask the employees at AirBNB / AirBnB / AirB&B / Air BNB / Airbnb and see what they say.

My frustration with Evan, sexual and otherwise, gnaws at me until the goat yoga class ends and it's time to eat. After getting a few snuggles in with our new furry farm friends, we thank our instructor and exit the barn to grab lunch at the picnic tables. There's already a long line as the other half of the team must have wrapped up their activities early.

I hover around Evan, holding my sweater up to my chest to avoid getting nipply in front of his colleagues until the breeze cools me down enough to put it back on. People engage him in small talk, genuinely enjoying his company rather than trying to butt-kiss. It's heartening to see. As grumpy as he can be with me, it's obvious how much he cares about his team. I'm a bit jealous, to be honest.

But then he finds ways to loop me into conversations, introducing me to every employee and highlighting all the amazing work they do. At first, it felt like I was Evan's shadow, but after hitting it off with so many folks, it's starting to feel more like he's mine. My shadow, that is, despite how nicely a ring *mine* may have in the more definitive sense. How tantalizing we'd be attached at the hip, or maybe further south . . .

"Hey, Casey." Max startles me from my shameless fantasies, nudging my elbow as we reach the utensils station and grab our sustainable bamboo flatware. "I'm thinking you can help us with something while you're here."

The buffet line splits down the long stretch where the picnic tables have been pushed together, and Evan lifts his head toward me, curious at the exchange. Folks are grabbing items from identical trays of artisanal, mostly plant-based deli sandwiches, bags of 'healthy' chips that are just regular chips with hipster packaging, and bottled tea and kombucha. Having worked in fashion, I'm used to dealing with people's BS diets, but there's something about being on a so-called farm that makes me crave some good, ol' fashioned Texan barbecue. Oh well.

"Sure, is it about your attire for First Party? Because I've been bookmarking some options that could work."

"No, it's not a clothing-specific question," Max hedges, "but I figured with your experience, you would be someone worth consulting on this fashion analogy we're using with the product we'll be announcing at the event."

By now, we've filled our plates and make our way over to the table where the rest of the leadership team is eating. It's not until we take our seats on the picnic bench, Max motioning to the others to scoot over, that I realize I've made a grave mistake—sitting between Paul and Natasha. Evan's smug on the opposite side, gloating at the predicament I've found myself in.

Is it more common for executives to congregate than to socialize with their respective teams? I find it strange how everyone in business is always talking about 'having a seat at the table,' when it's clear there's no room for anyone new when the table is already full of people who don't even like each other.

Considering I'm getting paid to do yoga with goats, I

might as well settle in because there's not much else I can do about it.

"So what's this analogy?" I ask Max, careful to keep my body language open to the entire group. "I can't imagine software having any similarities to fashion, but you've got me intrigued."

Paul snaps his head in Natasha's direction, even though Max was the one who initiated the conversation. "Did you bubble this up again?" he accuses her. "I thought we settled this weeks ago."

With a thorny topic rising to the surface, the remaining execs caught in the crossfire start finding excuses to jump tables or be anywhere else. Kevin Elmore goes to check in with his on-call team, and the Johns light up a couple of cigars for a smoke break around the grounds. I look around for Laura, but she's nowhere to be seen, so there's no one to play HR referee in case things get out of hand.

So the remaining witnesses to Paul and Natasha's bickering are me, Max, Evan—who must be enjoying his front-row seat to this shitshow—and Drew, who's absent-mindedly feeding tiny pieces of sandwich crust to Bigfoot, sitting next to him on the bench.

But I'm used to being the mom friend in the glam fam, at least up until Alex detonated a bomb in our group's dynamics. I'm plenty experienced stomping out petty squabbles, so I'm determined to make Max proud and be the fashion tape that holds the Habituall leadership team together, if that's what it takes.

"I'm happy to weigh in." I take a sip of iced tea, regretting that I forgot to refill my stash of Sweet N' Low in my bag. Fitting, I guess, that I don't have any sugar to make this corporate medicine go down.

"It's a ridiculous matter, and there's no reason you need to be involved," Paul says. "It wouldn't make much sense to you anyway."

"Try her," Evan butts in, sterner than he's been all day. I thought he was pissed when I was taunting him with my ass in his face, but this is a different kind of anger entirely.

"EC's right," Max agrees gravely. "If you can't explain the benefits of our metadata store to Casey, then I don't know how you'll manage during the keynote with hundreds of marketers, reporters, and other non-technical folks."

Paul sighs, sitting in silence until he accepts that Evan and Max are aligned for once, both refusing to change their minds. I want to tell him not to bother if he's so put out, but watching Evan dig in his heels with someone besides myself is hot as hell, so I follow suit.

"Alright, then . . . um, Casey, what do you know about metadata?"

Can't say I've ever given the subject much thought, but there's a time for everything. "It's data about data, right? Like when you right-click on a file and select 'Get Info.'"

Paul nods. "Yes, that's definitely part of it. When we work with consumer brands to personalize their marketing communications—email, text messages, push notifications, and the like—we can store the metadata on their products for them, so it's easier and faster to recommend items to their customers. We're calling this metadata store Collections."

"Collection," Natasha interrupts, "singular."

"It's plural because you can create multiple Collections!" Paul rubs his eyes with his palms. Out of the corner of my eye, I catch Evan smiling. How many times will Paul double down on this argument until he spontaneously combusts?

"So what's this product have to do with fashion?" I ask, hoping to get him back on track so we can end this bizarre conversation and get back to shooting the shit on whatever blockbuster movie everyone's watching.

"Fashion collections inherently have metadata," Paul says. "When you're shopping online, what info do you typically use to filter your search?"

"Hmm." I ponder the question, considering how to frame my answer in a way that will satisfy the C-suite. "There are so many factors. First, whether the item is available and, if needed, ready for pickup at the nearest location. Then the basics like size, color, and occasion. And depending on the client, I narrow further by specific brands or preferences like neckline, sleeve, or hem length. Make-or-break decisions might come down to average rating and the quality of the reviews."

"Exactly," Natasha says. "Those criteria are metadata, so each product can have dozens of unique data points. Multiply that by every single SKU—every item with a bar code, that is —and you can imagine the mountain of data that a major retailer stores. The personalized recommendations you could deliver to an individual consumer's inbox are endless."

Paul isn't enthused. "But the problem is that the engineering team has no way to include all of that data in a single collection. It's not possible on the backend, and it's not even sensible for a customer's marketing or merchandizing teams. So it's deceptive to use the singular in this instance."

"So this entire debate is whether the product's name should have an 's' at the end of it?" I ask less-than-innocently, a smile trying its hardest to tug at the corner of my lips. Evan's expression matches mine, but I understand why Max is taking this matter seriously. The dynamic between Paul and Natasha is downright comical in isolation but can potentially torpedo the company's productivity—and profits. How can anyone get any work done when so many billable hours are being wasted on an issue of semantics?

"Well . . . yes," Natasha concedes. "That's why we wanted your thoughts, Casey. You're the expert. How many collections you must have styled, after all!" She's going for flattery, that's obvious, but the joke's on her because it won't work on me.

"That's correct," says Paul, agreeing with her against his every instinct. "I bet that number is more than one, right, Casey?"

He can try to build rapport, but I'm not taking his side either. And the faster I rip off that bandage, the better.

"I think you're both wrong."

Okay, I could have dulled the sharpness of that verbal dagger. But while it's gratifying to watch their faces fall at neither coming out on top, it's more thrilling to watch Evan and Max's approval in the background.

"What do you mean?" Natasha asks, munching nervously on a veggie chip.

"You keep talking about online shopping, but what's the first thing you think of when you hear the word 'collection'? I think about the Southern antiques my mom hoards, like she is waiting for her home to be randomly featured on the cover of *Country Living* magazine. 'Collection' may adequately describe what you're selling, but it's not exactly innovative. And isn't that what Habituall is supposed to be as a tech company? Cutting-edge, bleeding-edge, and all the other phrases that seem more at home on a Hot Topic sweatshirt?"

Whoops, that last part slipped out, but Evan spits out his drink, coughing up his amusement, so I take that as a win. Even Drew has paused his attempts to get Bigfoot to stop stalking birds around the picnic table, so he can listen in on our conversation.

Paul harrumphs. "First Party is six weeks away, so it's not like we can go back to the drawing board now. Removing an 's' is one thing, but a brand-new name would change the whole concept."

"I hate to agree with him, but he's right." Natasha looks disappointed, as if she can't decide who's the lesser of two evils in this situation. "We're full speed ahead on the user interface and already partnering with the marketing team on the launch campaign."

"What other names do you have in mind?" Drew asks me with the same curiosity Bigfoot is showing a roly-poly he's batting around in the grass.

Paul sighs, cutting me off as I'm about to share my ideas. "Look, Casey, I'm sure you're great at your job. Those options you sent over for the product keynote are fantastic. But we're creating software not outfits here, so forgive me if I'm not in the mood to entertain suggestions in the eleventh hour."

Ouch, okay then. I try to get back to my lunch, but unsurprisingly, I no longer have an appetite. It's nothing I, or any other woman, hasn't heard before. Stay in your lane, ladies. Be seen but not heard. Here's a twenty—go to the makeup counter and buy yourself something nice while Daddy's on the phone, sweetheart. That last one was a bit specific, I know. No matter how much I love my father, it was hard not to take his brush-offs as personal whenever my mom needed to run an important errand or catch up on work on the weekends, leaving him on 'babysitting duty'—gross.

"Sounds like this must be everyone's first product launch," Evan says slowly, glaring at Paul, "if you think six weeks counts as the eleventh hour. I've seen your engineering team produce more lines of code in a single sprint than most do in an entire quarter. And weren't you tweaking your demo for last year's conference the night before? In fact, if holding to that rigid attitude is how you're showing up as a leader, then I bet any alternative name Casey comes up with will be infinitely better than Collections, regardless of whether it's singular or plural. Do you disagree?"

The way Paul is white-knuckling the edge of the table makes it clear he very much does, but it's also clear Evan's question is rhetorical. If a CEO asks for your opinion like that, he's not making room for healthy debate—he's giving you rope to hang yourself. Paul may have a couple of decades on Evan, but that means he knows when to back down.

Paul sighs, admitting defeat. "What other names do you have in mind, Casey?" He repeats Drew's question through gritted teeth.

I consider the best possible options, trying not to let Paul's reluctance get the best of me. "I understand why you'd want to appeal to retailers using terms related to fashion, but if this product's going to be used as a recommendation engine, then there's no industry that does personalization better than streaming. Designers and brands are artists in their own right, so how about Playlists instead of Collections? Habituall can collect that metadata so your customers can curate trending items, giving each shopper the equivalent of an on-demand Billboard Hot 100. You could even use a tagline like, 'Introducing Habituall Playlists: Personalized Experiences. Just Press Play.'"

The execs' eyebrows raise simultaneously, Max and Natasha's with delight and Paul's with surprise. It's not a perfect suggestion, of course, but watching Paul reevaluate his first impression of me gets me grinning. And when Evan locks eyes with a twinkle of pride, I feel like a hit song rising meteorically to the top of the charts.

"Great, Playlists it is. Glad that's decided," Evan says without a hint of irony around his unilateral decision. "Thanks, Casey, for weighing in on this. I'm sure Paul and Natasha can take it from here. Now, if you'll excuse me—"

"Wait—what? Hey, Evan, hold up . . ." By the time I can pull my legs around the picnic bench and grab my things, he's thrown the last of his lunch into the trash and walked off. I toss my tote bag over my shoulder and mall-walk as quickly as possible without looking like I'm chasing him, but I can't keep up with his long, muscular legs.

"Evan, stop!"

"I'm going to meditate." He doesn't stop or turn around, but once we reach a wooded area, he slows down as the trees get denser and the sun gets more obscured.

"Bullshit. There's not enough room to meditate out here. Can you stop for a second and talk to me—ow!"

Evan pushes a branch out of the way, which snaps back and whips me in the face, scratching my cheek. To his credit, Evan immediately ends his goose chase to check on my well-being. He leans in to evaluate the damage, tracing the abrasion, which fortunately isn't bleeding. He's standing so close I can feel his breath on my skin, and I have a feeling my cheeks are red for a different reason.

"Always getting into trouble, eh, Holbright?"

"Always getting *me* into trouble, you mean. Why the hell would you leave your product's name up to me? As if I didn't have enough work to do, now your team will curse my existence."

His mouth contorts into something resembling half a smile, half a frown. "It's nothing to stress about, which was the point I was trying to make when I told Max to loop you in. That trivial argument had been going on way too long. It's embarrassing. You contributed more in ten minutes than they did in two years."

As tickled pink as I am that Evan pulled Max's strings to request my guidance, I'm not reassured it was the best move. "I threw out the first thing I could think of on the spot. Evan, I coordinate outfits for a living—I've never even bothered to give a formal name to my business. It's Casey Holbright LLC!"

"Stop it. Do you get that you're treating yourself like Paul treated you?"

Realization slowly sinks in. Well, shit.

"I shut Paul up because I couldn't stand the thought of

him discounting you, but it's even worse when you discount yourself. The only person who should enjoy giving you a hard time should be me."

Flattered by his territorial side, I smile meekly, but he powers through before I can provide a rebuttal.

"I'm sorry we got off on the wrong foot, but you're not 'just' a stylist. My company hired you, so you have every right to be a part of this team and throw your weight around. Paul, Natasha, and the rest of them do it all the time, and now that I've seen you in action, Casey, I know you're not any less smart or talented than them. In fact, none of them have ever called bullshit whenever I left to meditate, so for that reason alone, you're already running circles around them."

I look down at my ballet flats, all scuffed up and dirty. While it should feel fantastic that someone outside the glam fam believes in me, the affirmation feels as unnatural and uncomfortable as imitation wool.

"I'm a contractor, not an employee. I'm not complaining. I prefer it that way, but I was hired for a very specific reason for a very limited time, so you can't blame me for treating myself like an outsider. I am one, plain and simple. Heck, I didn't even know the purpose of this offsite because you didn't tell me, and I don't get Habituall's emails!"

Evan nods firmly. "Done. I'll have IT issue you a company email address by the end of today. They'll harass me about it, because everyone with a Habituall email has what we call 'Boss access,' which means you have the unfettered ability to log into our platform and message our entire customer base. I keep telling Drew to put up some security guardrails, but you've seen the man. He's a cat-loving space cadet. Anyway, the point is if an email address will make you feel like a real extension of the team, it's the least we can do. Moving forward, think of yourself as my strategic advisor."

I laugh, but Evan doesn't join in, which throws me for a bigger loop. "Wait, you're not kidding?"

"Our target audience is enterprise retailers. You know retail, right?"

"Of course, but—"

"And retailers want to sell to consumers, which look to you and your very famous friends as the trendsetters?"

Just like his brand-dropping in the zen room, the comment catches me off-guard. Evan Chen always manages to know more than I assume he does. But he's not wrong, considering all the times a business got a huge boost after getting the 'Princess Alex shout-out.' "You could say that . . ."

"Then that settles it. You are our ideal customer's ideal customer. Why wouldn't I care about your opinions?"

I tug on his tank top, which is hugging the outline of his abs like it can't bear to be apart from them. "Because you've yet to give my fashion sense the time of day!"

His eyes crinkle in amusement. "I selectively listen to your advice . . . but in all fairness, you've been ogling me in athleisure, so you can't be complaining about my clothes."

I stop absent-mindedly tracing his stomach the same way Evan touched my face, flustered that I can't even maintain a proper amount of personal space. "This shirt is hideous," I say, more to convince myself to take my hands off it, but it's not working.

Evan leans down dangerously close to my ear. "Then go ahead and take it off . . ."

Holy hell, that is tempting. Images flash in my mind—Evan taking me up against one of these trees, bark scratching up my back as much as my nails dig into his, his hand covering my mouth to keep my moans under wraps—and my brain nearly short-circuits.

"That sounds unbecoming of a strategic advisor," I gulp.

He tilts my chin up, his thumb brushing against my

bottom lip. "I think it's about time we call a spade a spade and stop resisting the gravitational pull between us. You said it yourself; you're not my employee. Sounds like all the reward with none of the risk."

Although I don't buy that for a second, he sure makes me want to. But before we can succumb to our pent-up desires, a bunch of branches shakes out of the corner of my eye.

"Ow! Casey—are you out here? Everyone's boarding the bus!"

Tania walks into the clearing, and I shove Evan behind the nearest tree, so she doesn't catch us in a compromising position.

"There you are! What are you doing out here by yourself?"

"Um . . . I was meditating." I hear that fucker snorting with laughter, so I fake a coughing fit to drown out the noise.

"Oh my, here, take this," she says, handing me her water bottle. "Sorry to interrupt your session, but the team's getting restless and talking about taking the offsite to karaoke instead. And Evan's up and left. Can you believe he bailed like that?"

I thread my arm through Tania's and walk with her toward the farm. "Wow, what a dick. You know, you never spilled the tea on EC, so we've got a lot to discuss on the ride back."

Feeling a tad guilty for leaving Evan to fend for himself, I hope he's not waiting long for the team to depart so he can sneak off to wherever he parked his car.

Once we've taken our places at the back of the bus, Tania suddenly starts in her seat. "Oh! I completely forgot to bring this up—are you, by chance, free on Sunday?"

I consider my typical weekend plans: some cardio with the glam fam, followed by undoing that progress with bottomless mimosas at brunch. But nothing's ever set in stone. Shamelessly, it's not because we're scatterbrained, but because we never need to plan ahead. It's embarrassing to admit, but it doesn't matter where Alex goes—no one ever makes us wait.

Now that Alex isn't at the center of my social calendar, I should be excited that I'm free to make my own plans, but instead I feel adrift, like some loser who got her membership to the in-crowd revoked.

Checking my phone to give the impression that my schedule is fuller than it is, I say, "Nothing on the agenda, for once. What's up?"

"Thank goodness," Tania sighs. "The women in the Habituall volunteer group are having a Galentine's Day brunch with the organizers of Safe Harbor, a local nonprofit that operates a shelter for survivors of domestic abuse. They've got several activities available: making welcome cards for the residents, decorating journals for their support groups, and even building bracelets for teens to raise awareness of dating violence. I, uh, casually mentioned to the volunteer coordinator we were working with Princess Alex's stylist, and she said they would lose their minds if you could come, and I, um, might have told them that wouldn't be a problem. Is it?"

I laugh at her reluctant ask. It usually rubs me the wrong way whenever anyone name-drops my friends to make themselves more interesting, but it's hard to be annoyed at a noble cause like this. And it doesn't hurt that my second near-kiss with Evan has put me in a generous mood.

"Of course not. I'd be happy to help. I love working with women's nonprofits, and I'm sure I have a ton of clothes I can bring if they take donations."

Tania squeals, shaking my arm with glee. "Omigosh, that would be perfect. Our volunteers are taking care of the goodies for brunch, but I'll message the group and tell them to bring any lightly used clothes they'd be willing to part with as well. Yay, I'm so excited you're on our team!"

My phone pings, and when I see the notification, I smile.

> Your new email address, Casey [at] Habituall [dot] com, is now available. Please reset your password to access your inbox.

"Me too." And for the first time, I feel like it's true.

HABITUALL's #general channel in Slack – February 11

@TaniaBeecher: Hey Habituators! In honor of this month's theme, "Make Love a Habit," the members of our Habituat-HER employee resource group are partnering with Safe Harbor, a nonprofit here in SF that provides 24/7 domestic violence response. According to their impact report, last year they answered over 6,000 crisis calls and texts, and offered shelter to hundreds of women and children in need.

In case you missed the news in the #volunteering channel because you were too busy squee-ing over baby goats today, on Sunday we're hosting a Galentine's Day brunch at Safe Harbor's counseling center for women and nonbinary employees. If you'd like to join, please select an item to bring on the sign-up sheet below.

And you're welcome to bring lightly worn clothes as a donation in honor of our special guest @CaseyHolbright, who recently joined Habituall, contracted as our executive stylist for First Party. She needs no intro, but I'll drop her socials in case you want to see what she's been up to ;)

@CaseyHolbright: Thanks for the warm welcome, @TaniaBeecher. I'm so humbled to support this worthy cause. Many survivors are escaping dangerous situations with just the clothes on their backs, so any items you can donate would be greatly appreciated. I've been told before there are never enough socks!

@BrandonPeterson: What about the men? Can we come to brunch?

@WendyHoang: Are you serious, dude?

@TaniaBeecher: Thanks for the question, @Brandon-Peterson. The brunch is specifically to celebrate Galentine's Day, but men can support the shelter by donating on their website (click the link below).

@BrandonPeterson: Doesn't sound very inclusive to me. Why is the company sponsoring an event if not all employees can participate?

@WendyHoang: It's on a Sunday—just because you can't get a reservation at Zazie doesn't give you the right to hijack a safe space.

@LauraLackner: The employee experience team has a Valentine's Day happy hour planned the next day, and everyone is welcome!

@BrandonPeterson: I don't understand why we'd encourage such a double standard. Imagine the uproar if male employees hosted an event that women couldn't attend!

@WendyHoang: You mean like how the entire tech industry shuts us out? How many times did you invite the women on your team to your golf outings or bar crawls, @BrandonPeterson? Sounds like you're starting to understand how it feels . . .

@ITteam: Hey folks, a reminder to follow #general channel etiquette: if this isn't a conversation for the entire company, please take it to your DMs!

chapter
eight

That Sunday morning, I fret over what to wear, per usual, weighing my options like I'm trying to piece together the world's hardest puzzle.

A casual potluck-style brunch with a large group of ladies at a nonprofit organization dedicated to protecting women and families, where we'll be doing healing arts and crafts between bites?

My mind spins at the intersecting variables and contradictions of this part-networking, part-charity function until I settle on the outfit that makes the most sense: stretchy, high-waisted denim jeans to navigate a cramped space; a billowy, cream-yellow top that's warm enough for mid-February but bright enough to bring in the sunshine; camel-colored belt and matching ankle booties.

Having learned my lesson at the offsite, I tie my hair back into a voluminous ponytail to keep it from getting in my way or in anyone else's food. Then I finish the look with some 'no-makeup makeup' to appear fresh but natural.

I pack my car to the brim with clothes—most are leftovers from shoots I've worked on, but the glam fam also guilt-tripped Alex into donating a few pieces from her closet. I'm not sure how long that skeezeball Dominic is going to disrupt the impeccable style Alex and I curated together for years, but at least it means Safe Harbor has some stunning pieces in case they want to host a charity auction in the future.

With bags and bags of designer goods, I run the mental math in my head as I drive up the peninsula. I must be hauling the equivalent of at least two senior engineers' salaries, if my nosy search on Glassdoor yesterday was accurate. It's a good thing I gave Tania a heads-up before I left my apartment that I'd need a lot of help getting everything inside.

By the time I reach San Francisco's Mission district and grab an empty parking spot along the curb, Tania is already waiting with several women from Habituall, all of them wearing their company-branded T-shirts and jackets. Of course. I need to stop being so indecisive with my wardrobe choices and grab everything in my size from their swag closet. But then I immediately take back the thought because that dystopian dreariness would crush my soul.

Capsule wardrobes are hot among techies, who claim that wearing the same outfit every day reduces decision fatigue and cognitive overload. Call me a maximalist, but I wouldn't eat the same foods or rewatch the same movies again and again, so why would I restrict myself from enjoying the finer things in life, like a gorgeous ensemble? So-called experts swap productivity tips on how to turn yourself into a machine, but the last I checked, robots don't have clothes. To wear is human, you could say.

"Holy smokes!" Tania says as she and her crew start unloading my car. "You weren't kidding, Casey, when you said you had clothes to donate. At this rate, we'll be dragging bags inside until the cows come home."

My eyes squint, mainly because they're adjusting to the light after removing my sunglasses but also because my Southerner spidey sense is tingling. My twang may have faded except when I'm drunk or want to throw around the word 'y'all,' but I know me some country colloquialisms. Tania's accent sounds Californian, but you never know who's hiding their inner hillbilly.

"Did I miss you saying where you were from?"

Tania chuckles, breaking out into a flush, but that could merely be from the enormous bags she's hauled through the shelter's entryway and in the corner reserved for public donations.

"I don't think I mentioned it, actually. I'm from Fresno—well, technically a small town on the outskirts of Fresno, but no one knows where Sanger is. Why?"

"No reason—just realized I didn't know." Ah, that makes sense. I've lived in California long enough to know never to call it Cali and that Fresno is smack-dab in the middle of the state. I've never had a reason to visit, but I've heard folks from the Central Valley refer to it as the "Bible Belt" due to its large, conservative farming community. Basically, Southerners without drawls.

If we were out at a typical brunch with bottomless mimosas, I would love to ask Tania about growing up in the California heartland, but we're distracted, first with getting the bags in the building, then with taking a few flights of stairs to the large room where the rest of the group is eagerly waiting.

There's a large conference table in the center of the room where the arts and crafts will be done. There are notebooks, magazines, blank greeting cards, stickers, markers, colored pencils, and so many bits and bobs for jewelry making that I get flashbacks to the Seriously Fun team bonding from last week. My brain freaks out for a second, expecting dudes in baseball shirts to pop out of nowhere and start gushing about superheroes.

But thankfully, there are only ladies setting up the brunch

on smaller tables around the room's perimeter. They're peeling cellophane off trays of breakfast pastries and pitchers of juice, and pretty soon, an array of delectable treats await us. My stomach growls loudly, tired of being ignored after the long drive into the city, and thankfully everyone holds off on formal introductions so we can fill up our plates. There are no staff operating the food stations, but everything looks so sophisticated that it's hard to tell if the event was catered or if these women all have culinary side hustles.

I take a seat next to Tania and Wendy. It's a shame that nobody's wearing name tags because I'm terrible with faces, and there's no way to rely on my handy trick of remembering people by their outfits because they're walking billboards for Habituall.

I'm told the organizers of Safe Harbor's group volunteering program are wrapping up a meeting, so in the meantime, we make small talk and enjoy our meal. The bacon is deliciously salty, so before I know it, I gulp down my orange juice and need a refill. It's not the freshest, and there's a weird aftertaste, but there isn't any champagne around to cut it. I don't remember there being a ban against alcohol at this event, but maybe the team is being respectful of the nonprofit and sensitive to anyone who may be in recovery.

"Can you believe what a dick Brandon was being?" Wendy spits out, still pissed at their exchange on Slack two days ago. Part of me is embarrassed that someone would break decorum to insult a fellow employee at a charity function, one that's work-sponsored no less, but a much larger part is giddy over getting a seat for the drama.

"Omigod, yes!" Tania squeals. "I wanted to verbally bitch-slap him, but ever since Max joined, he's been going on about how I need to 'show up as a leader' and 'stay above the line.' Thanks for saying what I desperately wanted to."

Wendy nods in solidarity. "I was annoyed when Max

punted me under Gibson, but at least Finance is too swamped to give a shit about me running my mouth. Even if they had a problem with it, I'd like to see them fire me and take on the workplace vendors without my help. The first day they run out of those TCHO chocolate squares, they'd lose their damn minds."

I take another sip of OJ before breaking into my second scone. "Wendy, you used to report to Max? I didn't know you and Tania were on the same team."

She gulps down a mouthful of chocolate-chip muffin. "It sucked at first to be transferred, but it's better than fighting to be recognized among Max's dozen direct reports. All those dudes failed upward, and Tania here is the only one who wasn't given a VP title, even though she's practically carrying the marketing team single-handedly." She flashes her colleague a cheesy grin. "They love the shit out of her—no idea why!"

Tania tosses a grape at Wendy's forehead, which ricochets off and rolls onto the tile floor. They're super comfortable being sarcastic, but I can tell they've been through thick and thin, and they have each other's backs. Watching them makes my heart ache, missing the glam fam. The five of us couldn't be more different, and it hasn't mattered. Circumstances made us not work friends, but best friends.

Or at least I hope that's still true. Alex ripping the rug out from underneath me did a number on my ego, but I want to believe that regardless of her two-bit boyfriend's attempt to tear us apart, our friendship isn't irreparably damaged.

As we're wrapping up brunch, three women enter the room and introduce themselves as the volunteer coordinators guiding us through today's activities.

"Thanks so much for joining us for our Galentine's Day volunteer drive," says Rita Sanchez, who takes the lead role. "We've got thirty ladies here today, so we'll split you evenly to take part in one of our three programs: You can either make welcome cards for our new shelter residents, decorate journals for our counseling patients, or build beaded bracelets for the teens in our youth program. There's no right or wrong way to approach these crafts, so we recommend you put yourselves in their shoes, write messages from your heart, and think of what would inspire and empower you in your most vulnerable moments. And, of course, have some fun! Our line of work doesn't have to be dark and depressing, because we get to be the light at the end of the tunnel for so many women and families. If you're feeling good, that will show up in your art. We'll be circling around to check on everybody and answer any questions you may have about the organization, so flag one of us down if you need help."

It may be because Tania writes for a living, but she gravitates toward the notebooks, so Wendy and I follow suit after refilling our glasses of OJ. I'm starting to feel a little dizzy, and my stomach's a bit gurgly, but that must be because of the warm room and rich food. Orange juice is acidic, right? Perhaps if I keep drinking, it will break down whatever bug my gut may be battling.

We spend the next half hour shooting the shit while decorating notebooks to turn them from blank canvasses into journals of joy. Wendy plasters hers with washi tape, Tania folds colored card stock to fashion into notebook covers, and I decide to go full Y2K with Lisa Frank stickers and a handwritten note on the first page using glitter gel pens.

But before long, something's eating at me more than the acidic fruit juice. "Tania, what's your relationship like with Evan? If you've worked at Habituall since nearly the beginning, you would figure he would trust you to head marketing regardless of what Max thinks."

Tania gives the question some consideration. "I don't know. I mean, you've been around him. He's a weird dude. He spends as much time as he can in the gym or the zen room, and I've never seen him in a suit—even when some hella important people have come through for an office visit. When I first consulted him on how to approach the story behind our upcoming Series E fundraising announcement, he started going off on how he wasn't concerned about our competitors because the ecosystem we're in is like the Amazon rainforest, and there's plenty of space and symbiosis for everyone to thrive. He sounded like such a hippie caricature I thought he was high off his rocker."

I furrow my brow, so confused by this depiction of Evan. He's got to be pulling everyone's chain. "You don't think he's on drugs, do you?"

Wendy laughs, peeling off an adorable puffy sticker of a corgi butt. "With that much bullshit flying out of his mouth, I'd be more concerned if he wasn't!"

My question comes out more nervous than I anticipated. I've taken a THC gummy every now and then during those times when I wanted to chill out but had too much to do the next morning and couldn't risk a hangover. In the Bay Area, partaking in drug culture is seen as no big deal, but being raised in the conservative South does a number on you. After a childhood of fear-mongering D.A.R.E. videos and parental preaching about the dangers of 'the reefer,' I get uneasy at the thought of Evan waking and baking or taking part in an ayahuasca ceremony.

Tania must see the concern all over my face because she backpedals quickly. "Hey, I'm not about to start rumors about somebody. Even if EC is stone-cold sober, kookiness is part of his personality. And he may act differently with you, Casey, when we're not around. Maybe he dials it back. Or maybe pros like you and Max are bringing out the best in him and making him take things more seriously. I have to remind myself that he's four years younger than me, and while our brains are both fully developed by now, a founder's growth is usually stunted from the pressure they're under. That's why the board is pushing the company to fill out the leadership team. We're at the stage where we need adults running this thing, and apparently, we early employees don't count, as silly as that sounds since we're the same ones who built everything up until now."

I'm unsure if I'm more bummed at the idea of Evan being a drugged-out hippie or an incompetent child. What about the strong leader who has no problem putting an exec in his place when he's out of line? What about the smart charmer who keeps me laughing with a wit so sharp it could carve ice sculptures? And, most importantly, what about the man who makes me weak in the knees without his lips ever touching mine? The more I learn, the more I question whether I know anything about Evan. Nothing about this is sitting well with me, and my fifth orange juice isn't helping.

"What?" I blurt out, noticing Wendy staring me down between placing decorative embellishments.

She takes a sip from her glass, which she swapped out for ice water after we finished our first set of journals. "It sure seems like you're preoccupied with all things Evan Chen . . . does somebody have a little crush?"

"What? Nooooo," I insist with a few too many syllables. Did that come out a little slurred? My head's pounding, the room is much too warm with over thirty people cramped at a single table inside, and I wish I had an antacid to calm my upset stomach—or even better, my mom's cornbread. It always tasted like a buttery sponge that soaked up all my nerves and sadness.

"You two did look close when we were doing goat yoga," Tania says, which at first sounds like an observation but ends like an accusation.

If it was a Sunday brunch with the glam fam, I would have no problem admitting that I kinda-sorta-maybe have the hots for Evan. But it doesn't matter if I could get along with Tania and Wendy off the clock. The truth is they're still colleagues, surrounded by dozens of their coworkers potentially eavesdropping. Who knows how they would take the news—would they ask how his abs feel like Glen and Som would? Or would they question my judgment for getting involved with a client they described as an alleged user? Or worst yet, would they rat us out to their bosses and get us into trouble? I never even received detention in school, so the thought of being interrogated by HR makes me want to throw up more than I already do. What if those scrambled eggs I ate were bad, and I'm coming down with rapid-onset food poisoning?

"The only thing I want to crush is this job, which means getting as much time with Evan as possible so I can style him effectively. If that means hounding him to get his thoughts on colors or textures, then so be it."

I set my craft supplies down and push my chair back, desperate to step outside for some fresh air. If I'm feeling this bad, it might be worth cutting brunch short and getting back on the road. It's not even noon, and my bed is like a siren calling my name.

But as I stand up, Tania says something that makes my intestines twist into knots.

"Good, then I'm glad I invited him."

I whirl my head around, regretting it immediately when my throat burns with acid reflux. Maybe I overdid it on the OJ . . .

"What? Why?"

Tania's got this look on her face that's part incredulous she's having the conversation in the first place and part annoyed her thoughtfulness wasn't warmly received. "After Brandon threw his temper tantrum on Slack, I figured the leadership team should be here. The men say they want to be allies, so the least they can do is stop by. And EC was game when I told him you were coming. I thought you'd be happy."

I wave my hand, both to reassure her I'm not mad and to clear the path so I can make my way out of the room. However, I'm foiled yet again because when I go to pull the doorknob, someone's already pushing through.

"Hey, Holbright! Tania told me this is where the party's at. Are all those clothes downstairs yours? How did you manage to squeeze yourself into your car?"

Evan. No, no, no, I can't take his wise-cracking right now. I'm way too hot (the temperature kind), and he's way too hot (the just-left-the-house-after-taking-a-shower kind). My hands are shaking, the room's spinning, and I need to get out of here.

"Casey, are you okay? You don't look well. Do you need help?"

His arms are on mine, holding me up. With great concern, he starts blathering on about getting me some water and can someone please open the windows? But then he attempts to guide me back to my seat, and I shake my head violently, refusing to backtrack. Something's wrong, and all the acid in my stomach bubbles up like a geyser, and oh *no*—

I open my mouth to tell everyone to back up and give me space, but instead of words coming out, what I express is my breakfast all over the linoleum. Women are jumping up and shouting, and everything's a blur, but even though I'm mortified that I upchucked in public, I can still feel Evan's arms wrapped around me.

I'm just now taking in what he's wearing today: a white tee with gray joggers and nondescript sneakers. It's not his worst outfit, but I've officially ruined it. The stench of this morning's regurgitated meal hits me, but not nearly as strong as the understanding that he could have pushed me away to save himself, but he pulled me in closer instead.

"You feel better?" he says with a dimpled smile. How unhinged we must look, covered in vomit and thrilled about it.

"Much," I say, wiping my mouth with the back of my hand. "No idea what came over me, though . . ."

Wendy comes by, shoving wads of paper towels at me. "I'm not surprised since you had five or six mimosas."

"What?" I grab the towels out of her hand. "I didn't know the juice was spiked! None of the pitchers were labeled. Why the hell didn't you say something as I was pounding glass after glass?"

Wendy blinks blankly at me. "We're not kids on a school field trip, Casey. Of course, we're gonna have mimosas at brunch. Didn't you read the sign-up sheet?"

I decide against snapping back. I'm ashamed that I was so oblivious I didn't taste the champagne in the drinks—and that the liquid spewed back up that quickly. I swear I used to tolerate my alcohol much better when I was in my early twenties, but apparently now I'm a lush, and everyone's looking at me like I'm *that* girl.

"Hey, don't worry about it. These things happen—it's no big deal." Evan takes some paper towels and helps me clean up my mess. He could roast me mercilessly; instead, he's downplaying everything because he can tell that I'm awash with embarrassment. And while there's no guarantee he won't crack a joke once this ordeal has blown over, I'm thankful he doesn't punch down in my moment of weakness.

Once we've wiped up the worst of it, Rita and the other organizers bring over a mop, wet rags, and sanitizing wipes. I make a motion to shoo everybody off so I can take responsibility for my misfortune, but Tania pulls me from the ground and forces me toward the door.

"Come on, let's get you cleaned up. The team's got the rest taken care of." It's a tone I'm intimately familiar with, having used it countless times while partying with the glam fam. I'd bet my life savings she's the mom of her close friend group too.

"I think Wendy's mad at me," I say as Tania directs me into the nearest restroom.

She snorts. "Wendy? That's what she always sounds like, perturbed by the world around her. She's a total lightweight, too, so she's bummed you aren't Superwoman when holding down your liquor. She assumes all white women from the South were raised with whiskey in their baby bottles."

At the sink, I brush my teeth thoroughly with several of those disposable pre-pasted toothbrushes from their toiletry station, then chug heavy-duty mouthwash until I'm as minty-fresh as when I arrived. Next, I wipe my face the best I can without stripping off my makeup, but after a few attempts at getting the puke out of my blouse, it's a lost cause. "I wish I was Superwoman because I don't think this shirt can be saved."

Tania considers the situation for a moment, then runs out of the restroom with a hurried "I'll be back!" I bide my time, awkwardly saying hi to anyone who enters and witnesses me in my vomit-soiled outfit. I'm tempted to hide in a stall or even strip down to my bra and underwear because that can't possibly be worse for any bystanders.

Thankfully, Tania's not gone for long, and when she returns, she hands me a pink velour tracksuit, which makes me crack up instantly.

"What?" she huffs. "It was one of the first things I pulled from your donation stash. I figured it was comfy at least."

"For sure—I just wasn't expecting it. The last time I wore this was at Alex's Y2K-themed Halloween party—I was Paris Hilton in her peak Juicy Couture days."

I take off my top without thinking about it, and Tania turns around to give me privacy.

"Jeez, that's unnecessary," I blurt out as I zip up my fuzzy hoodie. "Remember, I'm a stylist—if everyone was modest in my industry, outfit changes would take forever."

Tania shifts back to face me. "Speaking of ladies, Habituall is sponsoring Safe Harbor's International Women's Day fundraiser, and it would be phenomenal if you could be involved somehow . . . maybe we can auction off a style consultation?"

Swapping my stained pants for the Juicy-emblazoned sweats, I consider the idea. I love being philanthropic, but selling my time to the highest bidder wouldn't be as fulfilling as supporting the people who need it most. "What if we were to do makeovers for the shelter residents instead? We've already got the clothes, and the rest of the glam fam should be back from Paris by then, so maybe I can convince them to bring their teams for hair, makeup, and nails. Could that work?"

Tania grabs my wrists, jumping up and down. It's like I told her I couldn't buy her a specific toy for Christmas, but I could buy the rest of the store instead.

"Omigod, are you freaking serious? That would be amazing! You are the *best*, Casey."

"Whoa there," I retort as she whips out her phone to share the news with god-knows-who. "Nothing's committed yet. Alex's schedule is completely bananas, so it's safe to say she's a no-go—" I leave out the part where our working relationship is on the rocks so as not to raise any concern. "But after seeing Safe Harbor for myself, I know the great work they're doing here, and I'll do my best to get everyone else on board. Slow your roll before making any promises, okay?"

With the way Tania's eyes are sparkling, I can already tell she's drafting the press release in her head. I can't blame her, though. It's not often you get an opportunity to bring a makeover montage to life—and do good deeds in the process.

After accepting the outfit I wore to brunch isn't worth

saving and dumping it into the trash, I reassure Tania I'll do my best to deliver the makeover experience the shelter deserves. She gives me a hug that nearly pops my eyes out of their sockets, and when we walk out of the restroom, she floats across the floor.

With today's chaotic turns of events in the rearview mirror, it's time I drive back home. "Hey, it's best that I get some rest. Do you mind if I take off?"

"Of course! Thanks so much for coming. Please take it easy, and I'll see you around the office." Tania's so happy that I could ask if I could commit homicide, and she'd give me the same response.

Before I can follow her through the door into the craft room to grab my belongings, I spot Evan already in the lobby with my purse over his shoulder. He's changed into an outfit that must have been from one of the many male models who's worked with Alex over the years: a too-tight Henley and too-short jeans that appear like they might have been intentionally cropped to show off some ankle. Despite the poor fit, it's already a massive improvement, and I'm imagining layering on a jacket and tossing out his stained sneakers for Italian full-grain leather low-tops. He's so good-looking that it's criminal when he won't put in the teeniest bit of effort getting dressed.

"I figured you had enough action for one day," he says.

"For one lifetime." I take my bag and make sure my phone, keys, and wallet are safely inside. "Sorry you had to witness that."

He chuckles. "That wasn't the first time somebody's thrown up at a work event—not by a long shot."

"Well, it's certainly *my* first time, and all I want is to crawl into bed and forget it ever happened. I can't believe I could ever behave that unprofessionally."

Evan has this strangely intense look, as if amusement and

concern are wrapped up into one expression, with a dash of smolder for the hell of it.

"What?" I demand, checking my watch. With this morning's meal and those mimosas out of my system, I shouldn't go the rest of the day on an empty stomach. If I leave now, I can pick up a slice of Hobee's blueberry coffee cake before the restaurant closes, so my brunch today isn't all for nothing.

"I was going to ask you something," Evan says slowly, jamming his hands in his pockets. "But I'm afraid it might also be . . . unprofessional."

"Go on then." The longer he stands there idling, the sourer a mood I find myself in. I exit through the front door of the building and make my way toward my car, Evan trailing behind me.

He laughs, like our attitudes are inversely related. "Is that how you always react when a guy wants to take you on a date?"

My heart tumbles into a somersault. Did he say what I think he said? "Excuse me, what? I puked all over you because I'm apparently so dense that I can't taste the difference between orange juice and champagne, and your first thought is to ask me out?"

He glances back at the shelter to check if we're being watched, then reaches out when the coast is clear to touch my arm, taking in the hoodie's velvety fabric underneath his fingers.

"Is that a no?"

He must have put that damn cologne on because there's no way he can smell that good post-upchuck. I cringe at how I must reek and take a step back subconsciously.

For a split second, Evan's face falls. "I get it—no big deal," he says, trying to sound nonchalant. "My apologies, forget I ever asked."

"No!" I close the gap between us, BO be damned. "I

mean, no, as in that's *not* a no. Not as in no way. Argh, you know what I mean. You just took me by surprise. I'm starting to think your timing is as poor as your fashion sense."

He laughs again, and I have to admit that I appreciate how he never holds back on sharing such hearty, indulgent joy. "You're right on that one, Holbright. I never had the patience to respect societal etiquette on scheduling. When I make up my mind about something, I see no point in waiting any further. So tomorrow night, then?"

I'm in the process of getting into my car, but hearing that outrageous suggestion makes me hit my head as I twist around to face him. "Are you out of your mind?"

"What? Monday or Saturday, what does it matter?"

I wait for him to comprehend, but he truly has no idea. "Tomorrow is Valentine's Day."

His eyes widen, and I enjoy watching him squirm as I close the car door and roll the window down. Will he backtrack or double down?

"Tomorrow it is. What's your address? I'll pick you up at seven."

I can't believe this man. "And what if someone runs into us? No one's going to buy that we're talking shop and chambray on the most romantic night of the year."

He takes a minute to mull it over but remains undeterred. "Not a problem. Just wear your fanciest outfit, and I'll take care of everything. No one else will know."

The audacity. I have a million questions, but his confidence that everything will work out shuts me up. And why wouldn't it? Nothing I've learned in the past week has made me doubt that this is a man who gets what he wants.

"You really are something, Evan Chen," I say begrudgingly.

He looks over the top of my car, another check against

prying eyes, before leaning down to tip my chin toward his gaze. What is happening? Is he going to—?

When his lips first make contact with my own, I'm expecting a chaste kiss goodbye. That mouthwash may have rinsed away the remnants of my earlier fiasco, but I assumed any potential mood would have been thrown out along with my sullied ensemble.

And yet, every part of Evan sets my skin aflame. His tongue runs across my lips before slipping past them, warming me up faster than my heated seats ever could in the winter. If I knew Evan could ignite me into an inferno with a single kiss, I wouldn't have been so quick to jump into my car in the first place. When he reaches back to tangle his fingers into my hair and tug on my ponytail, a moan escapes my throat. Eager for more, my heart races beyond backflips into full-blown barrel rolls, and I'm seconds away from ripping this door off its hinges so I can crush his body against mine. When he suddenly pulls away, I'm gasping for air. There's so much impatience in our kiss that I understand why he insisted on a date so soon. Having to wait even one day will be torture.

He smiles slyly, satisfied to leave me unsatisfied. "You don't know the half of it."

~

"4 V-DAY TIPS for Training Your Tech Bro" by SF Metropolitan magazine – February 14

SO LOVE IS in the air, but your new boo speaks in binary code? Girl, we feel you. You're on a strict timeline—and no, we're not talking about waiting for your big payout when honey's startup stops playing around with its alphabet soup (Series F, anyone?). You've got your own exit strategy to worry about, whether it's marriage and kids or affording a kickass backyard for all your plant babies.

To celebrate Valentine's Day, here are our tried-and-true tips for training your tech bro.

1. *Get him educated*. Don't let that PhD in Computer Science fool you, sweetheart. Universities don't teach engineers basic life skills, like how to load the dishwasher properly or where the clit is located. But the good news is if he can type faster than one hundred words per minute, he can be instructed to put his talented hands to work.

2. *No, not that kind of education*. There are only so many times a woman can hear, "I was listening to this podcast . . ." before her vagina dries up like the Sahara. There's an oversaturation of amateur white cishet male entertainment rotting your boyfriend's mind, so put him on an audio diet before it's too late. Tell him for every bad movie review or Apple fanboy unboxing he swaps for an intersectional feminist article, he gets a blowjob. It's what Steve Jobs would have wanted.

3. *Break in that beta*. If you're at least a semi-attractive single lady in Silicon Valley, you already know finding a date is like shooting fish in a barrel—super easy, but a little sad when you think about it. The trick is to avoid the fuckboys and go for the wide-eyed guy who lost his virginity at twenty-three. Sure, he's in need of a haircut, but he'll clean up nicely and treat you like royalty.

4. *Check out the goods*. And no, not that move where you 'accidentally' brush his crotch with your ass so you can get an idea of what he's packing. While he's following that recipe you sent him for date night, scan his bookshelf. If you see anything by Ayn Rand, *run*. Run like Whoopi just said, "You in danger, girl." You'll thank us later.

chapter
nine

It's no surprise that when someone gives me a fashion assignment, I take it seriously. But when the assignment is for a first date? Then I will put in the prep work required to pass with flying colors.

Which is why I'm now standing in front of my closet, so frustrated I'm afraid I'll need to wear a beanie to cover my head after pulling all my hair out.

Wear your fanciest outfit? What the ever-loving fuck did Evan mean by that? He couldn't even give me the benefit of clarifying such a general word as *outfit*—should I wear a full-length gown or my most expensive jeans?

Usually, our destination would give me clues as to which shoes to wear or what weather to expect, but yet again, Evan is no help. Despite my texts begging for the smallest hint, he wouldn't tell me a single thing, so I have no idea where we're going or what we're doing.

If keeping mum on the goat yoga offsite is any proof, Evan gets a sick thrill from putting me in situations I have no control over, and I'm not sure why I go along with it. Som, Glen, and Tori room together in the city, so if they weren't across the Atlantic right now, I'd head over to their apartment.

I'm sure they would have been more than happy to give me the makeover of the century.

So now I'm spiraling, afraid of attaching too much meaning or not enough to my potential options. I've got plenty of formalwear: gowns from award shows, galas, and other elite events. But every time I put one on, it feels sterile, like I took the assignment too literally. If I want to knock Evan's socks off—and who knows, maybe more than his socks—then I have to do my own interpretation of "fanciest."

When's the last time a garment took my breath away?

Peering toward the back of my closet, I squint at a rack of plastic sheaths and black bags containing pieces I never planned on wearing again but couldn't bear to toss.

I start unzipping the bags and set aside the unworthy choices—old Halloween costumes and theme party outfits. But then I pull out the last garment bag, recalling its contents, and bite my lip. Could this work?

My fingers tremble ever so slightly as I slide the zipper down. There was a reason I shoved this to the very back of my closet, after all, so I brace myself for the pain and sadness to bubble up. And yet, all I can do is break out into a grin.

Am I really going to wear my *prom dress* on a date? Have I lost my mind?

But while it is technically true that this is the dress I wore to my junior prom, it's much more than that. Yes, I can't forget why I abandoned it to collect dust, the daggers in my heart when I returned to the decked-out hotel ballroom after grabbing some air to catch my date slow-dancing with another girl. The shattered expectations of a good night kiss—and maybe more—while waiting for my dad to pick me up. It was a couple of years after my favorite song, Hunter Hayes's "Wanted," topped the country charts, and I spent the entire weekend bawling my eyes out with that song on repeat because I thought I would never get my happily ever after.

And while I'll admit that sometimes, even now, I throw myself a Hunter Hayes–sponsored pity party after a heinous first date, the only thing I don't regret about that night was this dress. It represents the moment that not only did I realize I wanted a career in fashion, but also that I had the vision and skills to pull it off.

This isn't just a prom dress. It's my *Atonement* dress.

I saw the movie when I was in sixth grade, during a post-Christmas school holiday I spent with Alex. We spent most of the week sneaking off to her theater room to watch whatever films my family deemed off-limits for an impressionable young lady. When I saw Keira Knightley wearing the most exquisite emerald dress, I knew one day I would make my own. By that age, I was already in love with fashion, but I became obsessed with the luxurious silk and how it flowed as she moved. The sensual library scene with James McAvoy may have catapulted me into puberty, but that dress ignited a different type of passion in me.

I quickly take the dress out of the garment bag, as if dawdling will turn it into ash. My breath comes fast and shallow because who knows whether it will even fit me a decade later? There's quite a bit more of me in every direction, which I remind myself is perfectly normal and healthy, of course. But now I feel strangely committed to wearing the dress and don't want to contemplate a backup plan.

I throw off my robe and step into the dress, not bothering with shapewear or even a pair of panties. As I slide the straps onto my shoulders, I relax, having heard no signs of stitches ripping.

Turning around to face my full-length mirror, I gasp. Even with the amateur stitching of a fledgling fashionista, it's so much more gorgeous than I expected. I must have sized the piece up quite a bit in high school to pull off Knightley's waif-like look, and now that I have curves, the dress cascades down them elegantly yet seductively. It's *perfect*, and I feel perfect in it.

Now that I think about it, it's also the perfect interpretation of Evan's prompt. My fanciest outfit isn't my flashiest or most expensive—it's the most beautiful thing I've ever made with my own two hands. And honestly, if this dress doesn't make Evan's jaw hit the floor when he sees me in it, then I don't know what will.

Several hours later, after I've done my makeup to the nines and followed a video tutorial on how to style a soft updo with finger waves, I get a text from Evan instructing me to wait outside my building. I spritz on my sultriest perfume and grab an understated clutch, feeling a surge of excitement at seeing him. But when I step outside, a driver with the nametag Rami opens the door to an empty limousine.

What the—a fucking limo? I guess part of me is relieved I'm dressed fancily enough for such transportation, but it's an awfully extra move for a guy like Evan, who spends most of his days at Habituall HQ, hunched over his laptop or hashing things out with the C-suite through games of ping-pong. And yet, as I take my seat, there's a premium bottle of brut rosé in an ice bucket, so perhaps tonight the debonair side of him is coming out.

"Your phone, Ms. Holbright." Rami gestures toward my clutch.

I instinctively hold my belongings closer to my chest. "Why on earth would I need to give you my phone?"

Rami smiles, sympathetic yet firm. "Mr. Chen is requesting that our destination remain a surprise. I will return your phone to you when we arrive, I promise."

Unnerved by the idea of losing my virtual limb, I stare at Rami for several beats before relenting and handing my phone over to him and closing the door. The limo peels away from the curb, and I take a few breaths to steady myself. The windows are tinted, and it's already nightfall, so I can't make out where we are going except for the general understanding that we're headed north toward the city.

I don't want to repeat my brunch mishap and get sick in this limo, but on the off chance I'm being kidnapped, I might as well get a bit tipsy. I help myself to a glass of bubbly and then another as the drive drags on. It frustrates me not to have my phone to dick around online and kill the time, but Evan was right to know I would have immediately tracked my geolocation. I've always been a planner, so I'm not sure what irks me more—that I can't predict what's coming next or that Evan is in complete control . . . again.

Finally, after I've lost track of space and time, the limo stops in front of a nondescript building. Rami opens my door and, true to his word, returns my phone before waving goodbye and slowly pulling back onto the street. It's dark outside, but there's quite a bit of open space and greenery, and I can see the ocean off in the distance. I'm guessing we're somewhere in the Presidio, but who's to say?

There's no signage or storefront, and I briefly consider blowing Evan's cover with a split-second internet search. But instead, I step inside the building and am taken aback that it's just as dark. I can barely see anything, save for a small podium where a woman is standing in the glow of a single candle.

"Hi, I'm Casey Holbright," I say to the woman, who's not wearing a nametag like Rami was. "I'm with Evan Chen?" I add for good measure, but it comes out like a question, partly because I don't know if she's a maître d' and partly because *with* sounds so . . . intimate.

"Ah, yes," the woman replies, checking a list in front of her. "Party of two. Mr. Chen has already arrived, so please put this on, and I'll lead the way."

She hands me an eye mask, dark and satiny like the one I bring on long flights. Oh no, what if I've got this wrong, and

Evan's invited me to a sex club? I've heard through the grapevine about a few in San Francisco, and a tech CEO like Evan must get solicited all the time. But on our first date? He must be out of his mind.

More people are starting to trickle in behind me, other couples presumably on dates, so I put on my mask less to throw caution to the wind and more to avoid holding up the line. As the woman leads me through the dark room, her hand on my elbow nudging me this way and that, it dawns on me that I spent hours upon hours agonizing over what to wear and then making the rest of my appearance flawless. My hair and makeup are impeccable, every inch below my waist is waxed smooth, even my fingers and toes are sparkling like diamonds—and this bastard won't be able to see any of it? I could have shown up in a T-shirt and sweatpants, and it wouldn't have mattered!

The lightbulb goes off in my head despite the lack of light anywhere else. What if that was the point? What if this was Evan's plan all along? If I find out he's dressed like a couch potato while I wasted my entire day to look Hollywood-worthy, I will murder him with a dull butter knife. At least I'll be able to escape the crime scene unnoticed.

Finally, in what must be the very back of this place, the woman stops and places my hand on a wooden table.

"Mr. Chen, Ms. Holbright has arrived. The first course should be here in a few minutes."

"Thanks, Rebecca. We can't wait."

Evan's voice sounds much closer than I expected, and then I feel his warm hand on mine as he gently pulls me into a leather-upholstered booth next to him. I assumed we would be sitting across from one another, so this arrangement is both comforting and distressing at the same time. But curiosity gets the best of me, and I use the seconds between placing my purse down and getting settled to brush my fingers along his leg, relieved to touch trousers instead of his ratty loungewear.

"Already trying to get into my pants, I see," Evan whispers, dangerously close to my ear, and I jerk my hand back before I'm tempted to punch him in the face.

"You wish you were so lucky," I hiss as if everyone nearby can hear our conversation, but the din of laughter and drinks clinking at the other tables gives me the impression that we're relatively secluded from the rest of the diners.

I'm about to resume my stylist-sanctioned pat down to verify his appropriate attire, but we're interrupted by a deep, booming voice in the dark.

"Welcome to Enigma, San Francisco's only Michelin-starred, fine dining experience where your sense of sight isn't on the guest list. I'm Josh, and I'll be serving you on this romantic Valentine's Day evening. Our prix fixe menu includes several surprise courses designed to be savored using your hands, so no silverware will be needed. Accompanying the dishes will be drink pairings from our delectable list of wine and cocktails. And if you need anything during your meal, press the buttons under the table where you're sitting, and someone will be over to assist momentarily. Do you have any questions?"

Evan says, "No, we're good—"

"Actually, yes. If the dishes are surprises, how do you address dietary restrictions?" Not that I had any, but the thought of coming across certain foods without knowing what they are gives me both the heebies and the jeebies.

"Of course, Ms. Holbright," says Josh. "Mr. Chen didn't list any restrictions on the reservation, but we're happy to take any of your preferences into account."

I pause, questioning whether to make a fuss and risk coming off too picky. But the anxiety over being in utter darkness wins over etiquette. And how do you never show your face somewhere again if they've never even seen your face?

"No oysters, please," I say with embarrassment. "Or mushrooms. Definitely no escargot if this cuisine is French. And I'm weird about toasted coconut in desserts and egg whites in my cocktails. But that's it." It wasn't, of course, but these were the worst offenders, for sure.

Josh chuckles. "I may not have anything to write that down, but trust me—my hearing is five stars! And those shouldn't be a problem, Ms. Holbright. Enjoy your Enigma experience, and let us know if you need anything else. We're just a button away."

I wait until the waiter's footsteps are out of earshot before addressing the elephant in the blacked-out room.

"Don't start, Evan—I can feel your judgment from here, and I bet your eyebrows have lifted so high they're on the ceiling."

He laughs. "I wasn't going to comment, but if you must know, I'm impressed you broke every Miss Manners bone in your body and actually spoke up for yourself."

I balk, doubtful. "You don't think I'm too picky?"

"About food? Absolutely, you're a madwoman because mushrooms are delicious. But this is the first time I've seen you be discerning about anything other than clothing. Makes me wonder what else you might be . . . *particular* about."

His fingertips dance up my arm, giving me goosebumps and making the hairs on my skin stand up straight. I haven't eaten much today, but even when the first course and round of drinks arrives at our table, I can't focus on our meal. My anticipation over where Evan's hands will go next suppresses my appetite.

He reaches the top of my shoulder and runs his thumb under the strap of the dress before tracing down my open back.

"Jesus, Casey," he growls, running his hand down to my waist.

"I didn't know you're a believer," I tease, basking under the radiating warmth of his palm.

"I'm not, but you wearing so little is igniting my faith in a higher power."

"And what about you? Is this really your fanciest outfit?" I reach out, expecting a ho-hum collared shirt, but when I grip his bicep, the softness catches me off guard.

"Is this . . . a velvet blazer?"

"Not sure if it's my fanciest item, to be honest, but if it gets you to feel me up like this, I'd say it was my best option."

I would never consider groping a date in a public place, but it's like the blazer is hypnotizing me, drawing my fingers in. It's not the satin lining I feel first, though—it's Evan's bare skin.

I gasp. "You're not wearing a shirt?"

"It's trendy right now, isn't it?" he murmurs, tensing slightly as I appreciate his washboard abs. He's correct—I have seen an uptick in celebrities like Jay-Z and Donald Glover wearing suits with only their birthday suit underneath, but I can't tell whether I'm more surprised that Evan is aware of fashion trends or that he'd try one out for himself.

Evan sucks in a breath through gritted teeth. "If your hand drifts any lower, it'll be considered cruel and unusual punishment."

My fingers hover above his waistband, as I entertain the idea of torturing him—running my hand along the front of his pants and down his inner thigh, everywhere but exactly where he's bursting at the seams to be touched.

For several beats, I don't hear Evan's deep breathing. Did the anticipation cause him to pass out in the dark?

But then his fingers dig into my exposed back. "Touch me, Casey, please. I can't take it anymore."

A vengeful thought occurs to me. I could stand up and walk out, leaving him to bumble around in a fit of sexually frustrated rage. I could make him pay for all the bullshit he's put me through.

The desperation in his voice gives me pause because it's proof that he knows he's at my mercy. He's relinquishing his power to let me make the first move.

"And if I give in now, what happens next?" I don't mean to say that out loud, but it's the power, not the sex, that worries me. I can't stand the possibility that we'd go back to the way things were between us—all sparring, no substance.

I brace myself for Evan to brag about rocking my world, but then his lips delicately kiss my shoulder.

"I can't predict the future, but I can promise we'll get through it together. You're not giving in, Casey. We're on the same side."

No idea when that happened, but I like how it sounds.

"This is the strangest olive branch I've ever received," I muse, tracing my fingers up and down his zipper.

Evan laughs. "Well, I also hope it's the largest."

Capturing my smiling mouth with his, he kisses me so deeply and invitingly that I can't help but release him from his punishment and wrap my hand around him through his trousers.

He groans and sighs simultaneously, grasping my face between his palms and pulling me closer, careful not to slide down our eye masks and break us out of the moment. Relief is pouring out of us, and it's like we're determined to make the most of this truce while we can.

Emboldened by our arousal, Evan isn't about to stop there. He slides my spaghetti straps down, and the fact that I'm not wearing anything under my dress is undeniable when it's pooled around my waist.

"It's criminal that I can't see this gorgeous body of

yours," he murmurs, cupping my breasts and brushing my nipples with his thumbs. I arch into him, urging him on, desperate for more. He leaves a trail of hot kisses down my neck and chest before taking one nipple into his mouth. I gasp as he rolls his tongue around it, making it a firm peak. Then he bites down ever so gently, causing me to yelp in surprise.

"We're going to get kicked out!" I hiss, yanking his head up by his hair.

"No, we won't," he says, nibbling on my ear. "We're in the most secluded booth, and it's pitch-black—as long as we're quiet, we'll be fine."

As Evan resumes working his magical mouth on my chest, I keep thinking that this is, hands down, the wildest thing I've ever done. Fooling around in public, knowing that at any moment the lights could suddenly turn on and expose my topless body to the entire restaurant? Really stupid. And really, really hot. But still stupid.

That said, it doesn't take long before I get so caught up in everything that Evan's doing to me that it would be even more unthinkable to stop. But before we can take it any further, my knee connects with the bottom of the table, and a current of pain shoots up my leg like it was electrocuted.

"Ffffu—" I groan, biting my tongue to mute the obscenities I want to release.

"Are you alright?" Evan whispers urgently. Now that I've clumsily cut our erotic experience short, we both remove our masks, to better assess where I've been hurt.

"Yes," I gasp, "I'm fine. Just hit my knee, that's all." I prod at the tender spot with frustration. "I'll have a mean bruise tomorrow, though."

Evan drops one of his hands to cup my knee tenderly while brushing my mouth with the other, grazing my bottom lip delicately under his thumb.

"Then I'll have to go easier on you next time," he says, replacing his thumb with his own lips and gently biting mine.

Even without our masks on, we can barely see anything, and the darkness is making it that much harder to resist temptation. I think I hear footsteps approaching our table, but it's probably my beating heart, which is pounding so hard as Evan's fingers snake up my leg that I'm not surprised if the sound has become audible.

"So, what can I help you with?"

I'm about to answer "getting me off" until I realize that voice is too cheery to be Evan's.

Shit—the waiter. What was his name again? I'm so horny it has escaped me, much like the straps to my dress I can't locate around my waist.

"You tapped the button under your table," he explains. "Is there something wrong with your food, or is it time for another round of drinks?"

"Actually, Josh," Evan says, wrapping his arm around me and pulling me closer so my bare tits are hidden from any potential view, "we have an urgent matter to attend to, so would you mind boxing everything up for us?"

I'm not sure what I'm more impressed by—Evan's ability to recall the name of somebody he's just met while he's rock hard, his protective nature making sure I feel safe and comfortable while topless in public, or his ingenious segue to finish what we started back at his place.

"Of course, Mr. Chen. I'll get these plates out of your way and pack up the remaining courses from the kitchen. You both can head to the front to close your tab, and we'll have everything ready for you in a few minutes."

Once Josh has removed our dishes of uneaten mystery food and it's clear that he's walked out of earshot, we share a nervous laugh.

"That was close!" I exhale, relieved that at no point did

our waiter reach out to grab a glass and get a handful of nipple instead.

"You're telling me," Evan says as he adjusts himself through his pants. "My junk is more tender than any meat they could have served, so let's hope the food is worth the interruption."

He buttons his blazer then slides the straps of my dress back on before taking my hand and leading me toward the entrance. I can tell my updo is coming undone, and my makeup is probably a mess, but I'm not about to fumble around the restaurant searching for a bathroom in the dark. I can only hope Evan finds me as attractive when he can see me clearly as when he can't.

Ew, what a ridiculously disparaging thought. The man would have risked an indecent exposure charge, so there's absolutely zero chance that he'd lose interest because my eyeliner's smudged and my lipstick's smeared. I can hear the glam fam shouting in my head: *Get it together, Casey. You are a goddess, and he should worship the ground you walk on. Now go fuck his brains out and report back, betch!*

"After you," Evan says, snapping me back to the present. While I've been giving myself a pep talk, my date has returned our masks and paid the bill. He leads me out the door with one hand holding our takeout bag and the other on the small of my back. It feels natural, like it's our fiftieth date instead of our first.

And when we stop at the curb underneath a streetlamp, his velvet blazer is the exact same color as my *Atonement* dress —a deep emerald, almost glowing under the warm light. When he said earlier that we were on the same side, I never imagined it would be this true.

"Wow . . ." he whispers, taking me in.

I've been in the fashion industry my entire adult life, so I'm used to hearing effusive compliments that demand as much attention as whatever they're praising. But the real sign I've done my job right is when all you hear is silence. And it's freaking the fuck out of me.

Evan drops the doggy bag on the sidewalk before cupping my face with both hands and kissing me. Gone is the hungry lust, replaced with a soft indulgence. He's content to linger on my lips, savoring every moment we get to taste each other. By the time he pulls away, I'm more light-headed than I was fooling around in our booth.

"Would you like to come over to my place?"

His words are hopeful but no longer desperate. He wants me, and I'm sure once we rev back up, I'd feel his wanton need again, but somehow the mood has shifted. I consider his offer, tempted to follow him home, because Evan Chen seems like a guy who would drive a woman wild all night long—a night you'd brag about to your friends because he was *that* good and everyone should know about it.

But then what? What about the following day, week, and beyond? After being so focused on proving myself in my career, I haven't confronted what comes next, and I'm sure Evan isn't thinking that far ahead either. Getting our rocks off would be fun in the moment, but I'm starting to think I might want an actual relationship with Evan rather than just a fling. And I'm not ready to face the reality if he doesn't feel the same.

I shake my head at his request. "I had such an amazing time, Evan, but I let myself get carried away back there, and I don't want to rush this." I don't want him to interpret 'this' as anything more serious than the sex, so I add, "It's our first date, and we Southern girls were raised to wait."

He raises an eyebrow as we both try to keep a straight face, knowing full well that giving a guy an over-the-pants hand job underneath a dining table isn't exactly the definition of modesty. He opens his mouth, and I can practically see the snarkiness rising to his lips, ready to call me out on my BS, but instead, he sighs.

"Fair enough," he says, wrapping his hands around my waist. He gives me a chaste kiss on the cheek, and I'm admittedly a little disappointed by his chivalry. I'm not sure what it says about me that I secretly want my boundaries crossed, but best not to dwell on it.

Evan leans in close to my ear. "You let me know when your answer is a hearty . . . jubilant . . . ecstatic . . . *yes*."

My breath hitches, and it takes a moment before I come to my senses and push him away. If he can't get between my legs, he'll get under my skin, and I'm doing a poor job convincing him neither is working.

"I hate you so much," I say, smiling.

"I hate you so much more," he replies with an even bigger grin. He points to the limo idling on the other side of the street. "Rami can drive you home; he'll even let you keep your phone this time."

"Oh no, thank you, but that's not necessary."

"How else are you getting back to Palo Alto?"

"I told some of my friends I'd stop by and say hi since they live nearby. It's no big deal." Even if the glam fam wasn't currently in Europe, they would never live in the sleepy Presidio. But Evan doesn't know them, and besides, who hasn't told a little white lie to get out of an awkward ride home with your date's limo driver? What if this is Evan's schtick, and he has this guy on retainer to send his one night stands on their merry way? "Tell Rami he can have the rest of the night off."

"At least let me drop you off at your friends' place, since I drove my own car here."

I turn my head where he's gesturing, expecting to see yet another Tesla, but when he clicks the unlock button on his keychain, the lights flash on a brand-new silver metallic Porsche SUV, easily a six-figure vehicle.

Evan must have seen my disbelief because he sheepishly adds, "It's electric, and I lease it as a business expense, so it's not like I own it—"

"You don't have to be embarrassed about your success, Evan. You really don't. Least of all in front of me."

The softness in his eyes hardens into skepticism. "What is that supposed to mean?"

I shrug. "I mean, in my line of work, I'm surrounded by millionaires and billionaires. When I first moved out here, I lived with one. Regular, working-class folks don't outsource their clothes shopping, so I don't know why, after all these years, I continue to be shocked that my clients are rich."

As soon as the words leave my mouth, I regret them. Lesson one of the lifestyles of the rich and famous: Never remind them they're rich or famous.

"I see," he murmurs, his mouth pressed in a firm, thin line. "In that case, why don't you take the leftovers from our *client* dinner, since I've imposed on you enough this evening."

He holds out the bag, and I take it, stunned. A minute ago, he acted so bold and confident in his shirtless suit, but now he's deflated, like he came to a Halloween party where everyone is wearing the same costume.

'Rich' wasn't the word that triggered Evan. I meant to alleviate his concerns about class privilege, but instead, I made him feel like nothing special. Like this was just another Valentine's Day for me, working overtime for a Silicon Valley CEO, pretending he's more than a paycheck.

"Evan, I'm sorry. That's not what I—"

"Save it, Casey. I'll see you in the office, and we can forget this night ever happened."

I reach for his arm and desperately try to explain the misunderstanding, but it comes out like an apology word salad. Evan briskly walks to his car without looking back and drives off into the night, and by the time I turn around, the limo's gone too. All the adrenaline has leaked out of my body, so now I'm standing outside in the cold February air, without a jacket and in a ridiculously fancy dress. Alone.

I should have learned my lesson the first time, wallowing to Hunter Hayes after my prom date broke my heart. This dress couldn't guarantee Keira Knightley's character a happily ever after, so I don't know why I ever thought I could break the curse.

Exasperated by my own delusions, I sigh and pull out my phone to hail a ride. It's going to cost me about seventy-five dollars to get back home, and while I could technically expense it, I'm not about to risk Evan seeing the charge and knowing I proved him right. I need to take this one on the chin and vow never to go on a date with a client—even if he's quickly becoming much more than that—again.

"If First Lines of Classic Literature Were Retold in Silicon Valley" by McSweetie's – February 18

1. *Pride and Prejudice*: It is a truth universally acknowledged, that a single man in possession of a good fortune, must be an angel investor with too many fucking worthless NFTs.

2. *A Tale of Two Cities*: It was the best of times; it was the worst of times. It was the age of being in the top one percent but still being too poor to buy a house in the Marina.

3. *The Trial*: Someone must have slandered Josef K., for one morning, without having done anything truly wrong, he was accused of forgetting to dilute the cold brew concentrate.

4. *The Catcher in the Rye*: If you really want to hear about

how I founded my startup, the first thing you'll probably want to know is whether I was an Ivy League legacy, and what my parents did for a living, and all that "being born on third base" kind of crap, but I don't feel like going into it, if you want to know the truth.

5. *Beloved*: The legal department that fucked up my deal with redlines was spiteful.

6. *Slaughterhouse-Five*: All this happened in the pitch deck we sent to that Forrester analyst, more or less. But definitely less.

7. *The Debut*: Dr. Weiss, at forty, knew that her life had been ruined by rampant age discrimination.

8. *Middlesex*: I was born twice: first, as an engineer who built things; and then, as a sales engineer, who got paid even more by promising to build things.

9. *Middlemarch*: Miss Brooke had that kind of beauty which seems destined to run the corporate social media accounts.

10. *Catch-22*: It was love at first tabs or spaces.

11. *The Great Gatsby*: In my younger and more vulnerable years, my father gave me some advice to stick it out at one company, and I've been job-hopping every single year since.

12. *A Frolic of His Own*: Justice?—You get justice in the next world; in this world, you have white women being counted as diversity hires.

13. *Doc*: He began to die when he was twenty-one, but late-stage capitalism is slow and sly and subtle when you're making six figures right out of college.

14. *Fear and Loathing in Las Vegas*: We were somewhere at Burning Man on the edge of the desert when the drugs we brought to figure out our next pivot began to take hold.

15. *The Color Purple*: You better not never tell nobody but your best work friend every time you come in without makeup and your boss asks if you're tired.

16. *A River Runs Through It*: In our startup, there was no clear line between religion and your preferred productivity app.

17. *Gone with the Wind*: Salesforce was not beautiful, but men seldom realized it when there's no decent CRM alternative.

18. *Middle Passage*: Of all the things that drive men to a mental breakdown, the most common disaster, I've come to learn, is the open-concept office.

19. *Jane Eyre*: There was no possibility of escaping on-call that day.

20. *Matilda*: It's a funny thing about startups. Even when their own founder is the most disgusting little blister you could ever imagine, Andreessen Horowitz will still think that he or she is wonderful.

chapter
ten

As the week crawls by, I get a lot accomplished making over the other execs, but Evan remains frosty after our Valentine's Day fight. It kills me not to demand a conversation and hash things out once and for all, but I force myself to give him space, throwing myself into my work instead.

At least by the time Friday rolls around, I convince him to send over a few bullet points detailing his style preferences. He's not cordial by any means, but he's civil, so I take it as a win and spend the evening shopping in Union Square for him.

In a way, it's like I'm using the outing to make up for our miscommunication, and I take great care to visit my favorite shops and pick out items that best suit him: luxurious, cozy cashmere from Vince; expertly tailored blazers from Theory; even a graffiti-styled, black denim jacket from Alexander McQueen for the ultimate pop of personality. The receipts are significantly higher than what I got for him and the leadership team last time at the mall, but hey, I'm doing my best not to get fired here.

Of course, refusing to acknowledge Evan as more than a client is what got us fighting in the first place, so I might as well admit the truth to myself. That I wouldn't be going to such great lengths if I didn't like the man and want him to like me back. Because if there was ever a time to treat my way into a man's heart, this would be it.

Now that I have a Habituall email and can peruse employee calendars, I already know Evan's occupied at a board dinner tonight, but it would be a nice gesture to deliver the goods myself. Thankfully, Tania has visited Evan's apartment several times for video shoots and impromptu karaoke happy hours, so she shared his address and key code. That way I can make the handoff without needing to wait to be let in.

While I'm coming down from the adrenaline after the stores close, I shoot Evan a heads-up text, trying to sound as upbeat as possible to prove there's no bad blood between us.

> Hey, it's Casey! I just finished the most intense shopping session, and you're gonna love what I got for you! I'd hate to lug it down to Palo Alto, and I already have your address, so would you mind if I swing by your place and drop everything off?

I brace myself for resistance, but surprisingly, he gives me a thumbs-up emoji. He mentioned hitting the gym before the last board dinner at State Bird Provisions, so maybe he had a gratifying workout beforehand, and he's still riding the high of an abnormally good mood. Regardless of the reason why he's not putting up a fight, I quickly order a car to pick me up before he changes his mind.

Evan lives south of Market Street, a few blocks from Habituall headquarters, so it doesn't take long before I'm at his place. I start to get butterflies because, for the first time, I'll get a glimpse of the real Evan, and it feels super intimate to enter his home. My brain goes into overdrive as I ride the elevator up to his floor and walk down the hallway, carrying my own weight in garment bags—will Evan be a dirty hippie, or a secret perv with a sex dungeon? Or both—what would a hippie's sex dungeon look like? Lots of hemp rope and CBD lube?

Punching in the numbers Tania gave me, I unlock the front door of his apartment, ready to face whatever comes next.

My first impressions are surprise and relief because when I step into the entryway, it's not the scent of dank weed hitting my nose but rather the smells of lemon and fresh laundry. Remembering to take off my shoes, I set the bags down and make my way into the open-concept dining room.

Holy crap. *This* is the home of a man who has his shit together. This is where a real CEO lives—one who's been leading Fortune 500 companies for years, not a quirky startup where they use coloring exercises to spur creativity.

I mean, look at this kitchen! All marble countertops and matte black fixtures—not to mention every surface is spotless. There's no cheap booze cart here, but a legit bar area with a temperature-controlled wine fridge and crystal glassware. I sneak a peek in one of the cabinets, relishing the idea that this *Top Chef*–worthy space is a façade covering his grubby snack habits, but I'm simultaneously disappointed and impressed when I see meticulously organized spices like saffron and turmeric, with no dingy yellow stains coating the interior.

I'm overcome with emotions: dismay that I don't know Evan at all; pride that his parents raised him right to keep his home so clean; bewilderment that his business must clearly be successful to pay for luxury down to every last detail; and envy at the long line of women he must have banging down his front door for a chance to be wooed by one of San Francisco's most eligible bachelors.

And when I step into the living room, my mouth drops, taking in the cityscape, featuring Salesforce Tower piercing through the clouds and the Bay Bridge jutting across the water in its brightly lit glory. Warm arousal makes my limbs tingly, and I squeeze my toes into the plush, cream rug, imagining Evan lifting my naked body and pinning me against the glass wall, thrusting into me with my legs wrapped around his waist, the city lights twinkling behind us in the background.

Damn . . . this is the home of a man who *fucks*.

I peer around the ceiling, searching for security cameras and embarrassed at the possibility of Evan watching me getting hot and bothered. But he either keeps his digital eyes in less conspicuous locations, or he's the only owner of a luxury apartment who doesn't have it monitored like Fort Knox.

A nagging thought keeps distracting me from leaving the shopping bags in the entryway and walking out of here.

Why does someone with a place like *this* choose to dress like *that*?

Go see what's in his closet, the devil on my shoulder whispers. *You know you want to.*

Absolutely not, Casey. I didn't raise a snoop, the angel on my opposite shoulder insists in my mother's voice.

You're not exactly on the best of terms. You might never get another chance like this again.

So if you have the opportunity to break and enter, that makes it okay?

You came to deliver a ton of nice, new clothes. It's your responsibility to hang them up, so they don't wrinkle. Your duty, even.

Is that in the job description, young lady? Digging through his underwear like some Peeping Tom?

Aw yeah, now you're talking.

My mind made up, I grab the bags before striding toward the main bedroom. When I turn the door handle, I pray for a pair of Tom Ford silk-blend boxer briefs.

The bedroom's as luxe as the rest of the house, with mid-century modern furniture in a muted color palette of grays, browns, and whites. Along one wall is a bookcase and a closet with Japanese-inspired wood paneled sliding doors.

I slide open the closet, and my lady boner deflates at the sight of his wardrobe: racks of T-shirts from tech conferences, ratty hoodies and sweatshirts, jeans without any shape, cargo shorts with an obscene number of pockets, and so many tank tops and basketball shorts that he could open a thrift shop dedicated to athletic wear.

I'm not sure why I'm so bummed out. He may have alluded to knowing certain designers when we met, but I've seen what he wears to the office. This is all par for the course. I shove the pieces aside to make room for my new finds and start hanging them, still in their plastic sheaths lest they become contaminated by the rest of this toxic waste.

I make quick work of it, not wanting to spend more time with these sins against fashion than I need to, before I check out his bookcase. Glossing over the stacks of boring management manuals and cliché CEO manifestos, I scan the gems that clue me into what Evan likes when he's not reading about work. The authors' names that pop out—Amy Tan, Kazuo Ishiguro, Celeste Ng—make me smile. Some of the best literary fiction, and no mediocre white-bro books in sight. At least Evan's capable of having good taste in certain areas of his life, namely interior design, liquor, and literature. It's a shame that level of discernment stopped at his fashion sense.

I put back a hefty tome in its place on the shelf, but the bookcase gives way suddenly, sliding on a hinge.

What the—a secret door! Am I about to fall into Narnia? No, wait. This is where he must keep the sex dungeon.

I push the door open, expecting a child's fantasyland or an X-rated fantasyland—nothing in between—but it's so much better than I could have imagined.

I've walked into my own personal fantasyland. If the

panoramic view of San Francisco made me wet, then this hidden closet is leaving me drenched.

Shirts—with buttons and collars! Cashmere sweaters and scarves, smart blazers and coats, and shoes that have been shined so well that I could use them as vanity mirrors to apply my makeup. And suits! So many suits! All the classics, of course, like Armani and Hugo Boss, but also Prada, Valentino, and even some far-out floral and geometric prints from Gucci and Versace.

Who the fuck does this closet belong to—Harry Styles? Is Evan able to afford this apartment because his side hustle is storing awards ceremony outfits for Hollywood's finest?

At this point, I'm crazed, pawing at the fabrics and admiring their textures and colors like I was given a VIP ticket to the world's most lavish petting zoo.

I lose track of time, overindulging in the opulence. I even come across the emerald velvet blazer that Evan wore on our dinner date in the dark and ease myself into it, enjoying the way the satin lining feels against my skin even though the sleeves are hanging off me. Then I start opening the closet's drawers, and it's like the petting zoo has expanded into a carnival with designer watches, sunglasses, and other accessories, making my eyes light up like prizes at the ring toss. I slide on a pair of Ray-Bans and put one of the Breitlings on my wrist, admiring my reflection in the full-length mirror like a Silicon Valley James Bond.

And then I find the jackpot, the equivalent of the best carnival foods—corn dogs, funnel cake, and cheese curds—all wrapped up into one. Tom Ford silk-blend boxer briefs.

"What the *fuck* do you think you're doing?"

My imaginary carnival comes crashing down, and I instantly go from salivating over accessories like they're deep-fried foods to dropping his drawers like I've been scalded with hot oil. I slowly turn around to see Evan dressed like a lackey in the Russian Mafia with his black and white striped Adidas tracksuit. His menacing look completes his mob boss outfit, as if he indeed plans to 'take care of me'—and not in a good way.

"I told you to leave the bags at the front desk, so why the hell are you in my apartment—in my bedroom closet—holding my fucking underwear?"

Evan's definitely been rude to me before, but prior to our Valentine's Day argument, there's always been an element of amusement, a sardonic joy from verbally sparring with each other. This time, however, when I turn around and see the disgust and contempt in his eyes, I can tell he's not being passive-aggressive anymore. Just plain-ass aggressive.

"I—I'm sorry—I lost track of time," I stammer, taking out my phone to confirm the now obvious. And lo and behold, there it is—the text I missed from him.

Shit.

"Evan, you have to believe me. I never saw your message . . ." I reach out to grab his arm, belatedly realizing I'm still wearing his emerald blazer, and my hands can't extend past the sleeve.

He recoils. "I don't have to do anything, Casey, when you're the one breaking and entering. Now take that off. You look fucking ridiculous."

Evan pulls on the sleeve, and I yelp—not because I don't want to take it off but because I'm afraid he's going to tear the delicate stitching. But he manages to shake me loose, lifting the blazer above my head and unceremoniously dumping me out as if I were the contents of a garbage can.

And when he rips his Ray-Bans off my face, I instinctively cover my eyes so he can't see the hot tears streaming down, but that makes things worse when we both notice it's the arm adorned with his Breitling.

"Are you fucking kidding me?" he growls, firmly grabbing my wrist and yanking the watch off, not caring if he pulled my arm from its socket. "I should call the cops for this shit, you know that? Are you even a real stylist, Casey, or do you trick unsuspecting, gullible guys like me so you can sneak into their homes and steal their most prized possessions? Do you even have any idea what this is?"

He pushes the watch too close to my face. "It's a Breitling . . . vintage, right?" I guess.

Evan chuckles darkly. "Vintage . . . you bet your ass it is. This is my great-grandfather's Breitling Navitimer, which he received as a retirement gift after forty years of bookkeeping at a law firm here in San Francisco. His grandfather was one of the thousands of Chinese immigrants who helped build the first transcontinental railroad in this country, so he could give a better life to his family back home and here in the Bay." Heavy with emotion, he pauses to admire its craftsmanship. "This watch has been passed down through four generations, a testament to our hard work and a stark reminder that no Chen should ever have to hold a shovel unless they're doing so because they want to—"

His voice cracks, and I almost lose it. Please, for all that's holy, let me plummet down this skyscraper and let the earth swallow me whole. I feel like the smallest, most primordial creature—some amoeba or bacteria, a microscopic speck with no functional brain.

Evan's standing with his shoulders back, his pride in his family palpable. What do I have to be proud of, in comparison? Look at me, acting like Daisy Buchanan in *The Great Gatsby*—fawning over beautiful shirts and behaving like a little fool. This obscene level of materialism and privilege isn't lost on me; rather, it weighs me down to the point where I want to be crushed by the guilt and shame. Maybe jail time is what I deserve—in this case, it's the adult equivalent of my mother sending me to my room to think about what I've done. And then I cringe at that hideous thought. There I go again, centering someone else's pain around me. Best not to think about me at all.

"When did your dad give it to you?" I ask meekly.

"Huh?" Evan lifts his head up as if he's lost in thought.

"Your watch," I clarify, hoping he doesn't remember how angry he is with me at the mere mention. "You said it's been passed down through four generations, so when did you receive it? It must have been a special moment."

"Yeah, it was," he replies softly, tracing the watch face absent-mindedly with his fingers. "Seven years ago, I told my parents I was dropping out of NYU to start a company. My mom was the daughter of Woodstock-going flower children, so she was always more of a free spirit and supported my dream of being my own boss. But my dad was traditional. I was deathly afraid he'd disown me and yell that I was wasting a perfectly good college education on some whim. He walked into their bedroom without a word, and I thought he wouldn't come back out that night."

Evan smiles at the memory, a reassurance that this story has a happy ending. "He returned holding the watch and said his grandpa waited for his entire career to wear something this nice. I figured he was about to jump into some speech about paying your dues first, but instead, he handed it to me and said, 'This watch represents raising the bar. He worked forty years for this gift, but the real reward is the opportunity you have to start where he ended, so that in forty years from now, you can look back and know you accomplished more than he ever could.'"

More tears pinprick my eyes, and I blink rapidly in a futile attempt to force them back, but I can't help but get choked up. Here I thought Evan was some privileged tech bro whose ego was so huge he couldn't even be bothered to wear a collared shirt, but I didn't just stumble into his secret closet. I discovered a piece of his heart.

"Evan, I'm so . . . *so* sorry for what I've done. And I'm also sorry for this—"

Before my self-consciousness can stop me, I reach out and envelop him in the sincerest hug I can offer. As anticipated, he seizes up, and I resist the urge to jump back like I've touched a hot stove. The last New York transplant I took by surprise with my Southern hospitality is the most talented esthetician I know, Victoria Townsend. It took persistence, but Tori no longer threatens to scratch my eyes out with her dangerously long nails—now, the pain she inflicts is when she's squeezing me back just as hard. And at that moment, I tell myself that I'm willing to win Evan over, no matter how long it takes.

A minute or two goes by, and while he doesn't hug me back, he doesn't push me away either. I wait it out, feeling him slowly thaw and relax into my arms. God, he smells good. Why didn't I make a quick pit stop in his bathroom so I could spritz myself with his cologne and be on my merry way?

We simultaneously let out shuddering breaths, and when I let him go, he suddenly grasps my arms as if to stop me. His hands graze over the back of my thin, striped top, making me shiver with anticipation.

"You took something of mine, Holbright," he whispers into my ear, his fingertips playing with the hem of my shirt and tracing the small of my back. "It's only fair that I get even."

Before I can spout off some sarcastic remark, he pushes me up against the wall with the full-length mirror behind me and kisses me like it's a punishment—one I accept with wild abandon. I would repent for every sin I've ever committed just to keep that tantalizing mouth on mine.

Evan only comes up for air to peel my shirt over my head. Thank the universe that I chose to wear my most luxurious, lacy black bra and G-string underneath. Not that it matters, because he quickly gets me out of my pants and discards those too, without so much as a second glance. First, he hooks up with me in the dark where he can't see my outfit, then removes my lingerie like it's annoying plastic wrap, stripping me nude in a closet full of clothes he doesn't even wear. At least the man's consistent in his utter apathy toward fashion.

"Not one for foreplay, eh?" I muse as he takes off his shirt, picks me up, and carries me into the bedroom.

He tosses me on the bed, a man on a mission. "There's plenty of time for that once our layers are off." He motions toward his drawstring, but I reach out to stop him.

"Wait—you're missing out on all the fun."

I shimmy across Evan's low-profile bed, so my face is aligned to his waistband while he's standing. Determined to make him overcome with yearning, I take my sweet time, slowly untying his track pants and sliding them down to his knees. His length strains against his boxer briefs, aching to be unleashed. But instead, I coyly trace up and down and around the seams. How wondrous that every stitch of a garment can both keep us constrained and set us free.

"You're one of those weirdos who takes forever to unwrap their gifts, aren't you?" he says, running his hands through my hair.

I kiss his hard-on through the fabric, pressing my lips delicately around the head. "Mmm . . . they don't call it a package for nothing."

When the tip of his cock has left a sizable wet spot, I finally relieve Evan of his underwear and take him in my mouth. Or at least as much of him as I can fit, my hand wrapping around the base in a soft fist. With my ass in the air and my other hand keeping his knees in place, I suck him eagerly. The way his hands grip my scalp urges me on, granting me the kind of power that world leaders could only dream of. I pick up the pace, meeting his unconscious thrusts in a perfect rhythm. Between his shaking legs and the moans that are becoming ever louder, I know I'm bringing my A-game. I'm congratulating myself on a blow job well done—that is, until Evan doesn't let me finish.

"As much as I hate for you to stop," he rasps, pulling out of my mouth, "I won't be able to live with myself if I come before you do."

He leans over to open the nightstand, but after rummaging around, he closes the drawer empty-handed.

"Shit! I ran out of condoms. I meant to go to the pharmacy to refill my stash, but—" He checks the time on his phone atop the nightstand. "It's after nine o'clock, and all the stores nearby are closed."

I smile, pleased to confirm my assumption of Evan's sex life when I saw how immaculate and luxe his apartment was. This is a man who fucks, indeed.

"Sounds like we've both been around the block, so to speak. I know it's a matter of trust, but I'm on birth control, and I was tested not long before I started working with you. There hasn't been anybody since. If you can say the same, I'm game to keep going if you are."

The expression he gives me is priceless: It's like I told him he won the lottery, the Golden State Warriors won the NBA Finals, *and* Christmas came early. He reassures me he's in the clear as well, kissing me in a tornado of excitement and gratitude. Although I'd argue I'm even more thankful: His abrupt shift in mood may be jarring, but at least he no longer wants to throw me out.

"I'm not worthy," Evan says. "Not even close. Seriously, you could ask me for anything—a first-class flight to anywhere in the world, a shopping spree at Tiffany's, a fucking Lamborghini—and I'd make it happen. No questions asked."

I laugh, pulling him closer to lay next to me on our sides. "All I could possibly want right now is this." I reach out for his hard cock and rub it along my slit, wet and warm with arousal.

But rather than guiding him inside, I press the tip against my clit, using him like my own personal sex toy.

"Fuck me, Casey," Evan groans into the crook of my neck.

I rub faster, surprised and delighted by how close I am to the brink already. "Oh, I will," I pant, "but not until I get mine first."

Evan's hands are everywhere, gripping my waist, caressing my breasts, and lightly squeezing the base of my neck every time he devours me in another kiss. He's desperate to close the space between us and slide deep inside me, but whether it's insisting he wear an outfit he hates or making him wait for his release, I relish the sweet torture of having him at my mercy.

As the tension builds, the tempo of my gyrations quickens, and I grind against him until I reach a fever pitch, moaning with abandon and babbling his name.

"Oh god, Evan, I'm so close—"

He flicks his tongue across my earlobe and down my neck, blowing cool air where his lips have landed and sending chills down my spine. "I know. I can feel you dripping down every inch of me. You keep using me." He groans as I trace his tip around my slick entrance. "*Fuck*, just like that. Don't stop until you take what's yours."

I bite my lip, amazed by Evan's restraint when I've got his dick pressed to my clit like my life depends on it. "Oh yes, I'm gonna come for you."

"Don't you worry about me, Casey. Come for yourself. Because you are the sexiest woman I know, and you fucking deserve it." He pulls me closer to increase the pressure. "Now let me watch you explode."

Cradling my body, Evan rocks me back and forth until I send myself over the edge, crying out as I free-fall. He captures my mouth, not waiting to catch me as I come down from my climax. There's no time for forehead kisses or full-body massages. Instead, he's ravenous, pinning me to the bed and finally seizing what's been a hairsbreadth out of reach. In one smooth motion, he throws my legs over his shoulders and thrusts inside my drenched pussy, and we both groan at the immediate fullness.

"Fuck, Casey," he grits out as he pounds harder and faster. "You feel too good. I can't hold out—"

"I know. I'm right there too," I pant. The friction has got us both in a frenzy, and it's all too much to handle. Before I know it, I'm about to burst. "Right there, Evan, yes. Yes!"

I come for the second time, much more intensely than the last, like an electric current radiating through every nerve. Evan follows soon after, bellowing in pleasure until he's utterly spent.

The bedroom's silent except for our heavy breathing from the comedown. "What *was* that?" Evan gasps, rolling over.

I wiggle my numb fingers and toes to shake feeling back into them. "You tell me."

We recover in quiet bliss, until I hear chanting coming from Evan's closet. Something about there being some whores in this house. At first, I'm indignant, thinking I'm getting straight-up harassed. That's when I recognize the lyrics of "WAP" by Cardi B and Megan Thee Stallion and realize it's my phone. Of course.

"Um . . . is that your default ringtone?" Evan laughs, pulling on his underwear and following me into the closet as I fish my phone out of my pants on the floor and send the call to voicemail.

"Ugh, no. It's my friend Som. She likes to prank the glam fam by stealing our phones when we're not paying attention and adding the horniest, most profane songs to her contact info so when she calls, she can achieve maximum embarrassment wherever we are. So mission accomplished!"

He chuckles, running his hand through his dark, deliciously rumpled hair. "Glam fam?"

I throw on my clothes. "Alex's glam family: Som's a makeup artist; then there's Glen, our hairdresser extraordinaire; and Tori, who's in charge of paws and claws, brows and blackheads, you name it. Up until recently, we were in the business of making our princess the most fabulous version of herself, but . . ."

After laying it bare in bed, there's no point in hiding from the facts. I force myself to get the words out. "We had a falling out. For reasons I still don't understand, Alex's boyfriend convinced her she can do better than be dressed by her best friend since birth. Now I'm stuck scrambling to make up for lost income because they decided to travel to Europe without me. All so she can try on other stylists like I try on clothes." I calculate the difference between time zones. "I'm sure Som's drunk-dialing me after an all-night rager if she's hitting me up this early in their morning. I don't see any other reason why they'd need anything from me."

"Hey," Evan says, lifting my chin up before the bitter sadness can consume me. "In case I haven't explicitly told you, I have no doubt you're the best in the business. And regardless of how unlikely it may seem, I'm not alone in thinking that. Of course, Wendy and Tania sing your praises all the time, but you've even got the leadership team putting aside their egos to admire your handiwork. The other day, I heard Paul and Natasha begrudgingly compliment each other's outfits while practicing their keynote, and honestly that's a more impressive feat than anything on the product roadmap." He cradles my cheek. "I know I'm not the easiest to work with, but you're doing a fantastic job. Even if Alex doesn't see it right now, she'll come back around. Because whether it's the Habituall team or your glam fam—everyone you meet is lucky to have you. Especially me."

I step back, stunned. "Wow. That's the nicest you've ever

been to me, and I'm not just referring to the words of affirmation. That also includes the multiple orgasms."

"Are you sure you don't want to stay the night?" His hands linger on my hips. "Because there's much more of both in your future if you do."

After ogling Evan's bulge in his boxer briefs, I take in the rest of the eye candy in his closet, inhaling the stale, musty air like it's an antique shop full of hidden treasures. "As much as I love compliments and climaxes, what would make me the happiest woman in the world is if you brought back this wardrobe."

Evan sighs, rubbing his face. "Look, I just had the best sex of my life, so I don't want to ruin the mood. Trust me when I say I'm not going to wear any of this anymore."

"But why not?" I plead. "Our sexcapade could have been cut abruptly short, but I let you play at the waterpark without floaties, remember? You said I could ask for anything I wanted—and this request is much easier to fulfill than a Lamborghini! I'm sure these clothes still fit you like a glove, but if it's a matter of sizing, I know several great tailors in the city—"

"As much as I appreciated the all-access pass, I'm not getting into this with you right now," he says through gritted teeth. "So drop it."

I gesture at the racks of art. "I don't understand. It's such a waste to let these masterpieces hang unworn for this long . . ."

Snippets of our conversation replay in my mind, and something about them isn't adding up. "Wait a minute, you said you've had your watch for seven years, when you started your company, but Habituall was founded five years ago. I'm confused."

His glare bores a hole into my skull, but I refuse to lose this staring contest. I learned from my dysfunctional parents to give the silent treatment, not take it.

Evan breaks eye contact, his gaze falling to his feet. "I said I started *a* company, not *this* company."

My brow furrows. "But in all the interviews I read for this gig, you made it sound like Habituall was your first startup."

"It might as well have been," he mumbles, digging his toes into the carpet. "The first one never got off the ground—didn't even last a year. I was able to secure some angel investors and hire a few employees, but I was a college dropout and wanted to be taken seriously, so I wasted tons of cash on looking the part of CEO. Even had a fashionista girlfriend who loved taking me and my credit cards out for a joyride—in the name of coaching me on the differences between Dior and Dolce & Gabbana. And for a while, people believed the act, but that's all it ever was. I was in way over my head and buckling under the enormous pressure. Suits and ties may get you meetings, but they don't keep customers happy or make the paychecks magically clear when you're in the red. The business was a trash fire, my ex dumped me when I cut up the cards, and I was forced to walk away from everything."

I reach out to hold his hand, careful not to squeeze too hard from my anger at his shallow ex-girlfriend. I, too, love to shop til I drop, but in no circumstance would I encourage someone to spend beyond their means and go into debt. No wonder Evan tossed me out of the zen room like I was a washed-up reject on the clearance rack—he took one look at me and assumed I would stir up as much trouble as she did.

"I'm so sorry you went through that. It sounds like you've been through hell and back. But you did what all Texan parents teach their kids about resilience: You got back on that horse. And now that horse is destined to become a unicorn! At least the silver lining of that setback is it brought you the success you have now, right?"

He pulls his hand back, scowling. "Yeah, and it took everything I fucking had to climb out of that rubble. I was so ashamed I wanted to give my dad's watch back and sell my designer shit to a consignment store, but he wouldn't let me. Told me I would need them again when my next business made it big. After all that, he still believed in me, but I couldn't even look him in the eye. I felt like pond scum in his presence. So I packed everything up and moved to San Francisco, determined to start from scratch like my ancestors and learn how to do things right. And this time, I was going to be unapologetically myself. No more CEO cosplaying and posturing. I was going to win over Silicon Valley in cargo shorts and flip-flops, or I wouldn't play the game at all."

I've attended fashion shows around the world and become familiar with the unique styles of so many cities, so I can understand Evan's reasoning behind exchanging buttoned-up New York workwear for laid-back California casual. It's stifling to pretend to be someone you're not.

"Sounds like you made the right move because you're in great company. The kooky tech founder who doesn't give a crap about his clothes is so common it's a Silicon Valley cliché. No offense," I add, smiling.

He chuckles, putting his hands up in the air. "None taken. That's what I thought too. And for a long time, nobody cared what I wore. They encouraged it even. I was Evan Chen, the hippie wunderkind, the gym-rat genius. Reporters were fascinated, and it made for great headlines. But then we raised our Series D, opened our first international office, and the board started changing its tune about my image. Everybody loves eccentricity in the early days, but they're embarrassed by it when they're ready to ring the bell of the New York Stock Exchange. That's why you're here."

I recognize how the pieces of this puzzle have come together, but I'm still frustrated by the final picture. "I get why Habituall hired me, and I get why you disagreed with that decision, but what I don't get is why you continue to let mistakes you made over half a decade ago dictate not only how you dress, but how you live your whole life. I'm not saying anybody should force you to add these specific items back into your wardrobe, but you wore that velvet blazer on our date, so it doesn't seem like they cause you that much distress—"

"That's different," he hedges, pacing around the closet like a caged animal.

"Why is that different? Because you wanted to get into my pants on our first date—is that it?"

He stops in his tracks, fire flashing in his eyes. "Technically, you were the one trying to get into mine, but if that's the reason you think I made an effort, then I guess it worked."

My phone interrupts us as Som calls for the second time, taunting me with "WAP" as if that's all I'm good for when I'm around Evan. My face flushes with heat, and I can't tell if it's more from anger or embarrassment, but I tap *decline* and start collecting the rest of my things. The silence is more claustrophobic than these narrow closet walls, and all I want is to shake some sense into Evan, but the fire in his eyes has gone out, and I know I've lost him.

"You may think I'm overreacting," I say, standing at the closet doorway, "but to me, you're not just being stubborn. You're being incredibly selfish. It's one thing to refuse to let your board of directors pull the puppet strings. They're probably a bunch of old stooges who don't need to work for a living. But in your hands are four hundred people who definitely do, and you're letting them down. You're not making some last stand like you're Davy fucking Crockett at the Alamo—you're dying on a hill of designer clothes. I've got to go, but let me know when you're ready to be a real leader."

I stride out of the closet, across the bedroom, through the hall, out of his apartment, and down the elevator, not stopping to look back until I exit the building and gulp in the cool evening air. Every minute I wait for my rideshare to arrive, I hope Evan follows me to apologize, perhaps even donning the blazer as a grand gesture proving how much he cares about me —about *us*. But until my driver shows up, I'm left alone on the sidewalk, wondering how it went so wrong.

~

OBLIGATORY "HAPPY INTERNATIONAL WOMEN'S DAY" *corporate blog post from yet-another-tech-startup – March 8*

HAPPY INTERNATIONAL WOMEN'S DAY! We're flabbergasted this diversity holiday happens annually, and yet every year, it surprises us. Thank goodness we have a twenty-two-year-old social media girl—we mean gal, that's okay to say, right?—reminding us to pretend to give a shit.

This article will feel redundant because we already used our platitudes a week ago to celebrate Women's HER-story Month, but here we are again. The engineering team desperately needs to hire more women, but they're not so desperate to do the work to recruit them, so they've delegated the job to the ladies in HR and marketing. Cross-functional synergy!

It's a shame it's *International* Women's Day, because we don't hire non-US citizens since paying lawyers to deal with visa sponsorships is an expensive pain in the ass. But we know diversity is supposed to be important, so we'll plaster our website with stock photos to pass off as the tokenized employees we don't have. We claim to never discriminate, but it's a guarantee you will be asked ridiculously backward questions, like, "When do you plan on getting pregnant?" "Why don't you smile more?" and "Can I touch your hair?"

Anyway, we're building technology to change the world. Tech is a progressive, disruptive industry—not stodgy and sexist like Wall Street or the oil and gas industry. Instead of blatant *Mad Men*-esque misogynists who will call you 'toots' and demand you make coffee and take notes, we're the male feminist allies who will butcher your 'ethnic' name and politely ask that you bring them a kombucha and take notes, if you don't mind? Thanks for being such a team player!

Sure, we were the nerds you turned down in high school, but we're not resentful after all those years, don't worry. We don't intend to keep you in your place with a comically large gender pay gap and arbitrary reasons to deny your promotion. We don't intend to—it just happens. But we're totally a meritocracy, in that we don't think your work has merit until a man takes credit for it, of course.

Are we done yet? Great, the Grace Hopper conference is coming up, and we need one of you to take time out of your busy schedule and spread the word about how we're so dedicated to equality in the workplace. Take the extra swag bags from the storage closet. Bitches love a good swag bag!

There's one rule among the glam fam that has kept our friend group from imploding, and that's to never talk *about* someone when you should talk *to* them instead. It keeps the rumor mill at bay, especially when our queen bee is an A-list celebrity and the rest of us are on her payroll. Or most of us, I should say, now that I'm going solo.

And yet, nearly three weeks later, when the glam fam returns from Paris without Alex, I can't help but dig for dirt.

"You're sure Alex is simply de-stressing in Monaco, and it has nothing to do with the tabloids?" I ask from the driver's seat on the morning of International Women's Day. The blind items I read alluded to trouble in paradise between Alex and Dominic. I know they all hate Dominic as much as I do, but I can't get any of them to confirm the rumors.

"Nope, that's not what we're here to discuss," Glen says, riding shotgun. "You and Alex are way overdue on patching things up, but a whole month's gone by, and you owe us the play-by-play of what you've been up to."

As much as I want to know the drama from Fashion Week, he's right. I've been so busy with Habituall I've had no time to loop the glam fam in. I have revealed nothing—not Evan's secret closet, not the huge fight that resulted from me finding it, not the white-hot sex that the fight turned into, nor the heartbreaking reason why he kept the closet a secret in the first place. I'm like a gasket ready to blow.

Which is why I offered to carpool with the glam fam for Safe Harbor's fundraising event, bribing them with their favorite coffee and the hottest of goss.

"Spill it, sis," Som chimes in from the back seat. "This tea better be so scalding Bill Nye does a climate change PSA about it if you're waking us up this early."

"Does doing a B & E before a P-in-V count as scorching enough?"

Everyone simultaneously spits out their drinks in shock, before screaming at me to keep talking. After everyone's caught up, Tori's the first one to throw in her two cents.

"So you're telling us after weeks of driving you nuts, you find out Evan's been lying about his wardrobe, and you *still* decided to sleep with him? Casey, I've seen you swipe left on guys who didn't match their belts to their shoes. What has gotten into you?"

Glen wiggles his eyebrows with approval. "I think she told us exactly what has gotten into her—and out of her, and in and out—"

Tori leans forward to smack him upside the head. "We got it, Glen! But I don't care how good he is in bed, a secret closet doesn't automatically turn Mr. Khaki Cargo Shorts into Casanova."

Som nods in agreement. "That's what I like to call clitful thinking. You always used to say if a man couldn't be bothered to wear nice pants, then you'd never get him out of them."

I sigh, annoyed they're throwing my own words back at me. I'd like to see them turn down someone as magnetic as Evan in his velvet blazer. "What? So I can't have a little fun with a hot guy on a Friday night anymore?"

Glen reaches across the center console to rub my shoulder. "Of course not. And we've all had fun ourselves, so we're not ones to judge. But hot guys are a dime a dozen, and you, Casey, are priceless. Is Evan worth the fun? Because clients are expensive flings if it goes south—"

"Which it will if he keeps ignoring you and dressing like a beach bum," Tori chimes in disapprovingly behind him.

"You've made your point," I say, unsuccessfully holding back my defensiveness, "but you didn't see the hurt he's hiding in that closet. Yes, I'm upset he never told me about his old clothes or his hang-ups about them, but I can sympathize with him seeing fashion as a symbol of his failures. It's not easy to move on from something like that."

Never one to give any man the benefit of the doubt, Tori refuses to back down. "It's not like his first startup crashed and burned yesterday—you said it's been over six years. I understand you want to be empathetic, Casey, but if you go at his glacial pace, history will repeat itself. Evan can't keep making excuses why he's not doing what needs to be done for the sake of his team. The billion-dollar valuation, the future IPO, and let's not forget your own ass is on the line with your six-figure contract. There's too much at stake."

I think back to when Evan admitted to reading Brené Brown. You can't 'dare to lead' when you're too paralyzed by shame to take meaningful steps forward. Tori may not have the best bedside manner, but she's always been the most sensible one in the glam fam, so we accept her truth bombs even when they explode in our faces.

"I know that, Tori. And Evan knows that. He cares deeply about his company, and so do I—we just show it in different ways. I think I'm getting through to him, though. That night together was confusing as hell, sure, but it felt like we had our first real conversation. I'm positive he took what I said to heart, and his personal style will change because I believe he's capable of change. I'm not ready to give up on him yet. A lot can happen in two weeks—and no, Som, I see that twinkle in your eye in the rearview mirror. I'm not talking about sex."

She sucks down the last of her iced coffee. "Hey, I'm not saying that keeping a man between your legs will keep him in line, but it's worth a shot!"

Glen smiles wryly. "What she means is if Evan falls head over heels in love with you, we have no doubt he'll wear whatever you want to make you happy."

My heart pounds, and the butterflies in my stomach flutter in a whirlwind of agitation. "Yes, well, it's way too early to be thinking of the L-word. I'm taking it one day at a time."

He grips my shoulder again. "Like you said, a lot can happen in two weeks."

A COUPLE OF HOURS LATER, we're settled in at Safe Harbor, fully caffeinated and ready to go. Makeovers may be our business, but they're also the closest thing we have to a spiritual calling. As much as the glam fam complained about the early start, it didn't take any convincing. Doing their favorite thing in the world for such a great cause? Of course, they were in.

It's a tight fit when we congregate in the big conference room, the same one we used for the Galentine's Day brunch. Som, Glen, and Tori are directing their hordes of assistants; Tania and Wendy are leading the rest of the Habituat-HER volunteer group; Rita Sanchez and the other organizers are engaged with the nonprofit's board of directors, who have dropped by to show their support. Thank goodness Tania took it upon herself to have name tags created this time because there's no way I could keep track of everyone today.

Som slides over to me as we're putting the final touches on

our beauty stations, dressed in white go-go boots, a baby-blue miniskirt, and a cropped pastel pink top with the slogan TRANS WOMEN ARE WOMEN. "Ooo, how many madeleines do you think I can stuff in my purse?"

I look over to where she's pointing. The team has set up two tables, one with a delicious continental breakfast spread of fresh fruit and pastries and the other with a gourmet candy bar. Above the assortment of juices is a handmade sign reading NO ALCOHOL, and a matching one reading HAS ALCOHOL is set up next to the fancy champagne gummy bears.

Wendy nudges my elbow. "Like what I did with the signage?"

"How could I miss it?" I deadpan.

Som cocks her head to the side, befuddled. "Did Casey forget to tell us something?"

"Girl, you are in for a *treat*." Wendy grabs Som's arm and pulls her over to the candy bar, I'm sure to recount every embarrassing detail of my mimosa mishap over chocolate-covered nuts. If I'm not careful, by the end of the day, they'll be the best of friends, and I'll never hear the end of it for the rest of my life.

After the room is set up and we're properly fueled with sugar, Rita stands on a chair to get everyone's attention.

"It's T-minus fifteen! At nine a.m. sharp, we'll be kicking off our International Women's Day fundraiser. If you're unclear about where you need to be when, please consult the schedule in the lobby. We've got teams answering phones, covering social media, and drumming up buzz in the neigh-borhood. You are taking on the important work of giving the amazing women in our emergency shelter a much-deserved day of self-care. In order to serve all thirty residents, we've got six shifts of five women each. With hair, makeup, nails, and style, it's a packed itinerary, but we know you'll do a fabulous job!"

The crowd breaks out into whoops and hollers, at which point Tania reenters the room, this time with Evan. My immediate reaction is anger, partially at the Habituall team for not mentioning that he was making an appearance, but mostly at myself for insisting with the glam fam that he's capable of change when that appearance includes freaking jorts and flip-flops. How dare he show his face in a place like this, looking like that? Did he take nothing I said about being a leader to heart?

"Ah, right on time." Rita steps off her chair and gives the floor to Evan. "The ladies in the orange T-shirts already know our executive sponsor, but to everyone else, please give a warm welcome to Evan Chen, founder and CEO of Habituall!"

Evan brushes off another round of applause.

"Hey, I appreciate it, but today is about all of you. I'm fortunate to be surrounded by phenomenal women, from my mother who raised me to pursue my dreams to my teammates here who aren't afraid to remind me who's really in charge. I make mistakes often, but each day I strive to become a better version of myself because of the women who push me and hold me accountable."

A hollow laugh of sarcasm escapes my lips before I can hold it back, and Evan's eyes dart to me. From the way his face falls and his cheeks flush with embarrassment, it's obvious he wasn't expecting to see me here, let alone call him out on his shit. Which is ridiculous if you think about it. I'm the company's stylist, and this is a sponsored makeover event for charity. Where else would I be?

Evan clears his throat before cutting his speech short. "So, um, to celebrate the women who are the backbone of our communities, Habituall will match every dollar we raise. We're proud to further Safe Harbor's mission of providing refuge to survivors, and we can't thank you enough for the impact you're making today."

He walks off to make the rounds with his employees. Before I have a chance to speak to him, the first group of shelter residents arrives, and there's a flurry of activity making intros and getting them to their correct stations.

I keep glaring at Evan from across the room, trying to decipher his intent with his atrocious attire. Is he dressed so offensively because he doesn't see charity work as real work? Because he decided to make an impromptu pit stop on his way to Fisherman's Wharf? Or because he truly doesn't give a single shit?

"Casey! Why haven't we heard about your love life until now?"

Interrupting me from getting the measurements of my first queen, Wendy waves her arms with Som cringing behind her.

"It just came up in conversation," Som says, passing me a box of champagne bears with such a twinge of shame that the likelihood of it 'just coming up' is precisely zero percent. Either Wendy yanked the information out of her, or Som's as terrible at keeping secrets as I am.

"Whoa, careful there, Casey. You don't want to go overboard again," Wendy teases as I bite into a bear. "Now spill on this new boyfriend of yours!"

After a quick scan around the room, I don't see Evan, and Glen's already got his hair dryer going for blowouts, so there's enough noise and activity happening to keep people from eavesdropping on our conversation.

"He's not my boyfriend. Just a guy I went out with. It's nothing serious." That's my strategy—tell the truth but say it so dully that Wendy loses interest.

"What's his name, Holbright?" Evan enters my periphery, startling me.

Fuck. Of course, I didn't see him if he was standing behind me the whole time.

"Um, his name is . . ." The first thing that comes to mind are the brands I bought for Evan while shopping in Union Square. "Vince. I met him through work." God, this is so awkward. I turn my back away from him and try to focus on finding the right pieces among the racks containing the clothing I donated for Galentine's Day, but Evan won't drop it.

"That's interesting. Is this *Vince* a client?"

There's way too much to do today. I am straight-up not in the mood for this absurd line of questioning when he clearly knows who I'm talking about. I spin around and lock eyes with him.

"He could be. I could deal with him being a bad dresser, but he refuses to listen to me. That's why he won't work out —as a client, I mean. Or a date, who knows."

His fake smile breaks for the first time since he started this interrogation, and I grab another gummy bear from the box, pleased that I'm getting under his skin too.

"You make his fashion sense sound like a moral failing when the only thing wrong with him is he's failing to meet your astronomically high standards."

Som gasps, clutching a makeup brush to her chest. "Oh, girl, no, he didn't!"

Maybe it's because I'm surrounded by women—empathetic, selfless women who could be anywhere else but are choosing to dedicate their time and talents to celebrate, empower and dote on those who need it the most—but I can't stomach the thought of a man criticizing the reason why I was put on this earth. I'm about to vomit all over Evan again, and this time it won't be mimosas.

"Martina, was it?" I say, turning to the resident assigned to me. "Do you mind if I rip our esteemed guest here a new asshole? It'll just take a minute, I promise."

"Let it rip!" She grabs the box of gummy bears from me

with a smile, as if they're a bucket of popcorn at a blockbuster film premiere.

"Alright, EC, listen up." I point in his face. "You want to talk about *my* high standards? How about the unreachable standards of a racist, classist, patriarchal society that punishes women for existing, no matter what they wear?" I grab our marketing maven's attention as she walks past. "Tania, what's the most bullshit comment you've dealt with on the job?"

Tania quickly thinks it over. "I had a boss tell me I wasn't allowed to wear open-toed sandals in the summer even though it was over ninety degrees that day, and plenty of the male engineers wore flip-flops."

We look down at Evan's similarly beach-appropriate footwear. "Huh, how relevant!" I comment with a complete lack of surprise. "What about you, Wendy?"

She bitterly bites into a strip of sour candy. "I was told to show more cleavage at a conference because that would make me a better 'booth babe.'"

"Ugh, gross. And Martina, have you ever been judged or discriminated against for your appearance?"

She nods solemnly. "I didn't get a job years ago because they thought my natural hair was unkempt."

"Fuck, I'm so sorry. Your curls are beyond gorgeous, by the way. You're going to make Glen's entire day over there." I turn back to Evan, who has his arms crossed. "And that specific kind of bullshit was legal in California until the CROWN Act was passed in 2019. So the next time you want to accuse me of being high maintenance, remember what message you're sending when you're dressed like a slob while the women around you are fighting their hardest to be seen as equals in their Sunday best. It was disrespectful when Ed Sheeran did it next to Beyoncé at the 2018 Global Citizens Festival, and it's disrespectful when you claim to be a leader in athleisure. Allyship isn't about signing charity checks—you have to make way more of an effort than that. So yeah, that's why it won't work with *Vince*. Any questions?"

Evan takes in his outfit, and it's the first time I've seen anything close to regret cross his face. Seeing him gutted guts me, but I resist every urge to soften the blow. Knowing about his secret closet means I know he's more than capable of giving a damn. I'm not sorry for what I said, and if how I said it gets him to listen, I'm not sorry for that either.

"You're right, and I apologize," he says after a long while, not looking me in the eye. "I've been unprofessional, and it's dampening the spirit of the day, so I'm going to remove myself. I hope Habituall will be the perfect client to Ms. Holbright for the remainder of our contract. Thank you for everything, and best wishes to you, Martina. You're in the greatest of hands here. If you'll excuse me . . ."

I should feel smug that Evan is admitting defeat, but my heart is hollowed out as I watch him quietly walk out of the room. This wasn't how it was supposed to go. Our first night was complicated, sure, but also magical, and all I wanted was to share the swoon-worthy details with the glam fam. We'd finish the makeovers and toast to a job well done at the nearest dive bar. But there's nothing victorious about reducing my relationship with Evan to something clinical, something that will end the second the transaction is complete.

"There was no Vince, was there?" Wendy says, chewing on her lip.

She looks over to Som and Tania, who are reeling like I told them my dog died. I didn't think there was anything worse than having a fight with a client in public, but it turns out there is: Having a fight with a client in public when onlookers realize he was more than a client.

"I would, um, appreciate it if you could keep this . . ." What was this, an incident? An issue? "This . . . thing private."

Tania's stricken, our entire relationship flashing before her eyes as she reevaluates all the times Evan and I have been in close contact, but she nods.

"Of course," she says. "Do you need take a moment? Maybe walk around the block? Or, if you want, I can point you to the nearest cafe for a quick coffee break?"

Tears prick my eyes, but I refuse to cry and make an even bigger mess of this day. I take a slow, deep exhale, shaking my head. "No, I'm fine. Today is not about me. It's about Martina here!" I adjust the young woman's collar, squeezing her shoulders with a small smile. "We're already behind, and we're on a mission to make you into your most gorgeous self. Som, grab your glam bag, and let's get a move on."

The rest of the makeovers fly by in a flurry, and even though the pain of Evan walking out never dissipates, it dulls enough for me to get back in a groove with the glam fam. Despite putting her own beauty regimen on the back burner, Tania fits right in with the fashionistas, taking tons of photos for Habituall's social media accounts and giving Glen marketing advice for his haircare line. And with a dangerous combo of sugar highs and no filters, Som and Wendy become such fast friends that by the end of the day, they're practically a stand-up comedic duo the way they're keeping the residents bowling over with laughter.

When the fundraiser is wrapped up, I tell myself I should be proud. Dozens of women who deserve to feel confident and beautiful had their dreams come true. And not to discount the work of my friends, but unlike makeup which has to be removed before bedtime, or hair which has to be washed every few days, the shelter's residents get to keep their brand-new wardrobes for years and years to come. Now they have a variety of looks for any occasion: business attire for work or job searching, casual outfits for running around with their kids, and even LBDs and chic jumpsuits for nights out on the town.

Clothes open up and expand our worlds—they affirm that we're worthy of going anywhere and doing anything. That's ultimately the point I wanted to make with Evan, but I got too caught up in reacting to his condescension and trying to prove myself. In other words, I fought fire with fire and got burned.

"Hey, betch!" Glen calls out. "We're gonna grab a bite at El Techo. They've got happy hour from four to six—wanna come?"

I turn around from where I'm standing in front of Safe Harbor to see the glam fam waiting expectantly.

"Come on, they've got a sweet rooftop and five dollar margaritas!" Som insists, stomping her go-go boots.

It's a tempting offer, and I'm not talking about the drinks. I know how gratifying it would be to commiserate over how impossible Evan is with my best friends. I could retreat back into my comfort zone, telling the same inside jokes, reminiscing about the same good times, and giving everyone who drives us nuts the middle finger.

But growth happens outside your comfort zone, and however easy that would be, I'm not in the mood to take the easy route. Despite the rollercoaster ride that is my relationship with Evan Chen, I'm not done with Habituall. And I don't mean that my contract isn't up yet—although I'm not about to walk away without getting paid. I finally found somewhere outside of the glam fam where I belong, and I don't want to lose that. I want to stick around for the sake of the team, because there's a lot of good here that has nothing to do with this infuriating CEO. Not to mention, I am fucking good at what I do, so I owe it to the company and myself to finish what I started.

"Thanks for the invite, but I'm gonna pass. It's been a lot today. Go have fun, though. I'll catch ya later."

In any other circumstance, the glam fam would ignore my protests and drag me to happy hour, even if they had to handcuff me to the bar to keep me from bailing. But after my show-down with Evan earlier, they must know not to push it. Instead, they exchange pitying looks before going in for a group hug.

"Call us if you change your mind!" says Som, squeezing tightly. "We're here whenever you need us."

I shake them off and wave as they jump in a rideshare and head toward the rooftop bar.

Not a moment later, I hear Tania shouting, "Hey!"

I point to the car peeling down the street. "If you were looking for the party bus, you just missed it. The glam fam drove off to happy hour."

"Huh? Oh no, you were the one I wanted to talk to, Casey."

"Did we forget anything for the Safe Harbor folks?" I'm exhausted, but I wouldn't want to leave Tania in a bind. She's been an absolute trooper today, running around to keep the volunteers on task and serving as Safe Harbor's publicist on top of her marketing duties. After Evan left, Tania single-handedly steered Habituall's volunteers. So yet again, a woman does the dirty work, and Evan isn't around to appreciate it.

"What? I mean, there is one work thing we can hash out, but I came over mostly to make sure you're okay. How are you doing?"

I smile reassuringly. "I'm alright. This morning definitely could have gone better, and I'll find some way to get back on Evan's good side, but I know these things take time. I'm just concerned we don't have much of it left with First Party only two weeks away."

Not that I need to tell Tania. She's been counting down the seconds since last year's conference ended. "For what it's worth, you gave EC a lot to think about. No one ever chal-lenges him like you do. He may not enjoy getting called out in the moment—who does?—but he deeply respects you. That

Playlists name you came up with to replace Collections? Genius. Marketing was so jazzed to brainstorm new campaign ideas. To be honest, I've been putting my blood, sweat, and tears into this company for four years, and I wish I could influence the leadership team like you can."

I grip her shoulder. "That's a fucking tragedy, but I am happy to sing your praises to anyone who will listen, because after watching you run the show today, I know you can head up marketing. Evan may be CEO, but he clearly has a ton of growing left to do. You're a real leader, Tania, and I'm not ending my contract until Habituall knows it."

She pulls me in for a hug. "Thank you, Casey. That means the world to me. We're so lucky to have you, and Evan will see it eventually. I promise."

I squeeze her back, comforted by the citrus and jasmine scents from her ponytail in my face. We stand there in an embrace until I'm jolted by the vibration of my cell phone in my back pocket.

"What's Lola calling me for?" I say, catching her name on the screen and instantly worrying that Evan told Max to have me fired for my impassioned outburst.

"Don't answer her," Tania says flippantly, making a brush-off motion with her hand. "She and I just finished talking, which was what I was going to bring up, but I'm not surprised she doesn't trust me to relay her message myself."

I let Lola go to voicemail. Picking up would confirm that not only does she not trust Tania, but that I don't either. "So, what's up?"

"Nothing serious. It's just that Max is playing the emcee at First Party, so he's going to open and close the show. He'll only be on stage for ten minutes—fifteen tops—but he takes the job seriously, and he's requiring us to do a rehearsal on Friday."

"Us meaning . . . ?"

"You, me, Lola, of course, and I'm bringing Harris from my team to handle the videography. Max won't ever turn down a chance to see how he looks on camera."

"Good to know. That's not a big deal. I'll bring the preliminary options he's already approved, and we can use the time to nail down the winner. What time should I arrive at the office?"

Tania tilts her head, confused. "Office? Shoot, I left out a key detail. That would have been an epic fail. No, Max's schedule is a mess, and this was the only day we could squeeze in, but he's running around with his family right after—something about his daughter's softball game? I don't know, but the point is we're meeting at his house in Marin."

"Marin? He does that commute into the office every day?"

"Oh god, no, although plenty of the other execs who live in the North Bay take the ferry or an Uber Black across the bridge. But Max's also got a condo in the city and a home in St. Helena. Founders usually don't pull large salaries, but the rest of the leadership team makes bank. I heard through the grapevine that Max is bringing home at least a half-mil per year, and that's just his base. Who knows what his equity, bonus, and deferred nonquals are worth. Not sure if his wife works outside the home or if there's family money involved, but the odds are high if they can afford three Bay Area homes in prime locations."

Having been around the Waterston-Gardners for so many years, I'm no stranger to the one percent. But it never ceases to amaze me how much money you can make working for somebody else instead of yourself. I don't want to fetishize founders because, let's face it, too many are clueless twenty-somethings living off trust funds. But Evan's not like most of them, and when he's not pissing me off royally, he can be brilliant, talented, and sharp as a tack. After giving myself the grand tour of his apartment and learning he doesn't, in fact, live in a shack, I know he's plenty comfortable. But from what Tania's explained about tech founder equity, most of Evan's wealth is locked up at the whim of some venture capitalists while these career execs get to flaunt their compensation packages despite not shouldering any of the risks of everything going belly up.

But who knows? I haven't spent much time with Max. Maybe Evan is a stubborn man-child through and through, and people like Max deserve every penny they get for babysitting him. Tania had called Max the adult in the room, and now I'm not only going to be in the room, I'm going to his actual home.

Tania and I go over the finer details of Friday's agenda, and I brace myself for a long, taxing commute up the peninsula and across the Golden Gate Bridge. The selfish part of my brain kicks in and considers it a shame that Evan and I are not on good terms because if we were, I could start crashing at his place and save myself a ton of time. But men aren't meal tickets, and after the feminist rant I gave him earlier, it's only fitting I step down from my pulpit and drive my own damn self to Marin.

Tania sends me a calendar invite with Max's address attached as we make our way to her car. "One more thing before I forget!" she says. "Max's interested in leveling up his look for the investor meeting next week. Obviously, you can't say anything because you're under NDA, but Golden Pond is Habituall's top choice for our Series E. They're PE, not VC, so it's a big deal."

Talk about alphabet soup. "Um . . . what's PE stand for?"

Tania smiles sympathetically. "Sorry, private equity. I can't stand the jargon coming out of my mouth either, trust me. But that means the board thinks an IPO is imminent if they're bringing in a private equity firm. As we like to say, PE don't fuck around."

Not sure if that explanation clarifies anything since I'm no expert on Wall Street, but it sounds major. "So . . . super business formal, I assume?"

Tania nods. "The VCs on our board are younger and laxer, but Golden Pond is old school. They won't care jack diddly squat about our product if they think leadership isn't ready to take the company public. They will clean house, no questions asked."

"If that's the case, any chance we can get Evan to come to Max's too? Kill two outfits with one fitting?"

Tania laughs before the realization of today's spat sinks in. "I can try to get ahold of him tonight, but he may want some space. Why don't you bring your recommended looks for both of them, and we can get Max to be the messenger? Max may report to Evan, but he's a board observer and has a better chance of convincing him to take the meeting seriously."

I furrow my brow, not a fan of anyone taking the credit for my hard work. How many times has Tania unknowingly sold herself short like that?

"I'll try calling him too. I'd much rather have him there in person for any last-minute tailoring, but I'll come prepared no matter what."

She gives me a quick hug. "I wouldn't expect anything else. See you on Friday!"

For the second time, I watch a friend drive off into the sunset, and it pains me not to have someone to come home to. Someone with whom I can cook dinner, watch TV, and snuggle at night. Ironically, wearing comfy clothes makes sense in those picture-perfect moments. I don't hate Evan for his tank tops and basketball shorts, but we can never seem to bridge the gap and get to the point where we can unwind and under-dress together.

So instead of driving over to Evan's, laying claim to one of his sweatshirts, and arguing over what show to stream, I'm stuck at arm's length, wanting us to move beyond suits and ties as badly as he does.

I consider calling Evan up and telling him this, but when I pull out my phone, the uncertainty of not knowing what kind of mood I'll catch him in makes me chicken out. I can't interrupt whatever he's doing and demand his voice talk to my voice—what am I? A psychopath?

Asking permission to be a psychopath, however? Now that I can do. I shoot off a text before my cowardice gets the best of me.

> We're all wrapped up. Are you free to chat?
> I'd hate for today to end on a sour note,
> and it would be great to talk through things.
> I can even stop by your place if you feel up
> for it.

The read receipt pops up immediately. I stand there on the curb and wait ten agonizing minutes for those three dots to appear as he types his reply, but no dots. I could have chosen not to send my message and been blissfully ignorant of Evan's emotions, but in the face of such stark rejection, I feel much, much worse now.

A fiercer, more confident Casey wouldn't take no for an answer, but there are only so many rebuffs I can hear before I break. If he has nothing more to say to me, then I guess I'll take Tania's recommendation. I'll do the best I can choosing Evan's outfits from now until the end of the month, and Max can be our go-between. It's inefficient, sure, but it will get the job done.

And when the job is done, we will be too.

∼

"So You Wanna Be a Thought Leader?" by Random Schill, MBA – March 11

Gurus. Mavens. Ninjas. Rockstars. Whatever you call them, they've got opinions about their occupations, and they've been destined by the universe to share them. And if you've got a hunch you're the next Martin Luther to spout off his ninety-five theses on entrepreneurship, then read on and follow this step-by-step guide to ensure that you alienate your colleagues, past, present, and future.

Step 1: *Have a thought (or don't)*. Ideally, your point of view will be honed through robust research and years of specialization, but don't sweat it if your narrative isn't crafted to perfection—or even cohesive. The beauty of the internet means everyone can be an expert regardless of their pathetic attempts at persuasion.

Step 2: *Be a leader (or not)*. Gatekeeping of any kind is downright evil, so don't feel the need to abide by any laws, regulations, or general best practices. Who says your business has to be ethical or legitimate for you to profit from your perspective? If a former president can spew four years of pure bile without being permanently banned from the World Wide Web, then fair game for everybody else.

Step 3: *Start penning LinkedIn broetry*. If you've ever been on the platform where PowerPoint decks socialize, you know what I'm talking about:
The kind of post
That's just fragments
Broken over seventeen lines
And pats itself on the back
For giving a job to a homeless veteran
Before demanding $49.99/month to access their paid

newsletter. Sure, you could write in full sentences, but nobody beat the algorithm without sounding like a robot.

Step 4: *Inevitably self-sabotage by being a heinous asshole.* There's something about viral fame that makes thought leaders consider themselves invincible, like that CEO applauded for doing the bare minimum of giving his employees a living wage, who just so happened to (allegedly) waterboard his ex-wife. Make sure you get your book published *before* the accusations come out—because, let's face it, you would never be so successful pretending to be successful if you were a decent human being.

By some traffic miracle, we arrive at Max's Marin residence at the same time—me driving from Palo Alto and Tania and Harris carpooling from Oakland. Tania helps me pull the garment bags I brought out of my trunk, but before I can introduce myself to her bearded, hipster-looking team member, he's off carrying video camera equipment toward the house.

"Where has he been this whole time?" I ask Tania, watching Harris beeline back to the car to grab another box of camera accessories.

"Harris? He's always in demand at Habituall. One of the best content marketers I've ever had. An expert on all things video and a fantastically witty writer on top. Everyone wants to work with him, so naturally, he's one of Max's favorites."

Lifting up the bags so they don't drag across the ground, she hides a frown behind the hangers. "How pathetic that my own boss prefers one of my individual contributors over me."

I find that hard to believe given how amazing Tania is at her job, but before I can reassure her of that fact, she shakes her head as if to banish the negative thought.

"Whatever," she says. "Let's just try to get this over with as soon as possible."

We finish making our trips back and forth from our cars to the front door and ring the doorbell. The exterior of the house itself is as nice as the photos I found online, because you bet I looked up Max's address as soon as I got back from the International Women's Day festivities.

As much as I was hoping to come across a heinous McMansion to comfort myself for living in an exploded closet the size of a matchbox, it's an adorable coastal-style home. Each of the three stories has its own unique finish—speckled gray brick on the first, stark white siding on the second, and tan wooden paneling on the third—like a delightful, tiered cake you can live in. It's no Waterston-Gardner mega-estate, but it's four thousand square feet of West Coast cuteness—all for a cool $2.7 million.

"Welcome to our humble abode!" Max says, ushering us inside the not-at-all humble living room, with its luxuriously high ceilings and oversized windows with views of the Bay off in the distance. "Perfect timing—my wife and kids are taking our dog Daisy for a walk so we can film from anywhere in the house. Lola and I have been tinkering with the script, but we'll definitely need your eyes on it, Harris."

Harris answers in the affirmative, even though the only thing he has eyes for at the moment is the stack of boxes he's carrying into the foyer.

Tania grabs a box to lighten Harris's load. "I can take a look, no problem," she grounds out with a tinge of resentment. "I'm the one who crafted the narrative anyway."

Lola, who is sitting on a cream-colored couch, peers up from her laptop. "Of course. You have such a way with words, Tania. We just want to make sure it embodies Max's voice—you understand!"

I'm not sure how long Lola's been here, but she looks so at home that if there weren't photos of the Ericksons dressed like they came out of a J. Crew catalog, you would assume she's Max's age-inappropriate spouse, not his chief of staff. I know startups are fond of likening themselves to a family, but this feels a little too close for comfort.

Once everything's brought inside, Harris scopes out possible spots to film and lands on the area in front of the marble fireplace. While he moves furniture around and sets up the staging, I use the opportunity to consult Max on attire.

"So I know you said you wanted to appear 'enterprise,' but I'd advise against going with a full suit, because corporate events are so much less corporate these days. The conference's name is First *Party*, after all, so don't be afraid to have some fun with it!"

Max bounces on the balls of his feet. "Gotcha, gotcha, so should I keep what I'm wearing now?"

I scan him up and down, taking in his white collared shirt over blue jeans. Suitable for accommodating colleagues at home but with about as much pizzazz as using skinless chicken breast for Texan barbecue. "Don't get me wrong, that shirt fits well, but white doesn't complement most backdrops. It's best to have a pop of color, so you don't get washed out. Here's what Apple's leadership team wore at the last WWDC . . ."

I pull up my mood board on my tablet, and we go back and forth on options. Max's fortunately agreeable and open-minded to everything, but far too often, he turns to Harris to get a gut check.

"How 'bout this one?" he asks, holding up a brown leather belt. "Give it to me straight, man-to-man."

No one's ever given me the feedback that I wasn't direct enough, and yet here I am, an expert in my field (or at least in this room), but Mr. Indecisive would rather hear from Harris, a dude only half listening because he's preoccupied with his actual job of shooting this rehearsal. Admittedly, I haven't had a ton of face time with Max due to his busy schedule, so perhaps he's more trusting of his colleagues' opinions. His male colleagues, anyway.

As the rehearsal goes on, it becomes clear that Harris is Max's favorite because he's a yes-man—a character trait I can't stomach. I'd take Evan's incessant arguing over Max's fondness for flattery, because at least it means he sees me as an equal. And not once did Evan ever let anyone else discount me.

Ugh, why do I keep comparing Evan to every other man I encounter as if I'm stack ranking them like contestants on *Project Runway*? I can't even call Evan an ex if we weren't officially together. And yet, I find myself missing everything about having him around: the good, the bad, and the ugly.

"Tell us, Casey—how did the makeovers go?"

Talk about ugly. I flash back to my fight with Evan that day and resist cringing at Max's innocent question. He's not trying to interrogate me, I tell myself. I doubt he even cares about my answer and is only trying to make casual conversation.

"It went great," I respond, which is true if you don't count bickering with a CEO about appropriate footwear. I think of more ways to elaborate. "It's wonderful how Habituall fosters community by giving the team time off to volunteer. Most companies throw up an International Women's Day post on social and call it a day, but we made a real impact." Obviously, I don't mention the impact I made on Evan when I lit him up with my fiery attitude.

Max pulls his arm through a charcoal sweater that gives him college professor vibes. "Well said. Community is actually one of the tenets in my leadership manifesto because it's so important to give back."

I help him get the other arm in and check how the sweater sits on his shoulders. Speaking of giving back, I take the opportunity to segue and send some goodwill Tania's way. "You should have seen Tania in action, Max. She was a beast making everything run without a hitch. I think you've already got your VP of marketing right here."

I might have overdone it, but I've already learned that Max is the perpetually distracted type, always interrupting tasks to take a call or send an email, and subtlety won't work with him. Tania is debating with Lola about Max's script, but she clearly heard me, giving me a tired yet appreciative smile when I catch her eye.

On the other hand, Max's smile is frozen like he's tasted something off-putting, and now he has to pretend to enjoy it. "Ha, well, we are so lucky to have Tania. What a rising star! That's why I'm such an ally to women, championing their careers. It's why we gifted our Habituat-HERs a copy of Sheryl Sandberg's *Lean In*. Phenomenal book!"

Oof. That's what my dad would call a swing and a miss. Just like at the photo shoot, Max has an uncanny ability to say the right thing in the wrong way or vice versa. So close, yet so, so far.

"That's a good point, Max," Tania says slowly, as if testing the waters on how best to respond to her boss. "Lola here was telling me you promoted Brad to vice president of operations, which is great news, of course. It's like it was yesterday when we both joined Habituall in the same week, at the same level even, and to see how far he's, um, grown. He must have really leaned in."

Wow, I gotta hand it to her. That was some haute-couture corporate heckling. Tania could put my own mother to shame when it comes to passive-aggression.

"Yeah, Brad, he's such an awesome guy," Max says, his smile still frozen like he's on an episode of *Botched*. "Like you said, Tania, you've worked with him since the beginning. He has so much potential."

Ah yes, that elusive potential. Now I don't know Brad—never met him, wouldn't be able to pick him from a lineup—and maybe Max's right. Maybe he's a stellar leader who deserves every ounce of his success.

But that resigned look Tania's giving me is one I've seen from designers at top fashion houses. You would think an industry made up of so many women would be more immune to discrimination. And yet, the vast majority of luxury brands are headed up by men who were anointed early on as boy geniuses and kept failing upward because of their 'potential.' Meanwhile, the women around them are forced to prove themselves by doing the exact same jobs without recognition for years.

I had hoped with their reputation for being progressive and future-focused, tech startups wouldn't fall victim to sexist double standards so easily. Max has always been in my corner, telling me how important I am to improving Habituall's image. But here's a woman who has carried the weight of the company's reputation on her back since its founding, and Max doesn't seem to be fazed by her being passed over time and time again.

Checking out his reflection in the mirrored surface of the coffee table, Max is ready to move on. "How much did we end up matching at the fundraiser?"

Tania pipes up from her seat next to Lola on the couch. "We hit our goal of raising twenty-five thousand, so a total of fifty thousand went to the shelter."

Max claps heartily. "That's excellent! We should blog about it. And create a post for my LinkedIn too."

Tania's already pulling out her phone. "On it. I'll shoot over something by the end of the day."

"I heard Evan made an appearance. Hope he managed to put more effort into it this time around." He grins as if we're in on the same joke. "Especially as the only guy surrounded by all those ladies."

Ew. The Safe Harbor residents are escaping abuse, not auditioning for a dating reality show. Again, wild how he can make an innocent comment sound so gross.

Tania turns to me, hesitating on how to respond, so I decide to take one for the team.

"It was my fault for not sending Evan a dress code reminder beforehand, but the good news is he, um, learned a lot about gender discrimination that day. Unfortunately, he had to leave early." Keep it vague and hope he doesn't ask any follow-ups.

Lola wiggles her eyebrows, pointing at me. "I heard that Casey dished it to Evan. Called him out so badly he ran off, tail between his legs."

I should have expected the gossip mill to run amok after our spat. My cover blown, I brace myself for Max's disapproval for defying his superior, but he nods sympathetically. "Give him time. Sometimes we have to meet people where they are. I'm not perfect—it took me decades to understand the female experience."

Yikes on trikes. Tania and I give each other the side-eye, but then Max excuses himself to take another call, this time on his landline straight out of the '90s, and we're off the hook.

"Hey, Harris?" Tania calls out. "Where did you put that smaller box with the goodies? I think after all *that*"—she waves her hands around at everything and nothing in particular—"we've earned a break."

He points to the stack of boxes near the foyer, and Tania jumps up to retrieve the one she's looking for, proudly holding it above her head as if it's a game show prize. "Guess who brought the leftovers from the candy bar?"

We break into the box, and each grab a handful of sweet treats, with Lola going for the robin's eggs, Harris coveting the maple bourbon caramels, Tania taking the dark chocolate cashews, and me helping myself to some espresso beans.

Not long after, Max rejoins our group and picks up a box of champagne gummy bears. "Ooo, these take me back! I don't know about you, but when I was in college, my frat brothers and I would make all kinds of gummy bear shots—vodka, moonshine, you name it, we infused it. I bet I still have my gear somewhere in the garage . . ." He pops a bear into his mouth, chewing with delight. "Mmm, reminds me of the good ol' days before kids and taxes and climbing that corporate ladder."

Huh, that might have been the most honest thing I've heard Max say. It's difficult to imagine a straight-and-narrow exec and family man as a hard-partying frat bro, but I guess we're all hiding behind a mask in some way or another.

Harris clips a mic onto Max's final addition to his outfit: a navy blazer with a subtle plaid-like pattern that matches the gray in his sweater. "Sounds like someone needs to let loose—maybe on the last night of First Party?"

Max laughs uneasily. "Oh no, no, no. I've had my share of Vegas nightlife and even been to Burning Man a couple of times, but other than the occasional CBD tincture or microdose to unlock the ol' noggin, I prefer to keep it chill."

Yet another reminder that even though I've worked in Silicon Valley, tech startups are in another universe altogether. Alex's mother is the closest equivalent to my boss, and if I take the lord's name in vain around her, I'm in trouble. I can't imagine lightly tripping on the job for better brainstorming. Here I am ridiculing Max in my head for being an old fogey with a landline, but maybe I'm the one who's a square instead.

We set aside our munchies and get back to work. The rest of the rehearsal is uneventful, unless you count Tania's frustration every time Max mispronounces a speaker's name, despite the guide she provided in the text, or my terror when his family returns from their walk and Daisy almost tracks her muddy paws all over Max's First Party wardrobe. The kids naturally light up the moment they see the leftover goodies on the coffee table, and Max immediately grabs the boxes of gummy bears for himself, promising them they can eat the rest if they keep Daisy out of the way.

Fortunately, we wrap up not long after. As I zip the clothes back into their garment bags, I remember I still need to make the handoff with Evan's attire. I quickly help Tania and Harris pack their equipment and exchange goodbyes before making a dash to my car.

Hauling the last of the hangers, I hand them over to Max in the foyer. "Tania let me know you have a big investor meeting on Tuesday and wanted me to provide some options for Evan to wear. He left before I could confirm everything with him at Safe Harbor, but these should work. I'd hate for our, uh, tiff to come between Habituall and its fundraising roadshow, so would you mind delivering these to him? Maybe you can coordinate outfits."

Max takes a peek in one of the garment bags. "Yes, of course, but why don't I do you one better? You should come to the meeting and give him the confidence of a sharp-dressed man yourself."

I shake my head, taken aback. "No, I couldn't impose. Pitching an investor is a make-or-break opportunity, and I wouldn't want to risk jeopardizing that in any way."

"All the more reason for you to attend," he insists, hanging the bags on a hook in the entryway. "We have a billion-dollar valuation on the line, and I'm not sure how much you know about Habituall's Series E, but Golden Pond is exactly the investor to get us there. We need Evan to look the part, even if it means threatening to strangle him with a tie to get him to wear one. Whatever happened between you two at the charity event needs to be put aside for the sake of the company, or I'm afraid to say we may have to go in a different direction for First Party. I'd hate for it to come to that, Casey. Wouldn't you?"

I gulp, Max's message received loud and clear. It's not the first time I've been told by a client that they're prepared to move on, but it never sounded this threatening coming from Alex. How easily Maxwell Erickson shifts from being Dad of the Year doling out candy to lighting a fire under his subordinates' asses. "Of course. You can count on me, sir."

Evan hasn't responded to me since our falling out, so I have no basis for making promises, but I understand when no isn't an acceptable answer.

Max returns to his jovial state, giving me emotional whiplash as he leads me to the front door. "Wonderful. Thanks to you, we're gonna be rocking and rolling."

"A Step-By-Step Guide on How to Prep for Your Pitch Meeting" by Valleyslag – March 15

So it's been a few years since you dropped out of Stanford to focus on building your startup—congrats! By now, you've checked off the seed round milestones:

- You roped in a technical cofounder who just finished a six-week coding bootcamp and can be the bass player to your front man.
- You completed a prestigious accelerator program that can best be described as a daycare for computer geeks.
- You convinced your father to badger his friends at the yacht club to pony up your initial angel investment.

- You made your first eclectic set of hires, including a distant relative of the PayPal Mafia, a dude living out of his van, and a woman with the temperament of a kindergarten teacher who can take care of the office snacks and remind you not to use the word 'females' in a sentence.

Now you're ready for the big leagues! It's time to take the tour down Sand Hill Road and beg for someone to take a chance on you and invest in your Series A. If a global pandemic wasn't enough to rip the rug out from underneath the tech industry, that means there's still enough froth for your gig-economy-incumbent-meets-idea-that-already-exists business. Like Uber for flying cars (aka helicopters), Lyft for public transportation (aka buses), or WeWork for living spaces (aka having roommates).

So bust out your black turtleneck and get ready to be the next privileged prodigy because with these insider tips, you'll be well on your way to getting your headshot into TechCrunch.

1. *Make sure you've proved market fit.* This is business-speak for "guarantee real people will buy your product with real money." And that doesn't mean asking the dudes in your fantasy football league if they'd be interested in getting in early on the next big revolution. Your friends and family most certainly will blow smoke up your ass and tell you your startup idea is the best thing since sliced bread. But unless you've invented sliced bread and have thousands of folks already signed up on your sliced bread waitlist, you have work to do.

2. *Spend every waking moment perfecting your pitch deck.* Okay, so you've got market fit, but now you need to convince investors to believe you. Enter the pitch deck. This Google Slides (true neutral), PowerPoint (lawful evil), or Keynote

(chaotic good) presentation usually follows the same format that infomercials do:

- Painting the picture of the status quo by exaggerating the pain points of whatever you think your product can solve. This is the software equivalent of someone ripping out their hair or throwing things around the room in frustration.
- Exclaiming, "There's got to be a better way!" before imagining the utopian future where everyone has adopted your platform and made you filthy rich.
- Pausing for a moment to introduce yourself and your cofounder and share your superhero origin story, which must include at least two of the following three highlights: graduating from "a school in Massachusetts," paying your dues at Goldman Sachs where Daddy manages an entire division, and a childhood lemonade stand to exemplify your passion for entrepreneurship.
- Diving into the meat and potatoes of the presentation: growth metrics. If you're freaking out about your ability to deliver on these, remember your real job is to "puffer fish," aka appear bigger than you are by lying through your teeth. Repeat after me: "community-adjusted EBITDA."
- Concluding with a brief demo of the platform. And we do mean brief, like you're a host on an HGTV makeover show where everything may look fantastic, but that's because viewers can't see the duct tape just out of frame.

3. *Fake it til you make it.* Venture capitalists are placing

casino bets on hundreds of startups, hoping to find the next Facebook. This creates a top-heavy system where the company that gets the most funding succeeds. Be your own self-fulfilling prophecy by investing in world-class marketing from the beginning. After all, the winner isn't the business with the best product but the one who can tell the best story. Whether that story is fiction is inconsequential.

thirteen

I can't speak to the aesthetics of Golden Pond's headquarters yet since I'm waiting in the downstairs lobby, but it's obvious the private equity firm understands the importance of first impressions. San Francisco's Financial District doesn't lack skyscrapers with ultra-luxe interiors, but this office building is impressive even by Silicon Valley's standards. The ground floor, with its abstract artwork adorning the walls, looks more like the SFMOMA than an office building. The lobby is open to the public, and dozens of folks in fleece vests are seated at long, wooden tables working on their laptops while sipping their morning matcha lattes from the trendy coffee bar stationed inside.

My nerves are going haywire, so I chose to skip my usual caffeine boost. It's a quarter to nine, so any minute now Max and Evan will walk in, likely with Lola at their heels. I had expected to join them at breakfast beforehand to force Evan into one of the suits I had picked out, but Max texted that they got preoccupied with finalizing their presentation. Thankfully, he reassured me, Evan didn't put up a fight so a quick fit check should suffice.

I'm counting down the seconds, anxiously gripping the

oversized tote in which I packed extra accessories: a variety of ties, pocket squares, and cuff links in case we need to make a last-minute swap. It also holds my fashion emergency kit with supplies to trim loose threads, repair broken zippers, and the like.

My concerns about stains and mismatched socks vanish, however, the moment the group strides through the door, halting me in my tracks from the circles I've been pacing on the gleaming tile. I don't even have the mental capacity to wonder why Tania's bringing up the rear behind Max and Lola because I can't stop staring at Evan. Since I selected each piece, the outfit is familiar—a sleek navy suit over an impressionist-inspired floral dress shirt and textured dark gray tie—but I couldn't anticipate how he'd take my breath away in it. From his recently shorn hair to his polished shoes, he looks like perfection. It's like San Francisco's own Karl the Fog parted just to let the sun shine down on him.

"Jaw-dropping, isn't he?" Max slaps Evan on the shoulder. "You better watch out, Casey. You did such great work I think you styled your way out of a job."

I can't even absorb the ominous nature of Max's joke because Evan is grinning from ear to ear. After the fallout from our fight, I was afraid he'd never again be happy to see me. All that was left for me would be to complete my remaining work for First Party, close out my contract, and go on the hunt for new clients because my life very much depends on it. But that smile gives me hope that Evan isn't ready to call it quits yet.

"Casey, I'm so sorry for ignoring you after the makeovers," Evan gushes with genuine sincerity. "I was ashamed to let you down, but you told me . . ." He trails off, his train of thought abandoning the track entirely.

He could be hesitating because he's uncomfortable addressing past hurts he's caused, but something's amiss. I trade a look of concern with Tania, who shuffles Max and Lola off to the side to distract them.

"Evan?" I snap my fingers in front of his face. "What was it I told you?"

"Hmm?" He pinches the bridge of his nose, until recollection brings relief. "Oh yes, you told me growth happens outside your comfort zone." He breaks out into a boyish grin. "So I'm here, uncomfortable and ready to grow."

He grabs my hands, and I immediately pull him aside, pretending to adjust his sleeves. As elated as I am to receive my well-deserved apology, I'm more alarmed by his public display of affection right before a pitch meeting. I'm not sure I'll make a convincing strategic advisor, but nobody other than Tania is supposed to know my relationship with Evan is anything other than professional, and I need to keep it that way.

"Don't worry about that," I say, checking the knot of his tie. "It's water under the bridge. I'm not normally one to say you can turn your whole life around with one outfit, but damn it if you didn't crush it with this one. You're not cosplaying as a CEO anymore, Evan. You *are* one."

He leans forward as if to kiss me and I have to push against his broad chest to avoid getting caught acting inappropriately. With a quick glance toward his team, he gets the hint and relents. "You gave me the best gift, you know that?" he murmurs. "You deserve to be treated as amazingly as you make people look. Thank you for not giving up on me, Casey. After this is over, can I take you out to make it up to you?"

One date doesn't undo the ups and downs we've experienced—or will inevitably experience in the future—but Evan's earnestness makes me believe everything will work out. That no matter what happens, we'll be okay as long as we stick together. In his own way, Evan's asking me if I want to ride the rollercoaster all over again. My friends might call me foolish, but I can't imagine arriving at any other answer than yes.

I reach my hand around his neck, as if to check for an exposed shirt tag, and get a surge of sympathy for him when I feel the beads of sweat running down to his collar. It's more layers than he's used to wearing, and he must be nervous. "Forget making it up to me. You're going to go in there and nail that pitch, and then we'll celebrate."

BY THE TIME we get settled into Golden Pond's main conference room, I'm starting to feel perspiration collect on my brow as well. It's not because of my outfit, as I selected a breathable shift dress and blazer I know can keep me comfortable during a long workday. And it's not because of the room, which is cramped but not even close to claustrophobic. Lola and I take seats in the corner so the Golden Pond stakeholders can fit around the table. There's room to squeeze Tania in, but Max decides to direct her out of the room.

"Go introduce yourself to the Golden Pond PR team," he commands as her eyes narrow. "We'll want to make sure we add their contacts to our media list for the funding announcement."

Optimistically planning for a deal that's not yet done should be a good sign. But Tania being suddenly sent away causes me to overheat more, and I don't need any help in that regard. Because there's one thing that's putting me so on edge that sweat is pooling at the small of my back.

And that's Evan acting increasingly, inescapably *weird*.

At first, his behavior could be chalked up to the restless energy you get before giving a big presentation: bobbing his head from side to side, chugging from his complimentary bottle of water, and escaping to the restroom several times.

But when we finally get down to business and Evan requires assistance to plug in a dongle to project his laptop screen to the television at the front of the room, alarm bells in my head start going off. Evan's known as Habituall's CEO, of course, but that role wouldn't have been possible without his experience as a backend engineer. This is a man who used to pull all-night coding sessions after which he had to ice his hands. Hooking up an HDMI cable should be as easy for Evan as using double-sided fashion tape is for me.

"Alright, now that we've resolved our technical issues, let's get started," says Nigel Pittman, Golden Pond's managing director, without hiding his impatience. He wouldn't need to be seated at the head of the table or flanked by his associates for you to immediately identify him as the one in charge.

Like Max, he's on the younger side of middle-aged, but whereas Habituall's chief operating officer got the softer angles and baby blues more fit for a Hollywood executive, Nigel looks like he was given the Wall Street white privilege fast pass, plucked right off the lacrosse field and molded by the Goldman Sachs playbook. I'm fanning myself with my notebook, but Nigel's cool as a cucumber despite wearing a sweater vest over his dress shirt.

"We've already gone through introductory pleasantries and demoed the platform in previous meetings," he explains, "so it's time to get down to brass tacks. You've got the numbers we asked for, Evan?"

Evan gulps down more water from his bottle, precipitously less confident than when he arrived in the lobby. "Sure, sure. Last time, we went over our historical data, so today we'll forecast our growth plans based on our current MRR—"

"MRR?" Nigel scoffs. "You realize this is your Series E round, right? Habituall's not some rinky-dink seed-stage startup speaking in terms of *monthly* recurring revenue."

Evan coughs abruptly, spilling water on Max's notes as his hand jerks. The COO pushes his seat back to avoid getting his suit wet, and I jump in with the most absorbent material I can find: the extra men's dress socks in my purse. "It's all good!" I chuckle nervously, patting the table dry. "Once again, merino wool saves the day."

Nobody's amused by my attempted joke about moisture wicking, and Max speaks up. "Of course, Nigel. We meant ARR. Rest assured, our figures reference our annual recurring revenue. EC, you mind proceeding to the next slide?"

After too much deliberation, Evan taps the arrow on his laptop before fixating on the TV screen. "I think there's something wrong with the deck," he mumbles.

Max tries reassuring him everything's fine, but Evan's already abandoned his post, hypnotized by the television. He walks over, getting his nose as close as he can to the panel, waving his hands over the charts on the screen. "Do you see this? The numbers are moving!"

Oh, *no*. When I first met Evan in the zen room, I imagined the worst thing that could happen to Habituall was him showing up to an important meeting in grimy sweatpants. But whatever is going on here is much, *much* worse.

"That's it," Nigel commands. "I don't know what you're playing at, Evan, but it stops now. You know, this meeting was supposed to be simply a formality." He gestures to the folks at the table. "Our team was so excited to move forward with the term sheet, but when you consider the billable hours that are being wasted with your antics, we may need to rethink Golden Pond's involvement in this deal."

Max rises to his feet. "Whoa, there. Nigel, come on. After all the conversations we've had? Let's not throw out the baby with the bathwater here."

My fists clench at Max's insinuation that Habituall's CEO is disposable, but I let him fight for the chance to reschedule the meeting while I worry myself with the higher priority: Evan's well-being.

"Evan? Are you okay? Look at me." I make my way to the

front of the room and grab Evan to get him to stand still. He can't make direct eye contact because his gaze keeps darting to the presentation.

"Tell me you see them too, Casey. The numbers—they're floating around in circles."

I'm too distracted by his loopiness to answer him. I've never seen him this disoriented, and between his glassy eyes and the sheen on his forehead, I'm deeply concerned. What if he's fallen sick with something serious?

Maybe the immense pressure of running his company has caused Evan to experience a psychotic break with reality. Or if he's losing control of his faculties, he might have had a stroke . . . or something else? A change in behavior this drastic could mean he's suffering from a brain tumor—

"It's about time we wrapped this up," says Nigel forcefully, opening the conference room door. "We've had an eventful morning and could use a reset. Let's table this for now, and we'll be in touch, okay? I'm sure you can see yourselves out."

Max waves us into the hallway with a huff, barking orders at Lola to collect Tania and make sure a follow-up call is scheduled ASAP. Their blatant disregard for Evan's welfare makes me feel like I'm the one hallucinating.

"Um, hello?" I call out as they round the corner, gesturing at Evan hanging off my shoulder like a second handbag. "Shouldn't we be getting him to a hospital?"

Max stops in his tracks, crossing his arms. "For what, exactly?"

Taken aback by his heartlessness, I reach for possible explanations. "I don't know. It could be one of those mind-splitting migraines I've heard about, or the result of a stroke. Evan, do you smell anything like burnt toast?"

Evan clutches his stomach like he's about to throw up, and Max has the audacity to roll his eyes. "Casey, he's obviously on drugs," he says with distaste, annoyed he has to point out the obvious. "Given the way he was seeing nonsense on the slide deck, I'd guess he's on acid."

Acid. It's like the word hisses at me, making me feel like an assssss. It's at that moment Tania rejoins us, her confused questions cut off by Max's accusation. As she swivels her head to scan the cubicles, I can tell the silence in the office is more terrifying than the thought of her CEO tripping. I recall the saying, "You could hear a pin drop," but I'm convinced it should be "You could hear a pen drop," because I'm pretty sure that's what a random Golden Pond analyst is picking up off the floor, his eyes locked on the corporate car crash playing out in front of him and his colleagues.

"Why would you think that?" I ask Max, careful to keep my voice down. "It doesn't make any sense."

"Really, Casey? Don't be so naïve. You've seen what Evan's like. He's been a delusional hippie as long as we've known him."

It's a callous generalization, but I can't refute it without sounding just as deranged. Oh, don't worry, Evan's been putting on his crunchy granola persona this whole time. He has a secret closet full of designer clothes to prove it!

Sick of everyone talking *about* Evan instead of *to* him, I try getting him to explain what's going on, but most of the words that come out of his mouth are incoherent gibberish. I turn to Tania for backup, but she seems too shell-shocked to come to my aid. She may not have thought Evan would take things this far, but it must not be completely outside her imagination if she's not raising her hand to serve as a character witness to Evan's good reputation.

"We don't know a damn thing," I insist. "And if we don't take Evan to see a doctor, we're jumping to conclusions without any evidence." My voice is angry and shaking. While drugs are one possible explanation, I can't accept that Evan would have such an enormous lapse in judgment. Because if it's true, then what does that say about my own judgment?

"Fine," Max says, as if he's conceding my point while insinuating that I'd come to regret making it. "I bet the evidence has been on him this entire time."

Max yanks Evan off my arm and toward the reception desk. An admin abandons her post at the sight of the scene we're making, likely to enlist assistance from her superiors.

"Why don't we check his pockets?" He reaches around to Evan's back pockets, startling the founder from his mysterious haze.

"Hey, man! What are you doing?"

The first pocket indeed comes up short, but before I can breathe a sigh of relief, Max's moved on to the other side and let out an "aha!" in victory. He holds up not a wallet or phone like most folks would be carrying, but a sheet of blotter paper divided into little squares covered in colorful emojis. LSD tabs, plain as day. I might not have ever seen the recreational substance in person, but at least those D.A.R.E. videos I was forced to watch in grade school were good for teaching me something.

Evan's eyes are already dilated to the max, giving him a stunned appearance, but dismay spreads to the rest of his face. "I didn't put those there, I swear. Those aren't mine!"

Max laughs in disgust. "Sure. You're just holding on to acid for a friend. What do you think—we're stupid?"

Golden Pond's admin returns to the front desk with Nigel Pittman behind her, and no matter how much Evan denies that the drugs are his, the damage is done.

What do you think—we're stupid? Max's words don't sit right with me because that's the one description I'd never use for Evan. Sarcastic and stubborn as hell, yes, but never stupid.

From Nigel's repulsed expression, it's apparent the managing director doesn't agree. "Before you made a mockery of us this morning," he says, pointing at Evan, "we were prepared to bring the total of your Series E funding to $200 million—the largest round in Habituall's history, by far. But I don't care what Silicon Valley gurus say about the power of microdosing. There was nothing micro about what we saw today, and Golden Pond doesn't bankroll loose cannons." He shifts his attention to Max. "If you want us to be your lead investor, then you need someone else to run your company."

Panic courses through my veins. Evan has made mistakes in the past, but never in a million years would he commit such a monstrous fuck-up on purpose. "It's *Evan's* company," I argue. "He's the one who founded it. You can't just push him out!"

"That's enough, Casey," Max says sternly before addressing Nigel. "If you agree to the board seat we're offering, we can make that happen. We'll take care of it."

'It' being Evan, discarded like last season's rejects. Five years of his life—gone. Every line of code he wrote, every risk he took, every sacrifice he made to build his business, only for it to be taken from him.

To add insult to injury, Max grabs Evan's shoulder bag and orders Lola to confiscate his laptop and ID badge, despite my attempts to recover them. "You can't steal his stuff!" My speak-to-the-manager-voice slips out at the indignation.

"This is company property," Max asserts, "and Evan Chen is no longer running the company." He corrals me and Evan toward the elevator as Nigel directs the admin to call for security. "IT will wipe his equipment and disable his badge, so he won't have access to the office. HR will be in touch regarding the transition."

The transition. They've already moved on without so much as a conversation. Shut him out completely with no chance to say goodbye to anyone. And, worst of all, Evan's too dazed and confused to register what's happened to him.

I have too much pride and care too much about decorum to allow a security guard to throw us out on the street, so I stride over to the elevator and jab the button to take us back down to the lobby. "I'm taking him home," I declare, jutting my chin out in defiance, but it doesn't matter because nobody's listening. Max is planning to call an emergency board meeting, and his direct reports are somber, writing down his every word. Tania catches my eye as the elevator door chimes open, expressing enough doubt at the situation that it gives me hope I can convince her of Evan's innocence. I motion my phone near my ear in the universal signal to call me.

She nods, the silver lining on this shitstorm of a day. I have so many questions about where I fit into this so-called transition—what this means for First Party, how my contract will be affected, if I'm even needed at Habituall anymore—but all of my concerns are dwarfed by Evan's much bigger and more immediate problem: getting his company back. At least there's a chance Tania has my back and can be my ally on the inside.

Evan leans against the handrail in the elevator, fatigue setting in. "What's happening?" he exhales, rubbing his eyes.

We reach the ground floor and I half carry him outside. "What's happening is we're fucked, but I'm going to do whatever I can to un-fuck us."

FOR ONCE, I don't mind the bumper-to-bumper traffic from the Financial District to Evan's apartment in SOMA because it gives me time to evaluate this ordeal from all angles—even if nothing about it makes any sense. It's hard to accept that Evan took acid, but if he was hallucinating what was on the screen, it's at least plausible. We've grown close over the past couple of months, but I haven't known him that long in the grand scheme of things. He didn't have a problem with hooking up in public on our first date, so maybe he's got a wild side.

But if Evan has experience with psychedelics, surely he would know the difference between microdosing and tripping balls. And if he had never done them before, then why the hell would he choose the day of the biggest meeting of his career for his first time?

Something's not adding up, or he's more out of his mind than I ever thought possible.

No amount of theorizing will ever substitute for an explanation from Evan himself, so my best course of action is to wait for him to come down from his trip while sitting tight for Tania's call. Until then, the gameplan is to get Evan sober before it's too late.

Fortunately, Evan doesn't pass out completely, so I'm able to get him out of my car and into his apartment without too much trouble. I don't have any frame of reference on the effects of most drugs, as Glen and Som have always been the hard partiers of the glam fam, rolling on molly at raves and music festivals until the wee hours of the morning while I got my beauty sleep before hitting the doorbuster sales as soon as the stores open.

But I've been hungover too many times in my life, and if LSD works like Long Island Iced Teas, a cold shower should be a much-needed shock to Evan's system.

"Come on," I say, wiping away sweat from his hairline. "Let's get you cleaned up."

Despite my skepticism, Evan reassures me he's lucid enough to handle a quick shower on his own, so I get the water running and leave him to get undressed, keeping the bathroom door partially open in case he needs assistance.

While he's preoccupied, I take a seat on the sofa and boot up my favorite retail apps, scouring the latest deals in an attempt to calm my nerves. But when twenty minutes go by, and it's still eerily quiet except for the sound of running water, my spidey senses start tingling.

"Evan?" I call out, knocking on the bathroom door before pushing through. "I'm coming in."

A trail of clothes has been left on the tile floor: his navy suit jacket and matching slacks, a belt, the floral dress shirt, an undershirt, and, finally, his black socks and boxer briefs. That's when it hits me I'm likely to encounter Evan naked, but when I open the door of the steamed-up shower, it's empty.

"Evan—where the hell did you go?" I quickly turn off the faucet and jump to conclusions. What if he had an accident and slipped? What if he's collapsed on the floor somewhere with a concussion and a broken wrist? I got so distracted by online shopping that I never considered he might need immediate medical attention.

"Please be okay, please be okay," I chant, each repetition more desperately than the last, as I exit the bathroom and follow the drops of water from his wet footsteps into his bedroom.

"Evan!" I see him lying face down on his bed, his sheets askew as if he tried to tuck himself in and failed. Any other day, I would be admiring his tight rear end, but first, I have to confirm he's even alive. "Look at me!"

Sitting down on the edge of the bed, I tip his face toward mine. His eyelids flutter, and I remember to breathe again.

"Fuck, you're going to kill me. And from the way you constantly get on my nerves, it's supposed to be the other way around. Evan, can you hear me?"

He reaches up to hold my hand against his cheek. "Casey? You're still here?"

"Of course, I am." I resist adding 'jerk face' after giving me such a scare and lean in closer, as it's clear he's having trouble making eye contact.

"What happened?" I run my other hand through his wet hair.

I don't expect him to answer me, and he's quiet long enough that I assume he's fallen asleep again until he says, "You told me to."

Defensiveness bubbles up my throat. "What are you talking about? I'd never tell you to do something like that."

He tries rising onto his elbows. "You did. The suit . . . I wore it . . . for you."

"Oh, *that*." I crack a small smile. Even in his delirious state he's determined to prove he followed through and took my direction for once. Of all the things he could be thinking about with Lucy in the sky with diamonds, I'm touched he cares most about pleasing me.

"You looked fantastic, Evan. I saw a real leader, and I've never been prouder of you." I trace my fingers up and down his scalp. "That's why I need to know how it went so wrong. How you could go from reaching a billion-dollar valuation one minute and getting kicked out of your company the next."

The psychedelic haze dissipates for a moment, and I can tell Evan's looking past me, through me, getting lost in the thought of everything he's built vanishing, stripped away and strewn across the floor like his discarded clothes.

His eyes are glassy, a waterfall of emotion, and when I gently grab his face in my hands, the tears tip over the precipice and pour down his cheeks.

"I'm so sorry," I whisper, pulling the covers over his legs before squeezing his damp body in a tight hug.

"What do you have to be sorry for, Casey?" He grips me closer. "You weren't the one they fired."

"I know, but ever since you left during the makeovers, it's been weird between us. And if that influenced you to . . . I couldn't live with myself if that was the case."

My bottom lip quivers, and now I'm the one on the verge of tears.

"Hey, hey, hey," he says, comforting me as I cry on his shoulder. "We're okay. It's not weird between us. I mean, I feel weird right now, but I don't know how that happened, and that's not your fault. In fact, that gift you gave me was the highlight of today, before everything went to shit."

I stiffen in his arms. "Gift? What gift?" I vaguely remember Evan mentioning me giving him the best gift when we were standing in the lobby, but I assumed he was referring to my fashion sense. I never thought to interpret his words literally.

Evan's eyes are ping-ponging around, struggling to grasp onto any details. "The . . . gummy bears. Yeah, the champagne gummy bears. This morning at the breakfast place, when Max brought me the suit you picked out, he said you wanted to apologize for that day at Safe Harbor. That you were passing them along to me since I didn't get the chance to take any home after the makeovers. I thought that was really sweet."

"Are you sure? Because I wouldn't forget a gesture like that. Not to mention, Max kept the rest of the leftover candy for his kids." Although, now that I think about it, didn't Max take the gummy bears for himself? "Evan, do you still have the ones he handed to you?"

He shakes his head. "The box was empty . . . I think I ate them all while we were practicing the pitch at the restaurant. They were so good . . ."

"Fuck, fuck, fuck!" I pull myself out of Evan's embrace and start pacing the room, flashbacks of my mimosa mishap haunting my mind. "Did the gummy bears taste off to you?"

"Uh, not that I can recall . . . why, what's wrong?"

I sigh, reminded that Evan's synapses aren't firing on all cylinders. "What if you didn't take LSD? What if it was given to you, and you didn't know it?"

"Wait, wait, hold up. Are you saying Max drugged me?" Evan sits up, then looks down at his naked body. "Shit, sorry, has my dick been out this whole time?"

I chuckle, watching him pull the sheets up further and feeling flush at the brief sight. In any other circumstances, we could be getting it on, but instead, I'm having to decipher a drug-addled puzzle to make sense of the last few hours.

"If you ate the evidence," I say, pulling my attention above our waists, "we can't prove anything. Max 'found' LSD tabs in your back pocket, but what if he planted them?"

I think back to Max discovering the blotter paper, and I realize the grid was complete—there weren't any tabs missing, a clear sign that Evan ingested acid through other means. If only those other means weren't working their way through his digestive track.

I'm wondering how to come up with proof of Max's sick scheme when my phone blares from my blazer pocket. When Tania's name appears on the lock screen, I can't accept the call fast enough.

"Thank god. Give me the play-by-play—I've been dying over here!" I shout, desperate for details.

The din of city traffic and construction accompanies her voice. "I just left Habituall HQ. Are you still at Evan's?" When I answer in the affirmative, I can practically hear her begin to power-walk in our direction.

"Okay. Look, I don't know what the fuck happened in that meeting because I wasn't *invited*, despite being in charge of the Series E announcement, but whatever. Golden Pond holds the purse strings. We're *this close* to becoming a unicorn and going public, but we're burning millions of dollars every month, and we need their funding to make it happen. Max was only able to convince them to reconsider leading the round by having Evan removed as CEO."

"How though?" I exclaim incredulously. "It's his

company. If Evan agreed to step aside to be chairman or something, that would make more sense, but he's still the founder. Not to mention, he's Max's boss, not the other way around. How can a COO have the authority?"

I can't see Tania, but I can envision her shaking her head at me. "He's the founder, yes, and I'm sure he's still entitled to his stock options, but he was canned. Max is a board observer, so even though he doesn't have a vote, he was able to call an emergency meeting as soon as the pitch ended. With Nigel Pittman added as a new board member as part of the Golden Pond deal, Evan lost majority share, so he wouldn't be able to stop them. In fact, I heard from Lola afterward that the board thinks that's why Evan took LSD in the first place, because if he sabotaged the deal, then he'd retain ownership of Habituall."

"Is that what you think, Tania?" I interject, trying to keep my tone even so it doesn't come off as an accusation. But as much as I respect her as a colleague and a friend, if I can't trust her to have faith in the man she's followed into battle for four years, then I'm prepared to tell her to turn her ass back around.

She lets out a ragged sigh. "I'll be the first to admit I have questioned Evan's professionalism and maturity. Honestly, with the way he dresses, who hasn't? But I saw something break inside of him on International Women's Day. That's when I knew the only thing he cares about as much as his company is you, Casey. He knew you were coming today. He put on your suit to win you back. He might not have said the words out loud, but that man is in love with you. So no, I don't believe he'd tank the deal. Sabotaging Habituall's fundraising would kill our chances of going public. A move that selfish would make his own team lose faith in him—a team you're now a part of, which means he would lose your respect for good." She chuckles. "Even he wouldn't be that big of an idiot."

I bark out a laugh, tears pricking the corners of my eyes as they take in Evan, who's nodded off again and is snoring softly in bed. When I first met the tech founder, I wanted to kill him, and now I'd kill for him. Could that be love?

"I'm glad we're on the same page, then, because this whole situation smells as fishy as Pier 39." I give her the rundown of what Evan said about the champagne gummy bears. "Would Max go so far as to frame Evan in order to have him fired?"

Tania sucks in a sharp breath. "I did find it strange that nobody questioned Max for acting like he's second-in-command. It's not uncommon for founders to be replaced at this stage of a startup's lifecycle with CEOs who have experience taking companies public, but Max has never been through an IPO—shit, speak of the possible devil. That's him calling me. Sorry, Casey, I'm almost at Evan's place, but I gotta take this first."

She hangs up abruptly, and I'm left there reeling. Maxwell Erickson may have the executive presence a board of directors would be looking for, but he joined Habituall only a few weeks before I did, and I'm not going around pretending I'm an expert on the business. The business that Evan, Tania, and the rest of the team built from the ground up. Surely, someone would need more than a good tailor to be considered CEO material?

I turn to Evan, expecting him to be passed out, but he's leaning on his elbow, staring out into the distance. I'm not sure if he heard any of my conversation with Tania or if he's blanking from the comedown.

"Evan? Are you feeling alright?" I wave my hand in front of his face.

He perks up from his trance. "Hawker SF . . ."

"Huh? What about it?" I try to figure out why he's

bringing up the fusion restaurant all of a sudden. "Are you hungry? Do you want me to pick you up some of their crispy duck rolls?"

He shakes his head, rubbing at his temples. "No, after we finished breakfast, Max was in a chipper mood and mentioned something about going there for dinner to celebrate with the board. I thought he was asking me for recommendations like he always does when he's craving 'Asian' food, as if shumai and sushi are one and the same. I told him I was already planning on taking you out as thanks for your hard work, but we could meet them afterward." Whatever color is left in his face disappears. "He brushed me off, saying I didn't have to come."

Didn't have to, or wasn't needed? Setting aside the fact there's no way Evan could have passed off our date as merely platonic, especially if the acid had already kicked in at that point, in no universe would a board agree to celebrating a $200 million fundraising round without the founder present—unless the one who knew Evan wouldn't be coming was the same person getting him sacked in the first place.

At that moment, the doorbell rings, and I practically jump out of my skin, forgetting for a second that Tania was on her way. Evan bolts out of bed, while I speed-walk to the front door. "Coming!"

Swinging the door back, I catch the marketing director mid-knock. "Am I interrupting something?" she asks, eyes wide.

I turn around, following her line of sight, to find Evan in the hallway, fully nude and attempting to put on his slacks he picked up off the floor. Thankfully, as we watch him try to shove both of his feet down one pant leg, she must realize that nothing provocative was going on.

"Ignore him," I reply, ushering her inside. One day, we'll laugh about this, but until then, we've got a board dinner to crash. "Evan's staying out of trouble, but we're diving right into it." I pull out my phone and tap Som's name in my favorites. "And we're gonna need backup."

~

"8 Drinks for Drowning Your Sorrows" by SF Eatery – March 15

Some psychopaths only enjoy alcohol during the most joyous of occasions, like ordering a round of beers after Cal crushes Stanford in the Big Game or cheers-ing with champagne to celebrate a wedding or job promotion.

But that's like Kleenex only advertising tissues for happy tears. So when you need to cry it out for completely different reasons, these cocktails are for you.

1. *Pisco Punch-Your-Boss-In-The-Face*: when your manager puts an unannounced "Quick Chat" meeting on your calendar, and you realize you can't log in to the company's Facebook page anymore.

2. *Side-Chick Sidecar*: when you find out the woman that's too close for comfort in his photos on social media is *not* his cousin like he told you.

3. *Cosmo-Political Differences*: when you're trapped with someone who crashed your employee resource group and "wants to play devil's advocate."

4. *Treasure Island Iced Tea*: when you take your ex back only to learn their toxic behaviors became even more radioactive.

5. *Manhattanization*: when you can't afford to buy a home on the Peninsula because your elderly neighbors equate developing a few more mid-rise buildings with devolving into New York City chaos.

6. *Old Fashioned Pep Talk*: when your ignorant parents

respond to you telling them you're in therapy with, "What do you have to be depressed about? Cheer up. There are starving children in Africa!"

7. *Day Job Daiquiri*: when your tech salary still can't cover your student loan payments, so you have to moonlight as a blood boy, selling your life force to a billionaire who refuses to accept his own mortality.

8. *Painkiller*: 'nuff said.

chapter
fourteen

I'm glad I called in the cavalry by looping in the glam fam because just when I thought today couldn't get any worse, the news of Evan's disastrous pitch meeting was leaked to the press. Apparently one of the Golden Pond analysts took his eavesdropping straight to the tech tabloids, and Tania had to sprint back to Habituall HQ to do damage control.

When she returned, she was a wreck. The scandal caught like wildfire, stretching to every corner of the internet, so Max got a crisis communications firm and the PR hotshots at Golden Pond to take over Tania's responsibilities in the hopes of preserving the company's reputation.

Long story short, my best friends came to the rescue—and didn't even grill me on why I was bending over backward for a guy high off his rocker. Tori spent the afternoon comforting Tania, who feared a pink slip of her own, while Som and Glen used their experiences with illicit substances to bring Evan down to earth.

With Evan fired and Tania possibly next on the chopping block, we push our plans into overdrive, sending Habituall's loopy leader to bed and piling into my car to head to Hawker SF. As I drive around the restaurant, with Tania and the glam fam keeping their eyes peeled for parking, I channel my inner cowgirl like I did during the photo shoot in Chinatown and reflect on the good, the bad, and the ugly.

The good: Evan is disoriented but alive, and he didn't intentionally drop acid before the pitch meeting.

The bad: He was possibly drugged by Max in an attempt to discredit him and steal his job—even though I don't have a shred of evidence to support that theory.

The ugly: If I don't find some way to restore Evan's reputation, he will lose another business—this time, through no fault of his own—and his career as he knows it will be over. Not to mention, folks caught in the crossfire, like Tania, will be forced to fight their hardest to save their jobs and their dignity. So no pressure.

"There—behind that Range Rover!" Glen exclaims from shotgun, pointing to an empty space.

"Nice eye! Leave it to the Brit to find room next to the UK car." I manage to successfully parallel park along the curb and kill the ignition. "Okay, let's walk through the plan one more time."

Glen hands me his bomber jacket and pageboy cap. "I'll go in first so you can duck behind me and not get spotted."

I rub off my signature red lipstick and put on sunglasses for good measure. At nearly eight p.m., it's already dark, but I can't risk blowing our cover. I dig around my center console in search of another pair for Tania, before she stops me.

"It's okay. I won't need them," she reassures me, tightening the strings of one of Evan's baggy hoodies she threw on over her pantsuit to hide her gray-streaked curls. "If what you said is true, then for once I'm glad Max looks right past me."

She's right, even though I'm disgusted to admit it. In any other circumstance, I'd be empowering Tania to take up space and break that glass ceiling, but today flying under the radar is mission critical. "Alright then, we're set. You ready, Som?"

The makeup artist reapplies her own lipstick and fluffs up her hair, giving me a mischievous wink in the rearview mirror. "Born ready. I'm going to use my connections to deliver a round of drinks to their table. I sucked off one of the bartenders in the bathroom last time I was here, so he owes me one."

"Doing the lord's work!" I gush with gratitude. "And last up, Tori?"

She takes my keys from my outstretched hand and slides each one between her knuckles, Wolverine-style. "My job is to stay put, standing watch and shanking anyone who gets in our way."

If you didn't know Tori well, you'd assume she's joking, but I wouldn't put it past her if she plans on taking her role seriously. "Don't forget our exit strategy," I remind her as we hand over our bags and belongings for safekeeping. "I can't risk anyone recognizing me or Tania and giving Habituall a reason to can us, so you're our getaway driver in case we need to make a quick escape."

A pang of sadness hits me as I feel the absence of our social media princess once again, since this would have been the perfect opportunity for Alex to pitch in. She's way too famous to waltz into a place unnoticed, so she's usually the one who stays in the vehicle whenever we have to run an errand to avoid causing utter pandemonium wherever she goes. But until we find a way to work together like we used to, Tori's no-nonsense attitude is exactly what we need. If shit hits the fan, I trust her to get us out clean as a whistle.

Glen leads the way into Hawker SF, with Som and Tania flanking each side of me for 360-degree concealment. The restaurant is packed, which is underscored when a haggard-looking hostess welcomes us.

"Do you have a reservation with us tonight?" she says with an edge in her voice.

Som powers through, undeterred. "No, but Carlos is a good friend of mine," she purrs. "We'll squeeze in at the bar." She points to a man lighting a flaming mai tai, who waves us over. "Carlos! And here I thought you were the hottest thing in this joint."

She walks off to get her flirt on, while the rest of us edge away from the hostess stand and look around the dimly lit restaurant for signs of our targets.

"Ten o'clock," I whisper, gesturing to a row of booths behind a transparent partition wall inspired by Chinese symbology. Between the wooden decorative motifs, I can make out four middle-aged white men in business attire: Max and Nigel Pittman on the right, and two others I don't recognize who must be on the board.

Before I can tap Tania for details, Som returns wearing a black apron and carrying a large tray of cocktails. "Lychee martinis for you three and shiso gimlets for the suits. Carlos's break is in fifteen minutes, and I promised a bathroom stall sequel to remember in exchange for these drinks, so let's make the handoff quick before I report for duty."

I point to their table. "If we stand over by the partition and our backs are to them, we'll be able to hear what they're saying. But there's a chance Max will see us walking in his direction. So whatever you do, make sure they're too entranced by you to notice us taking our positions."

"Do you see how snatched my face looks tonight?" She vogues before balancing the tray of gimlets in one hand. "I dare them to take their eyes off me."

She struts over, treating the restaurant like her own personal runway, while we sneak as close to the partition as we dare for maximum eavesdropping.

"Evening, boys. It's your lucky day!" She thrusts the drinks into their surprised hands with the confidence and charm of a woman who's never been turned down.

"But we didn't order these," says a man with coiffed black hair.

"Of course, you didn't. You're our five-thousandth customer of the new year, so consider these tokens of gratitude. What's your name, sweetheart?"

"Hugo," he answers, his accusing tone dissipating thanks to Som's dazzling smile.

"Well, Hugo," she projects loudly in our direction. "I'm here to take care of you. I'm Darla Dragonfruit, Thai goddess of Hawker SF, and I'm here to please. Tell me, what brings you boys in tonight?"

I stifle a chuckle. Of course, Som would use any opportunity to plug her drag persona. All she needs now is Beyoncé's "Freakum Dress" to be playing, and she's right at home.

Som plays the perfect honeypot, hypnotizing the men with her effervescent charm, while the rest of us sip the martinis she brought us. The restaurant's packed waitlist provides the perfect cover, as if we're killing time at the bar until a table opens up.

Tania gives me and Glen the rundown. "You were right on the money, Casey," she says softly, "because every member of the board is here: Hugo Sandoval is partner at Dexin Ventures, and the man with the square-rimmed glasses sitting next to him is Byron Irving. Byron is a partner at Ronald Creek Ventures, aka RCV. Together Dexin and RCV own fifty percent of Habituall, and until his termination, Evan and the team owned the remaining fifty percent."

The weight of Tania's words is like a boulder forcing the air out of my lungs. Why does termination have to sound so . . . terminal? "And how do things change now that Nigel's involved?"

Tania frowns, fiddling with the strings of her hoodie. "After the pitch meeting, Nigel Pittman is now Habituall's newest board member when his team at Golden Pond were selected to lead the Series E fundraising round. Because of the terms of the deal, Evan had originally agreed to give up some of his ownership so the company could continue to grow with this influx of cash. That decision tipped the scale in the investors' favor and gave them the majority they needed to fire Evan."

That's it? Three men held the power to rip the rug from underneath him. When I imagined Habituall's board of directors, I pictured a packed conference room with a dozen faceless white guys. And while I was correct on the demographics, I didn't think there would be so few of them they could share one order of mushroom lettuce wraps.

"You gentlemen have a wonderful evening!" Som chirps, breaking us out of our conversation. "And don't hesitate to ask for anything at all."

Max takes a sip of his gimlet and grimaces. "Actually, I'm not a fan of gin—bring me a Moscow mule, will you?"

"Not a problem, darling. Darla Dragonfruit is here to fulfill your heart's desire."

Som takes his drink order and, as soon as their attention is diverted, reunites with us on the other side of the partition to tell us what she's witnessed. "There's some paperwork on the table," she says. "I couldn't make out the details, but a highlighted section was awaiting a signature, like some kind of business agreement."

Panic starts to creep in. "Find out what it says. Something nefarious is going down, and whatever is about to become of Habituall is there in black and white."

Som squares her shoulders. "You don't have to tell me twice. I'll get Carlos to make Max's mule extra special and report back."

While she makes her way to the bar, Tania, Glen, and I position ourselves so we can see the board's faces and listen in on their conversation without being caught.

"Not that I'm putting a rush order on this, gentlemen," Max says between bites of dumplings, "but now that the Series E is over and I'm CEO, we should get our IPO roadshow underway."

Byron raises an eyebrow. "Interim CEO," he corrects.

A flash of anger crosses Max's face before he recovers with a chagrined expression. "Of course. That's what I meant. But after today's events, it's obvious Evan was unfit to lead this company. You need someone with real executive presence, who's good for the Habituall brand and has what it takes to achieve a proper return on investment. I'm that someone, and I don't want to lose any more ground on going public due to EC's mishaps. What about all our talk about striking while the iron's hot?"

Hugo scoffs, setting down his scallop shumai. "The iron's hot all right—it's burning this company to a crisp. This drug scandal has turned Habituall into a laughingstock. Did you know that 'LSD CEO' is trending? The news is in every tech outlet and on every local subreddit. And now the Asian American community believes Evan's firing was racially motivated —the whole thing is absurd!"

Max's eyes practically bulge out of his head. "Whoa now —what in the world does that have to do with it?" He pulls at his collar as if he's overheating. "And where the hell is my drink, by the way?"

I wonder what's taking our dear Darla so long, but I can't get a visual of her or Carlos at the bar. Don't tell me they're—

"They have a point, though, Max," says Byron. "Steve Jobs and Bill Gates used to drop acid all the time, and nobody thought twice about it."

Max can't stop himself from rolling his eyes. "Any kid with a computer science degree can found a unicorn these days. When he builds a trillion-dollar business, he can get high all he wants."

The nerve of this two-timing bastard. I took everyone's characterization of Max as the mature executive at face value, but the more Max makes his case, the more strongly I believe he's been maliciously undermining Evan's authority. He's making it sound like Evan's a loser who chose to celebrate 4-20 too early, when he's the one who laced the gummy bears in the first place. I just have to prove it.

"Regardless," Nigel continues, "racism allegations are nothing to sneeze at. I'm unsure if now is the right time to pursue an IPO. Let's focus on damage control for now, and stir up some good press for First Party. After the conference is over, I say we consider an alternative exit strategy."

He pushes the contract on the table toward Habituall's new interim CEO. Max peers at it, stone-cold, before taking it in his hands. It's not the prize he wanted, but he's not foolish enough to turn down whatever consolation is being offered instead.

"Fine," Max bites off begrudgingly. "You said if we made you the lead investor in this round, Golden Pond would back up a truckload of cash. As long as I get my golden parachute, I'm not picky about what form it comes in."

My mouth sours like it's filled with battery acid, and my nails leave marks on my palms from being balled up into fists. Tania's looking at Max like she's about to slit his throat with broken stemware, and I might let her if I'm forced to listen to his bile any longer.

I'm caught up in my murder fantasy when Max suddenly stands up and tosses his napkin defiantly on the table.

"Where did that little waitress run off to? A Moscow mule only has three ingredients. What is the hold-up?"

He snaps his head toward us, and I pull Glen's cap further over my face, ducking behind him for safety. Holy crap, that was close.

Fortunately, Darla reappears in front of the board's table, holding out Max's cocktail with a flourish.

"Dearest apologies for the delay. There was a lemons versus limes fiasco to deal with—it was a mess. So we made yours super-duper special with a secret ingredient for a little extra oomph. I call it the My Phuket Little Pony. Cheers!"

As Max takes a hearty swig, Darla stacks the empty glasses haphazardly on her tray, until the opportune moment—

"Hey, watch it," Max barks before spilling alcohol down his shirt. The rest of the men hand over their napkins, distracted just long enough for Darla to swoop in and collect the contract on the table. As her eyes scan the pages, I hope she can get a good look in such dim lighting.

Max waves off the board, turning his attention back to her. "Where is your manager? I demand to speak to them."

"So sorry. I'm such a butterfingers." Darla bats her thick set of falsies. "The good news is I saved your paperwork. Still spotless—not a drop on it. Here you go, sir."

She shoves the papers in his hands before briskly walking toward the front of the restaurant, waving at us to follow her out the door. Once outside, we sprint to the car and jump inside, with Tori at the wheel.

"Step on it!" I shout at her. "Drive like we're about to miss out on Barney's semi-annual sale!"

Tori doesn't share my fanatical love for fashion, but she slams on the gas nonetheless, while Som catches us up between breaths. "I didn't have time to read much, but I definitely saw the words 'acquisition,' 'staff-cutting,' and 'intellectual property sales.' Whatever's about to go down at Habituall is bad news."

I gulp, my stomach twisting into knots. I'm no expert in finance, but I've seen *Pretty Woman* enough times to get the gist. Evan wasn't just fired from his own company: because of

Max's selfishness and Golden Pond's greed, he's been kicked out so they can steal it and sell it for parts.

Tania, in between me and Som in the back seat, looks crestfallen and we squeeze her hands in solidarity. She, Wendy, and four hundred employees around the world—people I've grown to know and love—are going to be thrown in the corporate garbage disposal in just a few weeks.

Unless I can team up with Evan and pull off a move as epic as the one Julia Roberts pulled on Rodeo Drive and show them what a big mistake they're making by fucking with his team. Not just a big mistake. Huge.

"We have to head back to Evan's," I urge, directing Tori to circle around toward the way we came in. "The quicker we make a game plan, the better a chance we have at saving his startup from being shut down."

As we twist through San Francisco's streets toward Evan's apartment, Tori turns around to Som, as if there's one more thing that doesn't make sense. "You said you were bailing to the bathroom to report for duty with Carlos."

Our Thai goddess chugs from a water bottle before reapplying her smudged lipstick. "That's already been taken care of," she teases with a wink. "What did you think I meant when I put a special ingredient in that dick's drink?"

SINCE I CAN'T GUARANTEE Evan isn't stumbling around in his birthday suit, I advise everyone to stay in the car. But with her livelihood on the line, Tania's much more invested in my scheming than the glam fam, and she practically falls out of the back seat to avoid being left out.

"Are you sure, Casey?" she presses, holding the car door open with one sensible block heel on the sidewalk, ready to bolt upstairs with me if I say the word. "I've got detailed notes on the board I always consult before I write marketing's performance reports. I can help."

I smile in sympathy. I can't imagine how hard it must be to put her trust in someone with less than two months' worth of startup experience, but Evan's already in a fragile state, and I don't know how he's going to react when I tell him what we saw at Hawker SF tonight.

"I wouldn't expect anything less, and of course you will help," I reassure her. "We're going to need your knowledge if we're going to have any chance of saving Habituall. But you saw how out of it Evan was today. Let me help him wrap his brain around this news, and then I'll loop you in, Tania. I promise."

After a few beats of hesitation, she relents, slowly closing the door in defeat. I can't say I can compete with her level of Habituall lore, but by now I've manhandled its CEO's cock twice, so that's got to count for something.

As I make my way to his apartment, I brace myself to deal with Evan fully tripping in the buff. And yet, when I let myself in, I'm surprised to find him on the living room sofa, dressed in cozy flannel pajamas and eating a healthy meal.

"If acid's anything like alcohol, I figured you would be face-deep in some nachos or a Mission burrito," I say, pointing to his fruit salad sprinkled with Tajín.

He swallows a mouthful of tea. "That would make me more nauseated than the LSD. But judging from the grim look on your face, whatever you're about to tell me might induce vomiting anyway."

Joining him on the couch, I relay what we witnessed at Hawker SF as delicately as I can. But there's no tiptoeing around the cold, hard facts. I may not be able to prove Max drugged Evan and plotted to have him fired, but now that he's been ousted, the board cares only about slicing Habituall into pieces and selling them off to the highest bidders.

I expect Evan to boil over in anger, throw fruit across the room, and demand retribution. But he instead drinks the last of his tea, sets it gently on the coffee table, and slumps back, defeated.

"Guess there's nothing more to be done, then."

My eyes bug out. "What the fuck are you talking about? When I found you passed out, your clothes tossed on the tile floor and the shower still running, I thought you *died*, Evan. You could have slipped and cracked your head open, bled out in the bathroom. All because you were drugged against your will. You have to go to the police."

"And tell them what, Casey?" He sighs, exhausted. "That I conveniently ate the evidence? I spent over half a decade leaning into the eccentric tech founder persona to avoid going bankrupt in designer suits again. Everyone assumes I'm some hippie druggie freak, and I let them. Now I'm reaping what I sowed."

He presses his palms against his eyes, until I reach out and grab one of his hands to stop him from rubbing too hard. "I don't care what you wear—I mean, I *do* care, but this wasn't your fault. Nobody deserves to have their business stolen from them because they show up to the office in basketball shorts. You can't take this lying down!"

Evan squeezes my hand to keep his tears from pouring over. "Maybe it's for the best. If my own board would go to these lengths to erase my legacy, why should I put up a fight? Failing one company could be a fluke, but failing two is a pattern. I guess I'm not cut out to be an entrepreneur."

I can't believe the bullshit coming out of Evan's mouth. Did the acid disintegrate his dignity? What happened to the man who stood up for himself and the others around him? The man who may have butt heads with me but stuck to his convictions? The Evan I met in the zen room wouldn't recognize this version throwing a pity party in his PJs.

I stare him down. "Do you know what I kept telling myself the first day of this gig?"

He shrugs, without so much as a witty retort, and I want to shake him.

"Only impostors don't get impostor syndrome. Up until I got hired by Habituall, Alex was my main client, and it's weird to call her that when we went to sleepaway camp together every summer. When she decided to go in a different direction and work with other stylists, it wasn't that we weren't seeing eye-to-eye professionally. It felt like a complete rejection of me personally. Like she was throwing away everything we built together. But I never wanted my legacy to be limited to one person, even if she was my best friend. Becoming a part of your team has been a dream come true, a chance to make a bigger impact, all on my own. But walking into that zen room, I was nervous to meet you and be seen as nothing more than a hack."

Evan cringes, guilt flashing across his face. "I'm sorry for being a jerk that day and for giving you such a hard time. You've been doing a fantastic job, and I've been in the way, acting like a chump. If anyone's an impostor or a hack, it's me."

"No," I push back forcefully, startling him in his seat. "That's not the point I was making. I remind myself only impostors don't get impostor syndrome because I am damn good at what I do. And in your own twisted way, you proved that. You challenged me to stop discounting myself and qualifying everything I say to the nth degree. You put up a fight with me so I would fight back harder as your equal. Habituall is the first client that's truly felt like mine, but more importantly, it's your business, Evan, and nobody else's. Max is the impostor—don't let him get away with this."

Evan pulls his hand away from mine. "He already has— and I'm not talking about tonight. Ever since he joined, he's convinced everyone—the team, the board, our investors, even the press—that he's more competent than me in every way. I hear what people say when they think I'm off in la-la land. He's the *adult in the room*, and I'm the college dropout who needs to be babysat. If I can't meet everyone's standards of a worthy CEO, why should I try?"

My heart is breaking faster than his resolve. "And what about me . . . about *us*?"

"Your standards were the highest of all, Casey, which is why it hurts the most." He blinks back tears. "You deserve to be with someone who isn't such a disappointment."

I can't quite tell if I'm mad *at* Evan or *for* him, but I'm irate, nonetheless.

"I get to decide what or who I deserve. You keep talking about my astronomically high standards, and you know what? You're right. I expect a lot from you, because I care a lot about you, Evan. Why would I keep coming back to headquarters, day in and day out, if I didn't care about you and want to be with you? I believe in you, even if nobody else does. You'll only be a disappointment if you quit believing in yourself."

I stand up. My hopes of devising a game plan tonight might be dashed, but I'm not giving up. As soon as Evan is sober and puts his head on straight again, we are going to run through First Party logistics and strategize how to take Max down.

"Go ahead," I say as I walk toward the door. "Sleep it off, lick your wounds, do whatever you need to do, but we're saving your startup, Evan. Together. I'm not taking no for an answer."

~

Transcript of Habituall all-hands Q & A, facilitated by anonymous "interaction app" Slido – March 16

. . .

Maxwell Erickson, interim CEO: Welcome, everyone, to today's Town Hall. Due to recent events, we won't be adhering to our usual programming. Instead, we'll be dedicating the entire ninety minutes to answering your pressing questions. We value honesty and transparency here at Habituall, but please understand the investigation is ongoing, and we will be limited to what can be discussed legally. It's also worth noting that because previous internal communications have been leaked to the press, we will only be able to be open with Habituators as long as there is mutual respect for confidentiality. So on that note, Lola, please get us started.

Lola Nichols, chief of staff: Thanks, Max. This is the most engaged Town Hall in the company's history, with over two hundred questions and comments submitted, which you can upvote to bubble up the most important to the top. The Slido is still open, and while we won't have time to address every question, we intend to share a spreadsheet with our consolidated responses by the end of the week. Even though Slido is anonymous, we ask that you keep our company values in mind: Practice Loyalty by assuming the best of intentions of our leadership, communicate your concerns through the lens of Teamwork, and keep an open mind with Balance. Alright, let's begin Town Hall with our first question: "What happened? Why was EC fired?" Our entire leadership team is prepared to participate in today's Q & A, so Laura, can you kick us off?

Laura Lackner, VP of employee experience: All we can officially say at the moment is Evan Chen violated our company code of conduct and was terminated by our board of directors. Because Evan was employed at Habituall, he is treated like any other employee, and we would never release confidential information about someone's employment.

Lola: Thanks, Laura. Next question, and please excuse my use of profanity: "Are the rumors true? Was Evan fired for microdosing? Since when did we become a bunch of fucking narcs?"

Laura: Please understand this matter is serious, and we all must respect Evan's privacy. We don't recommend fueling the rumor mill, and we ask that you do not contact Evan as he is no longer privy to internal affairs at the company.

Lola: We received this question many times: "Is Max really going to be our new CEO now?"

Max: Yes, great question, and as we explained in this morning's team-wide email, the board has instated me as Habituall's interim CEO. I wish this decision could have been made under more joyous circumstances, but we'll do our best to make the transition as smooth as possible. I'll be hosting an AMA next week to reintroduce myself to the team and lay out the tenets of my leadership manifesto. Lola will send out details later today.

Lola: Yes, keep your eyes on your inbox for more information. This next question is more of a comment: "Whatever happened, EC broke the rules, and he's not above company policy. He made Habituall a laughingstock. Good riddance."

Max: Thank you for your comment. We treat our employees equally, and we're looking forward to coming out of this incident a stronger team. I appreciate your support.

Lola: We've got another comment: "Sounds like the Silicon Valley playbook: supplant the Asian founder with a white man who fits the stereotype of CEO. Typical."

Max: Um, let's remember to keep our values in mind. We can assure you race had nothing to do with the board's decision . . . Lola, how about we move on to the next question?

chapter
fifteen

When I walk into Habituall HQ the next morning, I'm hoping that, with my disappointment ringing in his ears, Evan has come to his senses and is about to spring into action. That as soon as the acid stopped corroding his brain, he's raced through the grief cycle backward—going to bed settled into acceptance, but waking up this morning in a fit of rage.

If an entrepreneur is suddenly forced to face an existence without the company they've built, shouldn't their first response be flipping tables?

But as the hours tick on, there's no sign of him—either in the zen room or anywhere else.

I try to distract myself by focusing on my actual work—nailing down the C-suite's attire for the fast-approaching First Party—but without Evan around to make the hours fly by, my heart isn't in it anymore. Every minute I play a double agent wipes me out mentally, but I do what I must to make sure I'm not disposed of like Evan.

As I run through the final fittings, I spend half my time stroking Max's ego, reassuring him the worst is behind us, that not only is he made to be CEO, but now he also looks the part. I can't believe it took me this long to see his try-hard attitude for what it really is—narcissistic insecurity—but by the time lunch rolls around, I'm so good at making him feel smart, special, and important that Lola's getting jealous.

When the executives break for twenty-five-dollar green goddess salads even though the corporate catering rivals most restaurants and is completely free, I check my phone, hoping to see a string of texts from Evan going into fix-it mode.

But when the only notifications I have are the latest BOGO deals, it's time to enlist the big guns.

"Come on," I say, dragging Tania out of the kitchen, "we're eating out."

"But it's sushi day!" she laments, gazing longingly at the platters of gyoza and rainbow rolls.

We take the elevator down and exit the building at a brisk pace. "I'll buy you all the salmon and tuna you can eat, after you convince Evan to give a shit about saving Habituall."

Tania brightens, this new mission more motivating than any garlic edamame could be. "Aw yeah, time to take the anti out of the hero."

I look back at her, confused. "Is that a Taylor Swift reference?"

"What? Oh no, I'm more of an emo girl, but that's beside the point. I meant if EC is going to be portrayed as a villain, then we should make him see there's still plenty to root for."

"And how do we do that?"

With Evan's apartment building in sight, Tania power-walks ahead of me.

"The same way you inspire any tech founder. You remind them of their startup's origin story."

～

I'LL ADMIT Tania's Marvel-esque metaphor had me skeptical, but if anyone had the storytelling skills to convince Evan to defeat the Big Bad, it would be the woman in charge of PR spin and persuasion.

That said, it took some major faith on my part to keep my mouth shut. At every step—from yanking Evan out of bed to shoving him into the shower, then into clean, decent-looking clothes—I was overcome with exasperation, tamping down the urge to tell him to snap out of it.

But now that we're sharing a plate of veggie tempura from the closest Japanese restaurant in our delivery radius, the mood has lifted significantly. Southerners love to say you catch more flies with honey than vinegar, but who knew soy sauce works even better.

"Remember our old office, EC?" Tania asks, munching on a spear of fried asparagus. "When we moved in and didn't even have furniture?"

He chuckles at the memory. "Those were the days. We would race Razor scooters around the perimeter and bowl down the long hallway using empty wine bottles as pins. It feels like a lifetime ago. How old were we?"

"I was twenty-seven, but you had just turned twenty-three," she answers without missing a beat. "It was right before we announced our Series B. I was new to the team as employee number thirty, and that press release was my first assignment . . ."

Tania gladly skips down memory lane, recounting the day Evan interviewed her for her position, the adorably tipsy speeches he'd given at the holiday parties, and the late nights when ping-pong tournaments led to karaoke barhopping. In the midst of these stories, I realize that because she's worked for Habituall for much longer than I have, she's also known Evan for much longer. It's now obvious that no matter how much of a kooky hippie she assumed him to be, she thinks of him fondly. And that feeling is contagious.

"You're both so passionate about this company," I say with envy. "It didn't take me long to be proud to ride this rocket ship, but I can only imagine how you feel to have built it."

Evan's hand dips under the table to squeeze my knee, and it's nice not to hide displays of affection for once, knowing the space the three of us have carved out for each other is safe. "It took me losing my business to recognize it wasn't created single-handedly," he says, regret seeping through every syllable. "Habituall is the success it is today off the backs of hundreds of people. I may have gotten the ball rolling, but if I put the team at risk—intentionally or not—I don't blame them for moving on without me."

Tania spits an edamame bean at his forehead with surprising force. "Bullshit. We were already adults when we met, but in many ways, we grew up together, EC. Habituall made me the marketer and leader I am today, and I'm not about to let some straight-up sociopath and a soulless private equity firm dismantle our legacy. You owe it to us to see your vision through, to take us to heights we never thought possible."

She points at me with her soybean pod. "Casey's right. Everybody dreams of hitching a ride on the next rocket ship, and we actually did it: a team of four hundred across four offices in two countries—soon to be three if you count the plans to expand to Australia. It's because of *you* that we're headed to the moon, so don't you dare self-eject before we take off."

Tania's words sink into his psyche. The harder his lips settle into a firm line the more mine want to break out into a giddy smile. This is the Evan Chen I know, the one who digs in his heels with a dangerous glint in his eye. The one who won't back down from a fight, no matter what.

"Okay. What are we thinking then?"

It sounds silly to put too much meaning in a single word, but hearing 'we' gives me the camaraderie I've deeply missed. I know if Alex ever welcomes me back into the glam fam with open arms, I'm making Evan and Tania honorary members. We're a team now, and I can't imagine a life without them in it.

"I've been giving this a lot of thought," Tania says, "and I think we need to go straight to the top. The board holds the power now, and if they have the ability to fire you, then they also have the ability to undo that decision. Nigel Pittman's a lost cause, of course, because supplanting you with a new CEO is part and parcel of the Golden Pond playbook. Getting high as a kite just accelerated their decision, to be honest."

Steam comes out of my ears. "But Evan didn't get high intentionally! The board needs to know Max drugged him."

"We know that's what happened," she concedes, "but making such an accusation without any proof would be a major liability. Max would not be above suing for defamation, and duking it out in the court of public opinion would do further damage to Habituall."

Evan shakes his head vehemently. "I'd rather tarnish my reputation than the company's at large. If that means taking ownership of a mistake I didn't make, then I'll fall on that sword."

The idea of Evan paying for Max's crime twists my stomach into knots, but I have to trust their judgment when it comes to the cutthroat tech community.

Tania nods. "A board of directors is much more likely to forgive a founder for a one-time drug-induced oopsie than a targeted slandering of a colleague. And before the LSD fiasco, the other board members must have had faith in you, EC. They wouldn't have let you remain at the helm for five years if they didn't trust the direction you were taking the company."

"That's true," I add, recalling the board's conversation at Hawker SF. "And they didn't seem thrilled to let Max call the shots, given how they reminded him he's only interim CEO." I pause. "One of them even mentioned Jobs and Gates dropping acid like it was no big deal, so maybe they can be convinced this whole thing has been blown out of proportion."

"Exactly!" Tania gives my shoulder an enthusiastic shake. "They're venture capitalists for christ's sake. When you consider the chaotic early days of companies like Uber, WeWork, and Zenefits, they make the Golden Pond meeting look as buttoned up as a coat factory."

Evan chuckles darkly. "You've got a point. Hugo Sandoval and Byron Irving were no strangers to Habituall happy hours that devolved into all-night shenanigans. I always got the impression that early-stage VCs took 'work hard, play hard' seriously, so we weren't about to disappoint them when they swung by for a good time." He runs his hand through his dark hair, slightly damp from the shower we inflicted upon him. "But I was never on hard drugs then, and I don't want them thinking I'm on them now. We need to convince them that I'm better than the boy genius they invested in—that I'm the best man for the job of taking this business public."

Tania's gaze flicks to mine, her mouth curling up into a mischievous smile. "Sounds like you need a CEO makeover. I wonder who can help with that?"

WITH THE DAYS counting down before we have to catch a flight to Vegas for the conference, Tania and I move fast, careful not to be attached at the hip the whole time. Both our livelihoods are on the line, so as long as the C-suite is concerned, we're laser-focused on making First Party a massive success, and any conversation we have is merely keynote-related.

But behind the scenes we're in secret makeover mode. As I enlist the rest of the glam fam to give Evan the glow-up of a lifetime, Tania manages to pull a fast one on RCV and Dexin Ventures, booking a pitch meeting for an unnamed founder of a stealth startup. It takes a bit of lying by omission, but Evan's reputation isn't exactly stellar at the moment, and we can't afford to be turned down by the board.

"I took Evan's boy genius line and ran with it," Tania had explained once she got off the phone with Byron's assistant. "I had to pretend to head up comms at some hotshot PR agency pitching San Francisco's newest tech wunderkind, but everything I said about EC was true. *Forbes* 30 Under 30, the next Marc Benioff, the whole nine yards. I simply kept his identity a secret to maintain an air of mystery. Like I predicted, once they heard of his accomplishments, they wanted to invest immediately. We need to remind them that Evan Chen is the same in person that he is on paper."

Easier said than done when Evan's resume now includes a drug scandal gone viral. But I wasn't about to argue after Tania already achieved the impossible: getting two venture capitalists to agree to the same time slot.

Finally, Friday afternoon rolls around, and we put the plan into action. I didn't think my Silicon Valley bingo card would entail pulling a *Parent Trap* on two investors who don't know they've been double-booked by a founder already in their portfolios. But Tania reassured me that the tech industry is about winning at all costs, so even if Hugo and Byron are affronted by Evan's deception, they're likely to tip their hat to the ingeniousness of the maneuver.

I sure hope she's right, considering Evan and I are on our own pulling this off. While she's gunning for promotion to VP of marketing, Tania can't be seen in cahoots with Habituall's ousted founder. So I do what comes naturally when I'm lacking confidence: I fake it with an undeniable outfit.

For such an undercover operation, I dress us in matching monochromatic black suits. It's a tricky look to get right—without an impeccable fit you come across like a sleazy magician. But the look suits Evan's lean frame, with every angle cutting him in the perfect place. I ditch his tie to give the business attire a cool edge, and in a bold move, for my own outfit, I go for a curve-hugging turtleneck underneath a single-breasted blazer. It's both full-coverage professionalism and sultry sex appeal wrapped into one pantsuit. And from the way Evan's eyes are roaming over my entire body outside the meeting place, a healthy distance away from Golden Pond's headquarters, I'm optimistic that these VCs will hear us out and won't reject us immediately.

"Casey," Evan groans the second I come into his view. "It should be a white-collar crime to look that fucking good. Because I would let you commit a hostile takeover, no questions asked."

I swat his hands away, appalled he could joke about the very real danger his company is facing, even though it's been a month since our last hookup and my body is dying to give into its carnal desires. Between the contentious reveal of Evan's secret closet, the fight we had at the Safe Haven fundraiser, and his unceremonious firing, we've had more than our share of conflict get in the way of a good ol' fashioned roll in the hay.

"Let's get you off the board's shit list, and then we can relieve this pent-up stress from a horizontal position. Now, are you sure we won't have any problems getting in?"

We needed a meeting location that exuded exclusivity and innovation, without risking any intruders entering Evan's orbit, so Tania pulled all the strings at her disposal to book a reservation at the invite-only Opal Lounge, which isn't publicized anywhere online but according to word of mouth is apparently the spot for up-and-coming entrepreneurs.

Evan shrugs, opening the glass door without hesitation and ushering me inside. "It's in the same building as the startup accelerator program I went through, so at the very least, my alumni status should count for something."

The lobby has the industrial-chic interior of most coworking spaces: hardwood floors, exposed beams, and plush, leather furniture. But the low lighting and lack of typical startup accessories like foosball tables makes it feel more like a trendy bar at a four-star hotel. If tech bros are burning the midnight oil here, they're doing it with a nightcap rather than a mini fridge full of Red Bulls.

I smile as we approach the front desk, pleased that our surroundings have as much taste as our attire. If the Opal Lounge used the same interior designer, we'll fit right in.

The model-esque redheaded receptionist looks up at us expectantly, so I power through my nerves. I'm Habituall's stylist and strategic advisor, not a teenager trying to buy beer with a fake driver's license. "Casey Holbright and guest checking into the Opal Lounge for our meeting with RCV and Dexin Ventures." Tania put the reservation under my name since the board members haven't met me yet, and it doesn't help me get over the feeling that we're committing some kind of crime.

"Wallet ID?" the receptionist replies, waiting to type in my response. Puzzled, I scramble into my tote bag to grab my wallet. Did they need to search it in some kind of security procedure?

But the receptionist holds up her hand when I try to pass her the slim black case. "Your crypto wallet, ma'am. You can pay for today's reservation with Bitcoin, Ethereum, or the lounge's own token, Opal Bucks."

My heart seizes. Why wasn't this policy clearly stated when

we made the reservation? The only token I could possibly have in my purse would be from the last time I took my brothers' kids to their local arcade.

Before I can plead to pay double the amount if she could accept real damn money, Evan recites off a string of random letters and numbers, which the receptionist dutifully enters into her computer. She confirms Evan's digital identity has been verified by the blockchain and a receipt of the transaction has been emailed to him, but I'm half paying attention. The moment we're escorted into an elevator and told to take it to the top, I turn to Evan. First, his secret closet and now this? "You have crypto?" I accuse with disgust, as if I've caught him eating his own boogers.

He rolls his eyes—the universal expression for *doesn't everybody?* "I'm not one of those diamond-hand loons lurking on WallStreetBets, if that's what you're thinking," he hedges, like I'm not baffled by every word he just said. "But I'm a tech entrepreneur in SF, so it comes with the territory, alright? It's not that different from investing in a Birkin bag with the hopes that it will appreciate in value. You should be thanking me for diversifying my portfolio."

I'm able to save face without biting off a begrudging thank you when the elevator chimes to inform us we've arrived at our destination. Whatever bougie idea of a lounge I had in my mind vanishes when we step into what looks like a Victorian train carriage. Enclosed vestibules flank both sides of a narrow hallway, and the dark wood and dim lighting give the interior a hushed gravitas.

An attendant steps out of the shadows and introduces himself, then leads us to the compartment we've been assigned. When he opens the door, my first thought isn't to admire the ruby-red tufted seating but rather lament its inade-quate size.

"Um . . ." I start, hating to point out the obvious. "We

should be able to squeeze in just fine, but it's too cramped to fit our other two guests. Do you mind if we swap this for something bigger?"

"This is all part of the experience," the attendant reassures us. "Our guests value privacy, so everyone in each party gets their own booth. But don't worry—there's plenty of room in the metaverse!"

"In the what?" I blurt out, watching the attendant slide out a drawer from the table, pull out two pairs of high-tech goggles, and hand them to us.

"Everything you could possibly need can be requested virtually in the Opal Lounge. Just put these headsets on, and you'll be good!"

He leaves us to get settled in our seats, closing the door behind him. This entire floor is merely the loading zone to beam us up into cyberspace. Certainly an unconventional way to hold a meeting, but there's something exciting about witnessing the supposed next wave of innovation firsthand.

It doesn't take long, however, for my hope in technological advancement to crumble. Evan and I slide our headsets over our faces, and after selecting some physical characteristics for our avatars from a pitifully small number of options for skin and hair color, we're thrust into our virtual reality.

"You've got to be kidding me," I blurt out once our cartoon selves animate into a digital conference room—without pants. It's already an insult that eight-bit video games look more sophisticated than this metaverse, but its creators can't be bothered to give us legs? The whole reason I'm here is to make Evan look the part of a responsible, levelheaded CEO, not some reckless and entitled tech bro. If the board members can't see his appearance, then the thought and preparation that I put into it goes right down the drain, and that is unacceptable.

I'm about to pull the plug on this whole charade and

demand we get reassigned to an actual meeting room, but before I can log out, our guests appear on screen.

"Byron Irving with RCV, here." A gruff voice coming from the avatar with glasses infiltrates our headsets.

Recognizing the voice, the other avatar speaks up. "Byron? What are you doing here?" Apparently, we can't blink in the metaverse, so Hugo Sandoval looks as shocked here as I imagine he does in real life.

The men start talking over each other, asking who's in the room and what the hell is going on, so I decide to rip off the bandage and dive in. "Gentlemen, thank you both for joining us," I begin. "I'm Casey Holbright and while you may not know me, you obviously know each other from serving on Habituall's board. And the reason I know that is because the entrepreneurial prodigy I brought you both here to meet is none other than Evan Chen."

The Opal Lounge must have some way of tracking people's movements in each pod because their digital arms start pointing and waving wildly. It would be hilarious if the cartoons' body language wasn't accompanied with accusations of fraud and threats to get lawyers involved.

"You better explain yourself, Evan," Byron barks, "because if this is your idea of a sick joke, we haven't recovered from your last one."

The barb is laced with so much venom, it stings me, but Evan doesn't let it tear through his thick skin. "I completely understand why you're angry. So am I. I swear on my ancestors' legacy that I did not take acid, either that day or any other day. But I'm willing to take it on the chin and hold myself accountable if we can address the issue like adults, instead of blowing it out of proportion. We've partnered together since Habituall's founding. You know I'd never put the company at real risk."

When Evan pauses and the board members don't immediately log off, I'm relieved. Maybe he can convince them to see his side of the story.

"It did seem out of character," Hugo admits, not recognizing the irony that we're all out of character in this ridiculous metaverse. "But the problem is that it still seemed possible. You can't blame us for taking what's communicated to us at face value, Evan. Not when your overall appearance has veered into . . . unprofessional territory."

That's rich coming from someone who's conducting business in primary color hex codes, but Evan doesn't vocalize the same snark.

"Point taken." He sighs. "I dug myself into a hole on that one, but Casey here is working wonders to overhaul my personal presentation and that of my leadership team. I can't repair Habituall's reputation with a single suit, but I can make immediate strides with your support."

I steel myself to jump in and confirm that I'll do whatever it takes to get Evan back in good standing, but he moves on to make a pivot.

"That said," Evan continues, "at the risk of sounding cavalier, we've enjoyed some raucous times getting Habituall off the ground. On occasion, things got a bit wilder than anticipated, but that's the name of the game in Silicon Valley, isn't it? Sometimes you accidentally send a founder a calendar reminder before Burning Man to buy mushrooms that have nothing to do with the farmers' market."

Holy shit. Who would've thought he'd so easily segue to throwing the board's own hypocrisies back in their faces? To paraphrase a classic internet meme, it's a bold strategy, so let's see how it plays out for him.

It's so deathly quiet that I assume either our esteemed guests unplugged from the matrix or their mics got cut off due to the obscenities they must be screaming.

Hugo's avatar eventually breaks the silence. "What are you getting at, EC?"

If there was any confusion over who Evan was referring to, Hugo's defensive tone clears it up quick. If we weren't fighting for the future of Habituall, this verbal sparring would be fascinating to watch from the sidelines. Not to mention, there are few things sexier than a man who can command a boardroom, even one that's pixelated.

"What I'm saying is," Evan replies, "if we can't brush blunders off, then we're doomed. Don't condemn us to failure when we're so close to monumental success we can taste it."

The board members aren't preoccupied with the mental picture of Evan's tongue on mine like I am, because when Byron Irving speaks up, he's fixated on another matter. "Oh? Without you, Habituall is nothing. Is that what you're implying?"

"Absolutely not. The exact opposite, in fact. Without Habituall, *I* might as well be nothing. It may be just another business on the balance sheet to everybody else, but it's been my driving force for five years. The product, the team—they mean everything to me. It's not about ringing the bell on Wall Street, although that would be the honor of a lifetime. It's about standing alongside four hundred Habituators, through good times and bad, and seeing our vision through."

His voice wavers, reminding us that behind these legless cartoons are real people. In our vestibule with headsets still strapped to our faces, I reach across the tiny table and squeeze Evan's hand. So he knows I'm on his side, no matter what.

Chastened by Evan's emotional plea, Byron takes pity on him. "You haven't lost everything. You may not be CEO anymore, but you'll always be Habituall's founder. The board appreciates the sacrifices you've made, and you still own your stock options as a reflection of your hard work. At a billion-dollar valuation, you've become a very, *very* rich man, Evan.

Go sell off your shares and travel to some tropical island where you can spend the rest of your days sipping piña coladas. Wipe your hands clean of this mess. Max can take it from here."

At the mention of our adversary, Evan tenses. I know we decided not to throw around unsubstantiated claims, but it's the one time in this contentious conversation that Evan hesitates on his next move. Has he changed his mind about revealing Max's malicious scheme?

"Evan, you have to tell them," I whisper without thought. If we were conversing in an IRL conference room we could make asides without being overheard, but I'm thwarted by what must be the most sensitive mics on the planet.

"Tell us what?" Hugo says with a sharp edge. I've never been in a board meeting, but I can guess it's a cardinal sin to wait until the eleventh hour to bring up a matter of grave importance.

Gripping Evan's hand for encouragement, I wait for the bomb to drop. I don't understand why he's not exposing Max's treachery, because I would have dragged him by now. We didn't make all this effort for nothing. Walking away without recruiting the board to our side is as useless as window-shopping. I've never left a mall empty-handed, so why the hell would I give up now? My entitled baby sister energy surges through my veins. If we don't get what we came here for, I will make a *scene*.

Hugo repeats his question, and before I can change my mind, I step in. "The reason why Evan can't wipe his hands clean of this mess is because Max is the one who got them dirty in the first place."

The men's eyes are already enormous in the metaverse, so I can't tell if what I've said is shocking to them.

"That's a serious accusation, Ms. Holbright," Hugo says. "What is your evidence?"

I don't receive any indication from Evan that he wants me

to shut my face, so I power on ahead, recounting our experiences, both in the run-up and the aftermath of the LSD incident. The one part I leave out, of course, is our undercover mission at Hawker SF. The board doesn't need to know that we know about their plans for the business, especially when we spied on them to discover those plans. And now that Hugo and Byron are aware of Max's deception, that agreement should be null and void.

Byron's cartoon glasses stare blankly. "Do you agree with this summarization of events, Evan?"

He squeezes my hand back, and I hold back an audible sigh of relief. I've asked for forgiveness rather than permission before, but it's usually after adding an accessory or taking a hemline up. Nothing with do-or-die stakes like this.

"Yes. I have never taken acid, nor any illicit substance, either on the job or off. Considering that Max's career would significantly benefit from my removal and that he had the ability and access to spike the gummy bears, we believe he had the motive, means, and opportunity to frame me for this offense. We're asking you to reinstate me as CEO."

The board members' meta mouths frown, making me wonder what facial recognition technology is used in the Opal Lounge. "Even if everything you're saying is true," Hugo says, "without hard, undeniable evidence, our hands are tied. Evan, you retain your stake in Habituall, but you no longer have board involvement or voting rights. That power has been temporarily granted to Maxwell Erickson as interim CEO. Nigel Pittman will back his decisions because it's to the benefit of Golden Pond that they appoint a chief executive who serves their interests. So in the event that both Byron and I vote to open an investigation, Max and Nigel will block it. In a tie, whoever's leading the company wins the vote. That's the system that *you* created, Evan. It's what's kept you in command for so long, but now it's what will keep you from it."

The idea of guardrails like these failing Evan at a time when he needs it most is tortuous. "Is there truly nothing we can do?" I plead.

Byron's avatar strokes his chin, which comes off more preposterous than pensive in the metaverse. "Sometimes the best course of action is moving on. If it means anything, we're not fond of this transition either. For the sake of everyone involved, we'll keep this meeting between us private. But without proof, it's best that you mind your own business. And unfortunately, that business is no longer Habituall."

I motion toward the entrance, prepared to rip every vestibule door off its hinges until I find the real Byron Irving and Hugo Sandoval so I can demand to speak to their managers—as if board members had managers—but Evan clutches my wrist to stop me from going ballistic.

"Thank you for hearing us out, gentlemen," he says, resigned. "We appreciate your discretion on this sensitive subject."

Our avatars awkwardly wave goodbye as we log out, and I can't get my headset off fast enough. I bite my tongue until we exit the building and are safely out of earshot. And then I glance at our pantsuits of perfection and am immediately reminded that no venture capitalist is going to tell me how to live my life. Especially ones who put more faith in crypto and cartoons than real people in premium textiles.

"Alright, you heard 'em," I say, rolling up the sleeves of my black blazer.

Evan's eyebrows raise inches closer to that luscious hairline of his. "You mean, the part where they explicitly said to mind our own business?"

"It *is* your own business," I assert. "And we're not going to let Max take it from you. If the board says we need proof and you ate the only evidence we have, then we have to go straight to the source."

"And where is that, exactly?"

For being such a savvy entrepreneur, Evan needs things spelled out for him way too often. "At First Party—the whole reason I was hired. We need Max to confess to his crimes if it's the last thing we do. For once, what happens in Vegas isn't staying in Vegas—we're getting it on tape."

~

DATE: March 22

SUBJECT: "Being the Best Habituator You Can Be at First Party"

FROM: tania.beecher@habituall.com

BCC: team@habituall.com

HI TEAM,

It's showtime! It's been four years since our inaugural First Party, and I'm so honored that in that time, we've grown our conference from a couple hundred customers to thousands of innovators in the retail and e-commerce community.

Thank you, everyone, for attending the training on the event's logistics. By now, you should know what your role is onsite and what will be required from you during your shift. Whether you're coordinating the check-in booth, running demos at the Genius Bar, or guiding attendees as a human arrow, you are all essential to ensuring the day runs smoothly.

Remember: you are representing the company and must be on your best behavior, especially at the afterparty. Here's a quick reminder on how to conduct yourself.

- *Leaders eat last.* We've got a sold-out evening, so that means we must put our VIPs first. Give up your seat, let them have the last hors d'oeuvre, whatever it takes to ensure they are accommodated at all times.
- *Mind your mouth.* The audience will consist of our customers, partners, and investors, so watch what you say because you never know who may be listening. First Party is not the place to complain about your work or discuss confidential information. When in doubt, don't.
- *Drink responsibly.* You've worked so hard and deserve to blow off some steam, but while we want you to enjoy yourselves, don't become best friends with the bartender.

Overall, please use your judgment and remember you are on the clock. Habituall has a zero-tolerance policy for misconduct, and anyone found misbehaving will face swift and decisive action. What happens in Vegas can get you fired. So if you have any questions about what is expected of you at the event, please speak to your manager.

Now let's go out there and crush the customer experience!

Thanks,

Tania Beecher, director of brand and content marketing

S ome people can arrive at an airport with the bare minimum of time to spare before boarding, breezing through security because they can fit all their belongings in a carry-on bag.

Those people are not stylists.

Fortunately, I've become adept at rolling two oversized suitcases, while simultaneously carrying a backpack full of beauty products and layering on any bulky clothes or hats I can't otherwise make room for.

It's bright and early on Tuesday, the day before First Party, when I arrive at San Jose Airport, dressed to impress in a sixties-inspired scuba dress with a Peter Pan collar. As I walk up to the check-in counter at the cheapest budget airline traveling to Vegas, I try to count my blessings. Yes, it's been a while since I've flown coach, but the trip's only ninety minutes, and then I'll reunite with Evan at the Venetian hotel so we can come up with a foolproof Plan B to save his company.

Even if he wasn't closer to SFO, I would have insisted we take separate flights to avoid being seen together. It makes sense that I'm attending the event to be available for last-minute alterations and to enjoy the fruits of my labor, snapping photos of the best dressed leadership team during the conference keynotes. But I can't risk being caught with my co-conspirator and thrown out like scrap fabric.

"Casey Holbright, taking the 8:30 flight to Las Vegas," I inform the attendant, flashing my ID and mobile boarding pass.

"Ms. Holbright, yes," the woman behind the counter chirps, as if she's been expecting me personally. "Looks like you've been upgraded!"

"Amazing. I could use some extra leg room." Tania must have sprung for one of the bigger seats up front when she booked my reservation. I lug my suitcases onto the scale and pray I didn't pack more than the maximum weight. "What's my new seat number?"

"You don't have one assigned," she replies with an envious smile, lifting my bags onto the conveyor belt. "But our team will escort you to your plane and you can select whichever you'd like."

My brain short-circuits, thinking this 'everyone fend for themselves' open seating has gotten out of hand, until the attendant passes me off to a colleague, who leads me through a restricted exit. It's when we take a golf cart away from my gate and toward the charter terminal when it hits me.

I'm flying private.

I've circled the globe on Princess Alex Air so many times that I would be able to recognize its distinct shade of blush pink from thirty-thousand feet in the sky. And even though this is the longest I've gone without speaking to Alex herself, I smile so hard my cheeks hurt when I see her barreling down the airstairs, security risk be damned.

"Casey!" she screeches as she sprints in my direction. When we collide with a force that nearly knocks us off our feet, she crushes me in a hug to make up for all the hugs we went without in the past two months.

"Missed you harder than I served at the 2023 Met Gala," Alex says with reverence.

I laugh, flashing back to how we made a statement about that year's theme by having Karl Lagerfeld's most hateful comments hand-stitched into Alex's gown. "Missed you harder than that bigot deserved a smack across the face."

"So did I, Casey. So. Did. I. Let the punishment commence because I fucked up royally thinking I could ever find a better stylist than you. A better partner than you."

At five-ten and always in the most killer heels—this time in white suede thigh-highs under a cozy sweatshirt in the same hue as her private jet—she towers over me. And yet, whatever transpired at Fashion Week has knocked Alex down several pegs because confidence has leaked out of her like the inflatable mattress I used to sleep on at her house before her family upgraded to the mega-mansion.

I should feel triumphant as we board the plane, arm in arm, now that *the* Alex Waterston-Gardner, the princess who could do no wrong according to her hordes of fans, is admitting she was at fault for severing our relationship. But as much as I might have fantasized about giving her the smuggest 'I told you so,' all I can muster in the moment is immense gratitude that my best friend is back in my life.

That said, I'm not above wanting to hear every juicy detail of Alex's mishaps. "What went wrong?"

"Oh gawd, what didn't?" We get comfy in our cream leather recliners as several supermodel-caliber flight attendants come around, bringing us warm hand towels, glasses of brut rosé, parfait bowls with fresh berries, and anything else our privileged hearts desire. It's not like I've been roughing it without the Waterston-Gardners, but it's amazing how quickly you get accustomed to the finer things.

We've got time to kill until departure, so Alex catches me up while we're on the tarmac. Like I expected, without a thoughtful transition, Dominic's attempt to take Alex's style in a new direction backfired epically.

"It was too much, too fast," she explains, sipping her bubbles. "I went from Barbie doll to Bratz doll, and it was an utter disaster. We thought it would be great to sample a bunch of stylists during my time off the catwalk, but there were too many cooks in the kitchen, and not a single look was cohesive. Everybody in the industry wants you to experiment, but only in small doses. I found that out the hard way. No one even recognized me at my debut in New York, and it got worse each week thereafter. In London they thought I was experiencing an identity crisis, and when I attempted to rally in Milan, I got called a poseur—and that was the tamest insult! By the time we arrived in Paris I was dragged through so much mud, I needed to throw myself into the Mediterranean to get clean again."

She sets her glass down on the fold-out tabletop between us. "Needless to say, but I'm saying it anyway: I'm so sorry, Casey, for doubting you. There were countless times I spent drunk-crying in some overrated nightclub when I wanted to call you. At one point Som rang you twice because I was a blubbering mess, but I made the glam fam promise not to get involved."

That must have been the night Som's raunchy ringtone interrupted my first hookup with Evan. "Why didn't you reach out?" I ask, incredulous that she'd go radio silent for so long if she'd actually wanted to talk to me.

Alex stuffs her hands in the pocket of her pink sweatshirt. "I was ashamed by how I treated you. In some sick way, I felt I deserved the ridicule. That I should let the haters tear me apart for my hideous outfits because I committed the sin of leaving you behind. Now I know why you're my right hand, Casey. That's the one that pens my signature." She smiles, taking my hands in hers and batting her voluminous lashes. "Please, let's put this whole hiatus behind us and pretend it never happened."

The glam fam didn't accompany her to Monaco, so now one of her nails is chipped. The flaw is comforting, in a way. Alex is human like the rest of us mere mortals, and much like her manicure, our relationship needs a touch-up.

"I appreciate your apology. I really do. You left an Alex-sized hole in my heart, and you're the biggest, brightest, bubbliest personality I know. But severing ties even temporarily forced me to design a life that didn't have you at the center, and as hard as it was, I'm grateful for it. Standing on my own two feet was good for me." I pat her hands before pulling back. "I'd be overjoyed to style you again, but not exclusively anymore. I love you, betch, but you're gonna have to get in the back of the line."

The concept makes Alex laugh out loud. She hasn't waited in a line since she was thirteen, but she takes my pushback with good spirits. "That's a fair price to pay to work with the incomparable Casey Holbright. I'm proud of you. You must love this new client of yours if they've become such a big priority."

"I do love Habituall." My cheeks go warm, and my lips upturn in an embarrassed, giddy smile. "And maybe its founder too."

It takes Alex a split second to read between the lines, and then she squeals at the top of her lungs. I haven't mentioned Evan's name, and she's already babbling about future double dates. And that's when something doesn't compute.

"Double?" I repeat, disappointment sinking in. "So the tabloids were wrong, and you and Dominic didn't break up?"

She pouts at the reminder that she's the prime target for gossip rags everywhere. "We decided to take a break in Paris, but everybody took my vacay out of context. I just went to Monaco to clear my head. That's where I learned I need both my BF and BFF by my side. But I promise Dominic is not allowed to weigh in on my wardrobe anymore. If he wants to be with someone with more edge, he can go date a steak knife. Now tell me about your new lover!"

I chuckle, choosing not to be combative after reaching a truce. I find it hard to believe that douchenozzle Dominic can keep his mouth shut about anything he wants to mansplain, but if Alex isn't in the headspace to hear her boyfriend is a toxic waste of space, then it's not my place to harp on it. One day I hope she can find a man like Evan who learns from his mistakes and fights hard to earn her affection.

I'm about to bring Alex up to speed on Evan Chen and our mission to reinstate him as CEO, until a familiar not-safe-for-work ringtone blares through the cabin.

"You better make room onboard, betch," Som shouts on speakerphone the second I accept her call. "Because the glam fam is coming with you to save the day, and we sure as hell aren't flying economy."

A COUPLE OF HOURS LATER, we split up. Alex decides to use her time in Vegas to negotiate party appearances with nightclub owners, so the rest of the glam fam tag along to refresh her between meetings. Tori offered to strategize Max's takedown with me—because how often do manis need upkeep?—but I turned her down.

"The one time you stay behind," I told her as they piled into the town car, "is when our princess breaks a nail trying to open a can of seltzer. Go prevent a beauty emergency, Tori. I'll be fine."

It's too early for lunch, and my stomach is doing too many somersaults to keep anything down anyway, so I circle back from the valet station and walk inside the Venetian. If Alex is spending forty-thousand a night on us to stay in the Chairman Suite, I should try to enjoy it. Or at least try to calm my nerves until I can come up with Plan B.

"Casey!" a voice calls from my left. Evan's standing in the lobby next to the giant gold armillary sphere, wearing sunglasses, those hideous khaki cargo shorts, and a Warriors baseball cap.

"What the fuck—why are you here?" I hiss, glancing around for onlookers. We specifically planned for him to stay out of sight in the Palazzo tower. "Someone could recognize you!"

"You walked right past me without noticing, so I guess the disguise is working."

I sigh, reaching up to grab his cap off his head and shove it into his hands. With our luck, he'll blow our cover before we can even complete the mission. Seriously, did he have to make it obvious by wearing the logo of a San Francisco team?

"That's not the point. Let's get out of view before Max has you kicked out for trespassing."

I march toward the elevator, Evan rolling his carry-on suit-case behind me.

"It's not like I was trying to be conspicuous. I figured I'd meet you in your room, but the front desk said there weren't any under your name."

"That's because I canceled my reservation. Alex surprised me with an impromptu trip to reconcile, and booking the Chairman Suite is her way of making it up to me."

When we exit the elevator into the penthouse floor, Evan whistles. "Hoo boy, this is one nice apology."

I grab my gold-plated key card out of my purse. "I haven't even opened the door yet."

As soon as I let Evan in, he loses his mind, abandoning his stuff in the foyer to give himself the grand tour. Amused, I follow him from one outrageously ostentatious room to the next while he blurts out enough profanity to rival a *South Park* episode.

"Hot damn, a gym? Oh shit, a theater room? Fuck me, a massage parlor? If this is how you and your friends travel, then why the hell do you want to work for my tiny startup? Well, not mine anymore, I guess, but you know what I mean."

"Okay, that's enough." I pull him away from opening yet another cabinet in the fully stocked wet bar. "Let's not be flippant about your business when I'm trying my hardest to win it back—hey, what are you doing? It's like ten thirty in the morning."

Evan continues to grab bartending tools. "I know we've got a covert operation to conduct, but let's start with some cocktails. I have a feeling we're going to need them because Alex isn't the only one who owes you an apology."

He picks lemons from a fruit bowl and slices them in half on a cutting board, while I tilt my head. "What do you mean? The fight we had on International Women's Day feels like a lifetime ago."

"Exactly. We could be back in SF enjoying each other's company, but you've been dealing with bullshit this entire time. First, you put up with my petty, stubborn, immature ass for weeks, and then when I finally come to my senses, this scandal ruins my reputation."

He squeezes the lemon a little too hard in frustration, squirting some juice outside the shaker he's aiming for. "Anyone else would have given up by now—nearly everyone around me already has. After everything I put you through, I wouldn't blame you for wanting to be with somebody else."

As I watch him mix in honey and dark liquor, I'd be lying if I said I never questioned whether Evan was worth the heartache or if I'd be better off booting up the dating apps again. But as much as he drives me up the walls, I wouldn't want to sully what we have. Evan may be a stiff drink, but I'd never want to water him down and dilute our intensity.

Pulling him away from his task, I bring him close. "I'm not going anywhere. I'm here in Vegas, placing my bets on you. Even when the odds are a hundred-to-one, I'm all-in."

Joy pours out of him, lighting up his face. "Does that mean we're making our relationship official?"

Stroking my chin dramatically, I pretend to deliberate. "On one condition."

His eyes narrow as he recognizes how the tables have turned since he coerced me into goat yoga.

"I get to give you fashion advice any time I want, and you can't ever argue back."

Evan laughs, the joyous sound cutting through any unresolved tension between us. It's a tall order, but he agrees. "Every word that has come out of your agonizingly delicious mouth has been the truth, and I deserve to never hear the end of it."

He resumes straining the cocktails into two Waterford crystal glasses and sets them down on the kitchen counter. I haven't taken a single sip, and already I feel flushed at the thought of Evan putting his lips on mine. If that's not new relationship energy, I don't know what is.

"So what now?" I muse. "After we get Habituall back, we spend our time getting cozy on your couch and calling each other babe?"

He closes the space between us. "You're welcome to call me whatever you want, as long as I'm yours."

Elated to hear those words, I lean in to kiss him, long and slow, to prove how mine he really is. I could indulge in him the entire day, if it wasn't for the one remaining loose end distracting me.

"But how exactly *are* we going to get Habituall back?"

"Shhh . . . all in due time. First Party doesn't kick off until tomorrow, and I found the exact thing we need as the ace up our sleeve. But I haven't had you to myself in a long time, and I can't let this suite go to waste."

Evan takes a swig from his glass before pulling me in for another kiss. His hands firmly grip my ass, pressing me into his straining hard-on.

"Brandy sour?" I guess, tasting the familiar notes from his tongue. I turn my head, giving him more access to leave a trail down my neck, when I notice the liquor bottle on the counter.

"Did you seriously break into the Louis XIII only to sweeten it with honey from a plastic bear?" I'm laughing at the absurdity.

He shrugs. "Eat the rich."

Ignoring the fact that Evan is indeed the rich, I guide his hand under my A-line hem. "How about you eat this instead?"

Evan groans, gulping down the rest of his cocktail and setting his glass down hard enough that I fear he'll chip the fancy crystal. But before I can warn him to be careful with the drinkware, he picks me up and tosses me onto the counter. In record time, he yanks off my thong and kneels between my outstretched legs.

I gasp, reveling in the sensation of his cold tongue against my warmth as he makes a full meal of me. Between the smooth fabric of my dress gliding across the marble countertop and my bottom half becoming its own slip 'n slide, I'm afraid of taking a tumble on the tile floor. I grip Evan's head between my thighs, hands tugging his hair, holding on for dear life.

"Mmm . . . you're already close, aren't you?" Evan teases my clit with the tip of his tongue. "Tell me how badly you want to come."

I pant as he enjoys making me writhe with pleasure, the pressure building until I'm about to erupt. "I need you inside me. Now."

He stands up and turns me around, leaning forward to place my palms flat on the counter. I expect him to thrust unceremoniously from behind, but he takes his time, indulgently pulling the zipper down the back of my dress. He unhooks my bra and lets my clothes fall to the floor, leaving me completely nude. Thank goodness the glam fam are out all day—otherwise, they'd find out the only thing burning up to 350 degrees in the kitchen is us.

But it's me who's taken by surprise when Evan plucks a small ice cube from his glass and presses it gently on my neck, making me shiver as he traces down my spine, over every curve, until it melts between my legs.

"You spend all this time dressing me up, yet here you are, stripped naked and desperately wanting to get fucked by a man in cargo shorts."

He slides my legs farther apart with his foot and pushes his shorts and underwear down so he can rub his hard cock against my bare ass cheeks.

"It's a blessing that you're behind me, then, so I can't get distracted by your terrible outfit," I quip, unable to stop myself from pushing back and rubbing myself harder into him.

Evan chuckles, tweaking my erect nipples, his fingers still freezing from holding the ice cube. He warms his hands on my breasts as my back arches, my body wanton with urgency.

"Tell me you don't care what I wear when I take you, Casey. I want you begging for it."

He smacks my ass, pushing the tip of his cock against my entrance, while his hands slide down my hips, locking me in place so I can't impale myself onto him.

"I don't," I gasp, aching to be filled up. "I don't care. You could fuck me wearing a parka, a wetsuit, and a goddamn sombrero—at the same time—as long as you get your dick in me right now!"

"Mm-hmm . . . and don't you ever forget that."

He thrusts in one fell swoop, and my knees buckle in response. I lean against the counter, appreciating the cool marble as the heat inside me spreads like wildfire. He hits my spot, again and again, my moans reverberating through the suite. I thank every square foot of these soundproofed walls because this feels much more primal than the last time at his place. It's like the insecurities of where we stand with each other have fallen away, and all that's left is unbridled want.

"God, I missed you," I breathe. "Don't stop."

Evan curves his body over mine, kissing between my shoulder blades. "I'm never going to stop, Casey. Never going to stop bickering and bantering and driving you fucking nuts before I send you over the edge. You're mine, you got that? And I will have you every day for the rest of my life as long as you'll have me. Now lift that pretty ass up, and let's hear you scream."

He reaches around and circles my clit until I explode, yelling as the waves of my climax come crashing around him. The tightness squeezes out the last of his restraint, and he bucks forward with a heavy groan, rocking back and forth until utterly spent.

Beads of sweat roll down my back, and Evan gently tosses my hair to one side, exhaling slowly to cool me down before kissing my neck and pulling out.

I rise up and turn around, using his biceps for support, so I don't collapse like a pool of jelly in front of the fridge.

Evan scoops me up, enveloping me in an embrace that makes me feel more at home than I ever thought possible in a hotel kitchen.

"I better stay hydrated," he laughs, taking a gulp from my glass. "Because I counted fifteen rooms in this suite, and I am gonna fuck you in every single one of them."

About three hours later, we succeed in violating all nine thousand square feet—including rubbing each other down in the massage parlor, a steamy sixty-nine in the sauna, and getting dirty one last time under the rainfall shower head.

"Okay, I'm squeaky clean and thoroughly satisfied," I say after throwing on a plush white bathrobe and applying a fresh layer of moisturizer. "Now spill about this alleged ace up your sleeve."

He ties on a matching robe. "Hold up a minute. I'm starving. I'm guessing we can order whatever we want in this joint, and I'm craving sushi."

Out in the living room, I find the business card of our on-call butler and hand it to Evan so he can call in a prix-fixe delivery from Nobu.

"Food is on the way," he says, hanging up the phone. "Now for the big reveal."

He rolls his suitcase over to the living room before sitting next to me on one of the many Italian-inspired sofas. "When I went to pack the suit you picked out for the Golden Pond meeting, I checked all the pockets to make sure I wasn't missing anything." He unzips the bag and digs deep into the bottom under several outfits I recognize from my recent selections. "And that's when I found this."

He pulls out a clear box about quarter full of—

"The gummy bears!" I spring off the couch to get a better look. "I thought you said there weren't any left."

"Did I say that? Casey, I was high as a kite. I had no control over my motor skills that day, let alone the words coming out of my mouth."

"You told me the box was empty!"

He nods energetically. "That's the thing—it *was* empty. But I found a few in my jacket pocket. I vaguely remember holding onto the box like it was a lucky charm because Max told me it was a gift from you. I must have fidgeted with it during breakfast with him, and the lid came off while I was tripping. Some of the candy fell out, and I didn't notice, thinking I already ate them all."

I rub my forehead, confused. "But Max made you flip your pockets to reveal the LSD tabs he planted."

"Yes, my *back* pockets, which I never check. Who puts their hands on their own ass? Anyway, at least Max stopped me from eating the whole box at once. To his credit, he wanted me hallucinating, not hospitalized."

I turn the box over in my hands. It's obvious the gummy bears were custom made for Habituall in the way they're enlarged and embossed with the company logo, but you'd never be able to tell that they had been tampered with.

"But . . . so what? It's not like I can get Max back by drugging him. He won't fall for his own trick."

He looks at me soberly, without a hint of sarcasm. "He won't, but you can."

If I MISSED the chaos of Fashion Week, Habituall's First Party conference more than makes up for it. From styling the keynote speakers to keeping a close eye on the electronically enhanced cuff links I planted on Max, I can barely breathe. With so much nervous energy suffocating me, I barrel to the end of the event, so we can put our covert plan into action at the afterparty.

But I didn't expect to be thwarted before we can even enter the venue.

"What do you mean, we're not on the list?" I panic-shout at Wendy Hoang, who's staffing the check-in table at TAO, the Asian-inspired nightclub in the Venetian where Habituall is hosting its afterparty. "I was literally hired to style this event."

Wendy holds up her clipboard in self-defense. "Hey, I'm just stepping in for Tania here. She was supposed to sign everyone in, but Max said I was the better choice for *optics*." She spits out the microaggression with an eye-roll, gesturing at the giant Buddha statue backlit in red and gold lighting. "I'm sorry, but he was adamant that only employees and their pre-approved VIPs are allowed."

This is news to me. The show went off without a hitch, and every executive who went on stage was in great spirits. Even Natasha and Paul hugged it out after nailing their product keynote. Max especially was in his element, soaking up the adoration from the audience. If he was paranoid about being exposed, he wouldn't have allowed me to come and dress him in the first place. He seemed unsuspecting when I was busy securing bugged cuff links on him, so I didn't anticipate him guarding the guest list. Is Max bringing down the hammer now because he's afraid of the walls closing in on him?

"Come on." Som gestures to our group. "No one has more Habituall pride than we do. Casey has us decked out like billboards!"

She's not wrong. I painstakingly coordinated our dresses to honor the company's logo colors with me, Som, and Alex in red, orange, and yellow, respectively, and Tori and Glen in black suits with matching accents.

"And you look amazing," Wendy concedes, "but I'm under strict orders—employees and VIPs only."

Alex leans in. "Um, I don't wanna be that 'don't-you-know-who-I-am?' person, but I'm a Very Important Princess."

"Unless this princess wants to buy a hundred-thousand dollars' worth of enterprise marketing software, my hands are tied here."

No, this can't happen. From the moment the glam fam returned from their back-to-back meetings and got over the fact that Evan and I fucked in every nook and cranny of the suite, we hashed out how tonight's supposed to go down. This is my last chance because once the event is over, my contract is complete, and I have no reason to be involved with the company anymore. Plan B has to pay off—I don't have any other letters of the alphabet as options.

Wendy's preoccupied with the line growing behind us, ready to move on, but I summon all my belligerent indignity —not that difficult considering the three brandy sours I pre-gamed as step one of the plan—and get close to her face so only she can hear me.

"I can't get into it right now, but trust me, it's not just my job or yours on the line. It's *everybody's*. You have to let me in, or we are all fucked. This is Vegas, Wendy, so deal me in. Please."

She clenches her jaw, peering over at Alex, who I can tell is seriously pondering signing a one-year contract with a Habit-uall sales rep in line to get past the velvet ropes.

"Fine, but just you, Casey, because you technically have a company email address. But that's all I can do."

"Thank you, thank you, thank you." I turn to the glam fam in a rush. "Hey, betches, I gotta go on without you!"

Tori grabs my arm. "Are you sure?"

"Of course, it's as easy as A-B-C, remember? I've already got 'A' on lock."

She looks me up and down as I try to keep my balance on five-inch stilettos. "That's what I'm worried about."

I reassure her I'll be fine, then push them back toward the entrance before holding out my arm so Wendy can attach my wristband.

"And, um, we wouldn't want a repeat of your mimosa

brunch shenanigans," Wendy says, concerned at my wobbliness. "So go easy on the alcohol, okay?"

"Easy peasy." I give her a thumbs-up, wait until she's out of sight, then stomp over to the bar. "Double shot of Jack, please." If I had to 'A,' Act Sloppy, then I was going to make it count and get Casey-on-her-twenty-first-birthday sloppy.

With Tennessee fire shooting through my veins, I move on to 'B,' the Bait. Fortunately, with Alex's jam-packed party schedule every summer, I know most Vegas clubs like the back of my hand, so I head past the dance floor and up the stairs to the skyboxes. It's a more private area for extra-special guests, and you have the best view overlooking the entire space.

"Casey! What are you doing here?"

Like I anticipated, Max is with Lola and all three board members, plus another middle-aged man I don't know. From Max's tone, I can tell he's surprised but masking his displeasure, so I stumble into the booth, practically falling on his lap, confident he won't cause a scene and have me removed . . . yet.

"Looking for you, silly!" I slap him on the shoulder with intoxicated force, mirroring how he'd always get handsy with fellow Habituators. "I never got the chance to congratulate you on such a great job today—you were a fantastic emcee."

He mumbles his thanks while I try to identify the unfamiliar face. Lola, always so eager to help, jumps in. "Casey, have you met Rick Benjamin? He's the head of comms at Golden Pond."

"Pleasure," he drawls. "Can I offer you a drink?"

Rick's sharklike demeanor raises my hackles. Does Tania know he's here? Are they trying to poach him and put her out of a job?

"Why not?" I slur. "I'm already four or five in, so what's one more?"

Rick raises an eyebrow but proceeds to pour some Grey Goose and mix in cranberry juice from their bottle service.

"You sure, Casey?" Max says, nervously watching me chug the cocktail. "Lola can get you some water."

Classic. Even while the tech dudes are partying, they expect their women colleagues to run errands for them. Lola shoots him the briefest of dirty looks, then turns to Rick. "I'll take another too."

"Woo!" I squeal, a few decibels too loud. "That's the spirit. Come on, Max, don't be such a square—remember, you told us those stories of how wild you got in your frat? How you could turn any candy into a shot? Oh! That reminds me—"

I fish through my clutch and pull out the box, setting it on the table and feeling Max stiffen against me like I deployed a land mine.

"They're gummy bears—your favorite! They're the ones you gave Evan, remember?"

Max shakes his head, smiling. "I'm sorry, I don't know what you're talking about."

Push through the denial and don't let him change the subject, like we practiced. "Of course you do. Right before the pitch meeting, you gave them to him."

The men exchange glances, but Lola stares at the box, perplexed. "Wait, Max said they were a gift to Evan from you."

I scoff. "Oh god, no. I can't believe I came to his defense that day. I thought he would grow up after the International Women's Day fundraiser, but after I realized he betrayed everyone with his drug-addled antics I escorted him straight to his apartment to give him a piece of my mind. These were on his kitchen counter, so I took them. I didn't care. He didn't deserve your generosity, Max."

I open the box and offer it to him.

"Ah, no, thank you. I'm still full from dinner."

"More for us then!" I take a bear and slowly bring it to my mouth, waiting for Max to stop me, but Evan was right. I'm going to have to eat this thing because Max doesn't give a shit about me. Let's hope he has a conscience when it comes to the people who hold the purse strings.

I gulp the gummy bear down, praying I won't regret the high that's about to hit me—before holding the box out to the men across the table.

As expected, Nigel Pittman and his colleague Rick reach toward the gummy bears, not wanting to be rude, while Hugo Sandoval and Byron Irving watch intently from their side of the table. They must believe there's some validity to my previous accusation if they're hesitant to consume allegedly laced candy and follow in Evan's footsteps.

"Casey, can we have a moment to talk in private?" Max snatches the box out of my hand before Nigel or Rick can reach it and jabs me in the side to push me out of the booth. I make my way toward the corner farthest from the DJ, hoping to remove as much background noise as possible.

"Are you done?" he hisses. "Because I don't know how the hell you got in here, but your days of playing dress-up with us are over."

"Am I done?" I say, projecting loud and clear. "How about are you done tearing down Evan and everything he's built? How could you?"

"Whatever ridiculous ideas he's put in your head, he's the one who acted unprofessionally at work—not unlike how you are right now, Ms. Holbright."

"You *drugged* him—he ate so many of those gummies, he could have died! And you're clearly unfazed if I do the same."

"Please. Spare me the hysterics. All I see is some candy that was in Evan's possession and is now in yours. I have nothing to do with your recreational activities—including your secret relationship, by the way. It was almost endearing how much he was blubbering at the restaurant while he was high, gushing about how much he loves you and how he had to win you back before taking the company public." He scans me up and down. "I guess one out of two isn't bad."

I resist smacking his smug face, settling for shoving him out of my way and stomping back toward the booth. "Let's see what the board thinks about this then."

He grabs my arm hard, making me wince. "Are you that fucking naive? You think they'll take your side? That they don't benefit from me getting Evan fired? I am so sick and tired of running a startup full of delusional children. Now that Golden Pond's on the board, they can sell it off for parts. I don't care. I'm getting a nice golden parachute—because Habituall is getting dismantled and there's nothing you or Evan can do about it."

Bingo. Time for step 'C'—Catch and release. I whip out my phone and complete the last step.

"Oh yeah?" Max sneers. "What do you think you're doing? Texting your boyfriend to help you save the day? Whatever you're plotting, I'll deny everything. Who's going to believe a druggie and someone who picks out clothes for a living?"

It's jarring how fast someone you trusted can turn against you once you no longer serve their needs. I can't believe I ever looked up to him. If there's anything Maxwell Erickson has taught me, it's that even the most buttoned-up appearances can be deceiving.

"You're right, Max. But they won't have to. Because this" —I pull the mic out from my bust—"captured our little conversation, and this"—I twist his arm off mine and rip off the unsuspecting cuff link—"has been recording you the rest of today. So if Golden Pond is involved in your deception, I'm sure we'll find out soon enough."

"We? You mean you and your ditzy influencer friends? It's your word against mine."

"Technically, it's your word against yours. You're such an

esteemed member of the tech community and Habituall's new CEO, after all. It makes sense that your plan of supplanting Evan Chen, selling the company, and laying off its entire staff should come from you—delivered straight to the inboxes of every customer, partner, and employee subscribed to its emails. Habituall is a young startup run mostly by young, passionate people, but that doesn't make them inexperienced children. It just means the business is a bit rough around the edges. Like did you know that everyone with a Habituall email address has Boss access, giving them the power to deliver messages to any recipients from any sender? You should talk to Drew about that. It sounds like a security risk."

At the moment, not even the hip-hop music can drown out the sounds of hundreds of notifications pinging every-one's phones at the same time.

Max checks his phone and his face contorts with rage. "You conniving bitch!"

I blink at him innocently. "Who me? No, I just pick out clothes for a living. But I can't work miracles. I can make you look good on the outside, but I'll never be able to fix the ugly on the inside."

His head swivels around sharply, his nostrils flaring. "Where the *fuck* is Evan?"

The music suddenly cuts out, and the lights flash on.

"I've been around this whole time. I always will be. Can't say the same for you, though."

Evan strides up to us, flanked by the glam fam on one side and a handful of Habituators on the other, including Tania, Wendy, and other members of the leadership team.

"You see, Maxwell," I say, taking Evan's hand in mine, "you may have underestimated me, but we all underestimated this man here. Not only is his real fashion sense impeccable, but he also painstakingly built this business, created its code base from scratch, and hired the most talented, hardest-working people in the industry—you excluded, of course. Habituall's a unicorn, but so is he, and so is everyone else in this room. This company is worth a billion dollars, but this team is priceless, and I refuse to watch you steal their victory as your own. I love Evan too much to let that happen."

My boyfriend glows with pride, leaning down to grab my face in his hands and kiss me—to the hoots and hollers of the crowd behind us.

"Tania," Evan calls out, "why don't you escort Mr. Erickson downstairs where our legal team and the rest of the board is waiting. I imagine we have a lot to discuss to address these allegations and get ahead of the media circus I'm sure is brewing."

"I'm on it, EC." She smiles before giving Max the most withering look. "After you, sir—watch your step."

Som claps her hands. "Let's get these bops back! Princess Alex is in the house, and drinks are on her the rest of the night."

Everyone cheers and follows them back to the dance floor until Evan and I are alone in the skybox.

"So before I get my business back officially," he says, "I've got good news and bad news. Which do you want to hear first?"

I tense up in his arms. "After all that? Good news, please!"

He kisses me again. "I love you too, Casey. Thank you for believing in me when no one else did. If anyone's a unicorn, it's you. It's always been you."

I squeeze him in a big bear hug, mostly to express my love for him but also to help my balance as the room starts to spin.

"And what about the bad news?"

He laughs. "Oh, I'm going to have to demote you. You're still Habituall's stylist, of course, but I can't be dating my strategic advisor, especially after she's been seen getting sloppy at a work event."

I nod, amused albeit slightly embarrassed. "As long as I can stock your closet."

He leads me down the stairs, careful to ensure that I don't trip and fall. "Consider it yours—in fact, you should take half the space because if I expect my girlfriend to move in, she should be encouraged to make herself at home."

"Live with you?" My eyes widen. "Wow. I'll need to run it by Alex first—" My head swivels, searching for her bright yellow dress, then turns back to Evan. "You know what? No. As long as you treat me like royalty, the princess will be perfectly fine."

"Deal," he says, handing me off to my friends to take me back to the suite. "Now go drink a ton of water and wait up for me, because once you come down from your high, I will be at your majesty's service."

~

"SAN FRANCISCO EXECUTIVE Fired for Framing CEO in LSD Scandal" by Bloomberg – March 28

IT WAS ANNOUNCED today that Maxwell Erickson, chief operating officer at marketing technology company Habituall, has been fired for his role in intentionally drugging founder and CEO Evan Chen prior to an investor meeting in March. Chen had been removed from his position by Habituall's board of directors for violating the company's code of conduct after being under the influence of LSD, which is a Schedule 1 controlled substance and illegal for recreational use.

Sources close to the company report Erickson had tricked Chen into unwittingly taking LSD by lacing gummy bear candy. Erickson's alleged motive was to sabotage Chen during a meeting with private equity firm Golden Pond as Habituall sought Series E funding. These sources claim that once Chen was deposed, it was Erickson's intent to negotiate Golden Pond's dismantling of the company. Request for comment from the spokespeople at Golden Pond went unanswered at the time of publication.

"While I am relieved to be exonerated after this harrowing ordeal," said Chen, "our investigation is still ongoing. I look forward to getting to the truth and ensuring Habituall's board is reserved for those with the company's best interests at heart."

Erickson's firing was swift after news of his alleged crime was distributed to Habituall's email list during the company's fourth-annual First Party conference. Among the people who witnessed his confession was celebrity stylist Casey Holbright. Known for her longterm work with supermodel Alex Waterston-Gardner, Holbright had brought Habituall on as a client to style its leadership team, including Chen and Erickson, for the event.

Tania Beecher, Habituall's new vice president of marketing, released a statement thanking Holbright for her involvement. "The entire Habituall team owes so much to Casey for preserving our company's integrity and reinstating Evan as its rightful leader. We are grateful for her contributions over the past couple of months and consider her as one of our own. We look forward to continuing to work with her."

Holbright indeed seems close to the San Francisco startup in more ways than one. No party provided comment, but she and Chen have been seen on romantic outings around the city, and sources close to the couple say although it's early in their relationship, they're quickly getting serious.

As for Erickson, who also could not be reached for comment, the former executive is on the move. After escaping potential jail time when Chen refused to press charges, Erickson explained in a post on LinkedIn that he put his three

Bay Area homes up for sale and is in the process of moving to Austin, Texas, with his wife and two children. He did not address whether he'd be relocating to join a specific company but praised Texas for its "booming tech scene" and "tax advantages."

Habituall has since closed its most recent round of fundraising for an undisclosed amount. Based on market trends, business analysts predict the company will file its S-1 within the next year as it prepares to go public.

epilogue

"That's enough grounding today—we're gonna get kicked out!" I playfully push Evan off me, already missing his hands roaming along my curves. Our meditation exercise didn't last nearly as long as the first time we met; we didn't even get through the four things we could feel before succumbing to full-out groping.

"That would make two of us this time," he teases. "But if you've had enough of the ground, can I interest you in other surfaces? Perhaps take you home and push you up against the glass walls overlooking the Bay so those snoops can see how badly you want me inside you?"

Phew, the zen room was always warm, but now it's stifling with Evan's hard body pressing against mine and his hot breath in my ear. Don't get me wrong. I'm not a fan of reporters tailing us, but I'd be willing to give them a show if Evan keeps talking dirty like that.

I leap out of his arms before I get ahead of myself and check my watch. "It's three p.m.—you have summer Fridays in June, right?"

He threads his fingers through mine. "Even if we didn't, nobody in this office would care if we took off early. They're in vacation mode as much as we are. They're surprised I even came in today."

We walk out of the zen room and down the hall, past many familiar sights: the sales pod playing music and cracking jokes, folks snacking in the kitchen and chatting about weekend plans, and, of course, Paul and Natasha's incessant bickering. Even Drew's in town for a visit, letting Bigfoot roam around on a leash.

But much has changed since that initial walk of shame on my first day at Habituall. Now when I pass people's cubicles, they smile and say hi, showing off their new outfits and asking whether they're Casey-approved. First Party may be over, but now I feel like a true member of the team. They don't care if I work with celebrities or famous fashion designers, as long as I come by for Taco Tuesdays and compete in their ping-pong tournaments. I'm more than a stylist to them —I belong.

"You're still here, EC?" laments Wendy from the front desk. "Peace out already, will ya?"

Evan laughs, turning to me. "Told you they're ready to get rid of me."

With Max and Lola no longer in the picture, even the lobby is more inviting. I don't know how to explain it, but everything and everyone seems so much lighter these days, and it feels great.

"This just in!" Tania squeals, skipping up to us. "*Bloomberg Businessweek* is hot off the presses."

She opens the magazine in her hands to where she's marked the page with a sticky note.

"Omigosh, it's amazing. You look *so* good, babe." I snatch the magazine from Tania to see the glossy photos up close— Evan posing in front of Dragon Gate, like a debonair secret agent on a mission through Chinatown.

"'Tech Unicorn to Undercover Boss,'" Evan reads the

headline. "They must have had fun writing that one. But I thought they dumped me because of the incident?"

Tania chuckles. "Once the news broke on Max, they immediately re-added you before the issue went to print. Who knew Habituall's biggest scandal would also be our biggest PR boost?"

I smile. If anyone deserved a silver lining, it would be her. "The new VP of marketing won't mind if I keep this copy?"

Tania grins. "Of course, she wouldn't mind. If it weren't for you, I'd be updating my résumé, not my job title."

The thought of that alternate reality is too much to bear, and I engulf her in a hug, grateful that everyone is exactly where they're supposed to be. "Thank you, Tania. For everything." I slide the magazine carefully into my tote bag. "Not to mention, it'll make good reading on the plane."

She smacks her forehead. "That's right—your vacay's next week! Where are you headed?"

My new boyfriend winks at me.

"Don't say it, Evan. I swear I'll murder you—"

"We're going to Ibitha! I've got some beautifully colored roofs to show her."

THE END

thank you

Thank you for reading *Love Apptually*! It would mean the world if you'd consider writing a review on Amazon and Goodreads, as well as recommending the book on social media. Word of mouth has a huge impact on an author's success, and it helps other readers discover new books to enjoy.

Can't get enough of Casey and Evan? To gain access to a special bonus epilogue from Evan's point of view, visit alyssa jarrett.com/love-apptually

acknowledgments

This debut would not have been possible without the help and support of so many wonderful folks.

First and foremost, to Kristen Tate at the Blue Garret. Like so many writers experienced in 2020, the pandemic was a catalyst to realign my life according to my creative endeavors, and I'm so thankful it led me to you. You're more than an editor—you're a champion of my stories and my partner in bringing my vision to life. Thank you for improving my craft, holding me accountable, and keeping me from spiraling with anxiety all these years. And speaking of anxiety—

To the coaches, therapists, and medical professionals who guided me during a dark time in my life, especially to Daisy Cervantes and Liz Doyle Harmer. This book was therapeutic in many ways, so thank you for making space for my most important happily ever after—my own.

To all my critique partners, beta readers, and writing friends, especially to Sophia Le, Lindsey Lanza, Rebecca Wise, Joanna Furlong, Taleen Voskuni, and everyone who was kind enough to talk shop and share their insights on their own author journey. Thank you for your much-needed encouragement and feedback. Writing doesn't feel solitary when you have the right community.

To Susan Velazquez Colmant at JABberwocky Literary Agency. The paths of traditional and indie publication are not diverged in a wood, but instead intersected in the pursuit of readership. Thank you for your invaluable guidance after years in the query trenches. You may not be my agent, but *Love Apptually* is unquestionably a better book because of you.

To host Constance Hale, fiction instructor Linda Watanabe McFerrin, and all the organizers and fellow attendees of the 2022 O'ahu Writers Retreat. With your help, I was able to hone my voice, build confidence in my work, and complete the first draft of the book that would become *Love Apptually*. Thank you for showing me what it means for your writing to have heart.

To all my tech colleagues who have become fast friends. Together we've experienced the kind of hijinks that are ripe for romantic comedies—some so outrageous you had to be there to believe them. Thank you for giving me ~~fodder~~ inspiration for years and years to come.

To my closest friends and family, especially to Lily, Celia, Jill, Kit, and the ladies in the K.A.S.A. group chat. You have been by my side from the beginning and supported me through thick and thin. Thank you for listening to me blather on about my books, long after anyone else would lose interest. You're my ride-or-dies, truly.

To my brilliantly talented brother Nick Jarrett, who designed the cover of *Love Apptually* with a level of intuition I rarely experience outside of our collaboration. Thank you for making room for the added workload and tolerating my author eccentricities. Back when I took a marketing executive job, you told me not to forget my dream of becoming an author, and you were right. I'm glad our thirty-something selves can remind each other of what our eight-year-old selves wanted. I live to make you proud of your big sister.

And, finally, to my readers. Thank you for supporting me every step of the way. It is an immense privilege to live an artistic life, and I'm honored to share my stories with you.

a sneak peek

Please continue reading for an excerpt of Book 2 in the Glam Fam series, *Love on the Rocks*.

chapter
one

Unhappy hour. Drink your feelings hour. C-suite suck-up hour. I'm a marketing executive—shouldn't I be able to come up with better names for this event? All of my colleagues seem to be happy enough. It's the last day of our corporate retreat in Yosemite, and the presentations and brainstorming sessions are finally over.

You should be grateful, Tania Beecher, I keep telling myself. Everything in the bar at the Granite Grove Lodge spells luxury: the historic stone interior with exposed wooden beams along the vaulted ceiling, the warm lighting from elaborate chandeliers, the plush furniture perfectly arranged for cozy conversations.

If I'd stayed in journalism, I'd be in some grimy dive bar, commiserating over the latest round of pink slips at yet another dying newspaper. It took a decade for me to break into the tech industry and claw my way up to vice president of marketing at Habituall, one of Silicon Valley's hottest tech companies. But as I sink deeper into my tufted chair, clutching an exquisitely expensive Napa cabernet, I feel not satisfied, but suffocated.

Everyone on my team is giddy and getting along, clustered

together in a boisterous group near the bar—I just can't bring myself to join in the festivities. Harris Shepherd, one of my top content marketers, meets my glance and I quickly look away. Not just because I can't handle chitchat right now—*shit*, he's walking over—but also because his soft, gray eyes are so gorgeous that it's hard to make eye contact.

"You think you got enough there, Tania?" Harris clinks his wine glass against mine, nearly sloshing Silver Oak's finest on the hardwood floor.

Harris has that thirty-something hipster vibe on lock: a dark, full beard and equally thick hair with a silver streak that matches those eyes I have to avoid getting lost in. I cough, as if trying to hack up my lustful thoughts. I'm his boss, for christ's sake. Get it together. "The bartender got generous with the pours. It's not like I asked for a double."

He takes in my nervous laugh. "Maybe you should have a double. It wouldn't kill you to enjoy yourself for once."

"I *am* having fun." I take a defensive gulp of my drink to make my point. "I'm a little stressed over Q1 planning—that's all."

Harris squints his perfect eyes with disapproval. "Come on. That's bullshit, and you know it. I've seen that fifty-slide deck you've been obsessed with. You've had every *i* dotted, *t* crossed, and penny counted since Thanksgiving. There's no way in hell you overlooked anything, and I would bet my Hydrow on it."

Okay, that gets me to laugh for real. Habituall gives every team member a two-hundred-dollar stipend each month to spend on fitness, and I've been approving Harris's expense reports for over a year, so I know exactly how much his rowing machine means to him. And from the way his toned arms bulge in his black Henley when he crosses them, I don't blame him. I remind myself for the hundredth time that he has a girlfriend—whom he met while he was DJ-ing on the weekends, of course.

"The content team's jumping in the hot tub after happy hour if you want to join us. No mentions of AP Style or SEO allowed. Bring your wine, and come unwind."

I should want to say yes. I should want to sit in a hot tub with a ridiculously expensive glass of wine and celebrate our breakneck period of record growth with my team. But the only feeling I can identify is this one:

I don't want to be here anymore.

"Thanks, but you go ahead," I say, passing him my wine glass. "Take that, and don't let it go to waste. I'm going to go for a walk and get some fresh air."

"We're around if you change your mind." He frowns but doesn't press the issue, which makes me think it was a pity invite anyway, then walks off to rejoin the rest of the marketing team.

Although I would describe myself as an "indoor cat," Yosemite in early January is absolutely awe-inspiring: calm and quiet, pristine and pure, ideal for a tightly wound workaholic who has to remember to take a deep breath every now and then. Maybe I haven't spent a single dollar of my fitness stipend, but I can take a stroll in this majestic national park outside. My longtime therapist, Dahlia, suggested I go on a walk to recharge when I texted her earlier today, and for once, I'll be able to tell her I took her advice.

I stride out the door into an Ansel Adams photograph come to life and regret my decision as soon as the icy chill slaps me right in the face.

If I was anywhere else, I would have no problem abandoning my plan and sneaking back up to my room to watch rom-coms instead. But as the sun dips over the mountains, illuminating the peaks in deep orange underneath cotton-candy-streaked skies, I have to admit that it's not just the thirty-degree weather taking my breath away.

It wouldn't kill me to take a walk around and enjoy the view, I think to myself.

Would it though? The little hamster of anxiety in my brain —I call him Hammy—butts in. *You haven't reapplied your sunscreen yet, and just because it's freezing doesn't mean your skin can't get burned in the elements. And you don't even have your trusty water bottle—what if you get lost and die of dehydration?*

Calm down, Hammy. I'm only stretching my legs. You've been doing so many mental laps that I forget I need to move my actual body on occasion.

You sure about that? he insists, his imaginary hamster feet sprinting endlessly on the squeaky wheel in my mind. *You do know you're wearing Ralph Lauren leather riding boots, right? You look like you'd be better off playing polo than going for a hike in the snow.*

I hate when he makes a good point. Lord knows I'm no equestrian—I haven't been around horses since I was a kid living on the outskirts of Fresno, feeding carrots to my neighbor's mares—but I'm even less suited for real winters. I live in the Bay Area, after all, so the only cold-weather attire I own is a stack of corporate-branded Patagonia jackets and the Ted Baker peacoat I'm currently wearing.

It's fine, I keep repeating as I scuffle away from the lodge and down a dirt hiking trail. There's not much snow on the ground, nothing I can't stomp through. Setting my smartwatch to outdoor walk mode, I set off toward the sunset, surprisingly upbeat considering there's no hot cocoa or fireplace in sight. But nothing makes me feel more accomplished than crossing items off my "I really should" list: Visit someplace new? Check. Do some cardio? On it. Connect with nature? Hell yeah.

Look at me, Hammy. All the kids these days talk about touching grass, and I'm out here like a natural adventurer.

I ignore his stubborn squeaks and power through the nerves, enjoying the smell of pine as I breathe deeper than I have in a long time. The muscles in my jaw slowly loosen and my shoulders fall away from my ears.

It occurs to me then that my urge to flee the not-so-happy hour earlier was just Hammy fretting. I'm not having an existential crisis, and I don't need to escape my job. I just need to take that six-week sabbatical I've earned after six years with Habituall. Maybe a few months from now, though—or even next year. It's not like I can peace out after we just got back from winter break—even if I spent most of it working anyway. You can get a lot done when the office shuts down, you know.

I channel Dahlia again and tell myself to stop thinking about work and pay attention to my body. My skin tingling in the cold, my feet moving down the path. The farther I go, the more limber I become, and it's downright thrilling to break out of the sedentary cast my desk job has molded around me. Are these the exercise endorphins everyone's always going on about?

The air stings my lungs and the increasing incline burns my thighs, but I move quickly to keep myself warm, not bothering to keep track of which paths I'm taking as the trail forks off. I resist the urge to pull out my phone and check the same five silly apps, remembering an article I read that explained how our phones had effectively replaced cigarettes as our go-to distraction. They give our hands something to do, without the cancer risk. I've felt enough compulsive twitchiness on this work retreat to know that a habit doesn't need nicotine to be addictive.

The sun's in the west, so I keep hiking further and further into the forest, knowing I've got that molten ball in the sky as my compass.

Do you though?

I stop in my tracks, branches snapping ominously under my boots. It's always worse when Hammy whispers instead of squeals. But when I look to my left and no longer see the sun, I realize he's right. Everything is indeed not okay. When I stepped outside, the mountaintops were illuminated like lit cigarettes, but now they're being put out as fast and unceremoniously as butts smashed into an ashtray.

When I pull my phone from my coat pocket and turn on its flashlight, those four trusty bars have disappeared. Meaning I'm by myself, out in the stark wilderness without any cell service, and it's getting colder and darker every second.

Fuck. Fuck fuckity fuck. I whip around, hoping to catch a glimpse of the lodge in the distance, but it must be miles behind me. With the sun officially set, I can't tell east from west, up from down, and it's not like I can get Google Maps to point me in the right direction. How could I be so foolish? Hammy doesn't have to scream to wake me up to the dire circumstances.

It's pitch dark. The flashlight on my phone is rapidly draining my battery. And, worst of all, it starts to snow. At first, there are just a few flakes sparkling in the light from my phone. But after just a minute they're not sparkling as much as settling. Settling in a flurry on my frigid nose, incessantly blinking eyelashes, and gloveless hands. They're conforming to my increasingly damp coat and piling up around my boots— and everywhere else.

The snowfall is heavy enough that the path beneath me has disappeared. I try to double back and return the way I came, but with my footprints getting covered as fast as I'm making them, I can no longer orient myself. Wherever I go, it's white snow on the ground and blackness all around me. I've never experienced the weather take a turn for the worse like this. I mean, climate change is real, but changing this quickly? Fucking unreal.

"Hey!"

Leave me alone, Hammy. I don't have time for this. I need to get back to the lodge before I succumb to exposure. It looks like there's an area up ahead where the trees thin—maybe I can tell where I am from there.

"Stop!"

Absolutely not. That's how hypothermia gets you. You stop moving, and all of a sudden, the warmth of oblivion envelops you before you have a clue what's happening. It's why folks are found frozen in their birthday suits, and I am *not* about to die literally naked and afraid. I keep moving forward up a slight rise. There are definitely fewer trees ahead.

"Can you hear me? I said stop!"

"And I said leave me alone, Hammy!" Wait a minute. I said that out loud, which means I responded to a real person, not my imaginary hamster. I've got a vivid imagination—that's undeniable—but even I stop short of actual hallucinations.

Milliseconds later, an abnormally strong arm pulls me back with so much force that I collide into a sheer wall of muscle.

"I don't know who Hammy is, but if he followed you any further, you'd both be falling down that cliff."

I aim my flashlight in the direction my rescuer is pointing. Just a few paces away, the ground drops off precipitously into a pit of rock and darkness.

I whip back around, and he holds up a hand to shield his eyes from the flashlight. "Do you mind turning that off? I've got it covered."

Quickly tapping the screen, I adjust to my surroundings, settling my gaze on the person in front of me. A man, who looks like he's about my age, with one hand on his headlamp and the other braced against my waist to keep me balanced.

Normally, I'd be startled by being held by a stranger, but my body's too frozen in place to step back in surprise.

"Who are you? And why are you out here?" My voice comes out shaky but holds onto its edge, clearly not as comfortable as my extremities to discover a source of warmth in the wild.

"That's supposed to be my line." He chuckles softly, crinkling his eyes and immediately putting me more at ease. His voice is warm and deep, like his embrace shielding me from the snow.

"You didn't answer my question," I project loudly against the wind. My accusatory tone makes me cringe, but he's not at all bothered.

"How about we get you someplace safe before formal introductions, alright?"

He charges down a path leading away from the cliff, but it's difficult for me to keep up. He's properly suited up for snow in several hooded, waterproof jackets and well-worn hiking shoes; whereas I can't get any traction in these ridiculous riding boots, so I'm slip-sliding across the slush and at constant risk of twisting an ankle.

He doesn't say a word when he realizes I'm not right behind him, just comes back down the path and takes my hand to help me around the most unstable areas. In any other circumstance, this might seem like a chivalrous gesture, but I'm reminded of my mother, who would tug me along at the mall when I was little to keep me from dawdling. I don't care how warm his calloused hands are—there's nothing romantic about them gripping yours so you don't fall on your ass and bruise your tailbone.

After who knows how many minutes, the trees thin out and we come to a clearing. I expect to see his headlamp shining on a quaint log cabin or at least a bare-bones Airbnb, but the only thing I can make out is a large white van.

"Are you going to drive me back? My company's staying at Granite Grove."

His eyes bulge, and a scoff escapes his lips in a foggy exhale. "Not a chance. It's pitch-dark, the road conditions are already not ideal, and out here a small snowstorm can become a blizzard before you know it. We're better off hunkering down tonight, and I can take you back first thing in the morning."

"Hunker down . . . where exactly?" I ask, my head swiveling in search of shelter.

We walk up to the van, and he slaps the side of it. "In my humble abode, of course!"

~

"What You Can Learn From a Guy's OnlyVans Profile," by *The Send-It Sisters on Thursday, January 6*

We get it. You were minding your own business when suddenly you came across a hottie's OnlyVans page. And being the progressive digital citizen you are, you're tempted to support this intriguing #vanlife creator, if only to get a sneak peek of what's under his hood.

But before you impulsively commit to yet another subscription, pay close attention to these four key areas. If you're selective about your sign-ups, you can avoid the van boys and drive home with a new van man.

1. **A picture is worth a thousand groans.**
   Reviewing bios for red flags is essential, but a
   profile picture can fill in what's left unsaid
   between the lines. He may have the eloquence of
   Shakespeare, but he's no Romeo if his neck has

so much beard it looks like it's never seen
the sun.

2. **Perks worth every penny.** They say you get what
   you pay for, so don't cheap out with a lemon. If
   you want to evolve beyond van-surviving and
   enjoy van-thriving, pony up for premiums like
   sustainable energy, meals that don't require a
   microwave, and a bed big enough to unfurl from
   the fetal position.

3. **You can't spell GURL without URL.** Vans
   don't typically come with room for ring lights and
   tripods, so we don't expect dudes to be camera-
   ready influencers. But they better have a digital
   paper trail. So click those links, because a little
   cyber-snooping can be the difference between
   someone being all-American and on *America's
   Most Wanted*.

4. **Play a little game of "just the tip."** There's no
   ethical consumption under capitalism, of course,
   so we believe in supporting creators for their hard
   work. But if your van vagabond isn't adding more
   value than the space he's taking up in your
   driveway, might we suggest the only tip you leave
   is, "Get a real job."

about the author

Alyssa Jarrett is a romance author and tech marketer based in the San Francisco Bay Area. When she's not telling steamy, satirical love stories, she can be found drinking an iced tea or cuddling with her cats.

You can subscribe to her newsletter, Grumpy + Sunshine, on Substack, and follow her @authoralyssajarrett on Instagram, Threads, and TikTok.

alyssajarrett.com
alyssajarrett.substack.com

Follow Alyssa online:

instagram.com/authoralyssajarrett
threads.com/@authoralyssajarrett
tiktok.com/@authoralyssajarrett

9 781963 875010